WITHDRAWN
FROM
COLLECTION

# FUNNY ONCE

# FUNNY ONCE

Stories

## ANTONYA NELSON

B L O O M S B U R Y

NEW YORK • LONDON • NEW DELHI • SYDNEY

Published by Bloomsbury USA, New York
Bloomsbury is a trademark of Bloomsbury Publishing Plc

All papers used by Bloomsbury USA are natural, recyclable products made from wood grown in well-managed forests. The manufacturing processes conform to the environmental regulations of the country of origin.

Versions of some of these stories were first published in the *New Yorker*, *Tin House*, *TriQuarterly*, *Harper's*, and *Colorado Review* and anthologized in *Best of the West 2011* and *The Best American Short Stories 2013*.

LIBRARY OF CONGRESS CATALOGING-IN-PUBLICATION DATA

Nelson, Antonya.
[Short stories. Selections]
Funny once : stories / Antonya Nelson.—First U.S. Edition.
pages cm
ISBN 978-1-62040-861-2 (hardcover)
I. Title.
PS3564.E428A6 2014
813'.54—dc23
2013044001

First U.S. edition 2014

1 3 5 7 9 10 8 6 4 2

Typeset by Hewer Text UK Ltd, Edinburgh
Printed and bound in the U.S.A. by Thomson-Shore Inc., Dexter, Michigan

Bloomsbury books may be purchased for business or promotional use. For information on bulk purchases please contact Macmillan Corporate and Premium Sales Department at specialmarkets@macmillan.com.

To my mother

# CONTENTS

# LITERALLY

"SHE'S ALWAYS LATE!" THE sixteen-year-old sobbed. She'd set up the ironing board and all its accessories like a shrine to housewifery. Heat shimmered in the air, had already slightly compromised the plastic of the spray bottle. Only Bonita could master the pleats of Suzanne's ghastly uniform skirt. Other girls did not care. Still others had punctual housekeepers. Or parents who ironed.

"Suze is so anal," her brother, Danny, noted from the table, where he and his father were studying their computer screens over breakfast, sharing news items and a bowl of pineapple. "She takes three showers a day, which is more than some people take in a year. In the future that will be illegal. Seriously, I skip showers so that our carbon footprint won't be so terrible."

"Do you know there's a second part to that expression? The 'retentive' part?" his father asked. "It's amazing how comfortable people are tossing that around, *anal retentive*. Everybody very casual with the psychology. So blasé about the butt."

"God *damn* it!" the girl cried. "Please, please, please!"

"Also," Danny said, "she exaggerates. Constantly."

"Literally," his father said. Richard liked to make his son smile by using his favorite word incorrectly.

Suzanne had done everything she could: curled her hair, made up her face, donned her shirt and shorts and shoes and socks, packed her backpack, checked her assignments, opened the back door, cleared a path to the ironing board. She had spread the khaki skirt on the narrow end, where it sagged practically to the floor. Others at her school—the school she'd begged to attend, and which she worked at Dairy Queen to help pay for, a private, elite place run by nuns where boys were not allowed—had altered their uniforms, raising the skirt's hemline far above the knee. Still others arrived at the gate wearing sweatpants or jeans, and then pulled on the required garment like a burlap bag, something they'd kick to the floorboard of their car minutes after the last bell rang.

"*Lo siento!*" Richard heard, along with the clatter of Bonita's heels, "*lo siento, Susana, mija!*" And the hiss of steam as the iron met the cloth, and further Spanish as Bonita apologized and soothed, his daughter's name a shushing on her lips, *soos, soos, soos*. He could finally let out his breath. "Thank god," he murmured.

"Amen," Danny said.

"I have choir and then work," Suzanne called to her father as she rushed out the back door. These days she spent more time apart from her family than with them. That would be the story from now on, Richard thought, the incremental move away.

Bonita had brought her son, Isaac, with her, as she always did, but she let Richard know that the boy wouldn't be going to school today, because he was suffering a bout of what she had only ever been able to describe as "*nervioso*," rubbing her stomach to illustrate her son's mysterious and chronic affliction. His mother pronounced his name "Ee-sock," although the boy preferred "I-Zack." Unlike his mother, he spoke fluent English. He and Danny were the same age, eleven. Bonita used the family's street address as her own so that Isaac could attend the nearby public school. Most days, the boys would walk the three blocks together, the very fair Danny alongside the fairly dark Isaac. When they were younger, they'd held hands. For the past three years, since Richard's wife had died, the boys had been permitted to be in the same class, even though they distracted each other, communicating almost telepathically. No one challenged them when they requested a joint trip to the nurse's office; nobody admonished them when they were absent on the same day. There seemed to be an endless bounty of understanding at that modest brick building, the school located in the heart of a neighborhood populated by university professors and medical personnel, equitable two-income two-car two-children homes, nannies and gardeners and housekeepers, the insulated hub of bleeding heart liberalism.

Still, no matter how well-meaning a school it was, no matter how conscientious about having Spanish signage and notifications, Bonita was intimidated by its administration. Before, it had been Richard's wife who played intermediary; now it was Richard who phoned in the excuses for the boys, Richard who attended the parent-teacher conferences, too, Bonita sitting beside him nodding, listening but only half understanding what was being carefully noted about her son. She had five other children, older

3

than Isaac, a few on their own already, all of them independent enough. Where Isaac's siblings had gone to school, in Gulfton, there had been no counseling services or narrative reports. There had been grades and failures, expulsions and swats. Isaac's brothers and sisters had put Bonita through many trials—arrests, pregnancies, car accidents—but Isaac's trouble, its invisibility, was new to her.

He was tentative, alert to any little sound or look of disapproval; if you moved too quickly, he flinched, delicate and lithe as a water bug. He often cried; his stomach seized whenever he was confronted with something he was afraid of, and he was afraid of many things—loud noises and crowds and dogs and busy streets and elevators and balconies and the dark and his nightmares and chaos in general and change of even the smallest sort and, most of all, his father, who, during his rare appearances at home, was a drunken and brutal man. Bonita's other children had been toughened by their bad dad and their rough neighborhood and their overall hard luck, turned sturdy by duress, but Isaac had been made too tender.

"You want to play hooky with Isaac?" Richard asked Danny. Isaac smiled shyly from the doorway, his silver front tooth catching the light. Whenever Richard spotted that tooth he had the same thought: if his wife had still been alive when the tooth was knocked out, she'd have seen to an ivory replacement.

"This morning, but not this afternoon," Danny said. "Can you go this afternoon?" he asked Isaac. "It's pizza party day, remember?"

Isaac's panic often eased after a few hours of an ongoing game the boys called "town" on the living room rug. Isaac loved Danny. Next year would be the heartbreaking, stomach-aching change from the sanctuary of elementary school to the hormone hell that was middle school; Richard hated to think of it. He suspected that Isaac would eventually recognize himself as homosexual, that others might know it sooner than he, that Bonita's challenges as mother to this boy would become only more overwhelming.

Richard had an urge to play hooky himself—to seize Suzanne away from the nuns, then bar the doors and hunker down. "Be good, boys," he said to them as he reluctantly put together his backpack and travel mug. Only now did he notice that Bonita was wearing a pair of jeans that his wife had given her long ago, hand-me-downs. Every year, another plastic bag of last year's clothing had made its way to Bonita; when his wife had died, Bonita had shaken her head at the offer of the entire closetful, turned her face as if to keep from witnessing further shameful behavior from her employer. "No," Richard had agreed, swiftly closing the door on the dresses and shoes. Also: his children sometimes visited those dresses, which smelled, they said, like their mother.

The trio before Richard made a pretty picture, the two smiling boys and the kind, hardworking woman. "*Adiós*," he told her. "*Hasta luego*."

"Bomb threat?" Richard joked when he arrived at the *Chronicle* to find a group of co-workers milling and muttering outside. But indeed that *was* why everyone had been evacuated.

"Credible," they kept repeating. An official bomb squad was rumored to be on the way. When rain began falling, Richard and his advertising staff headed across the street to the breakfast place they liked. There'd been layoffs in editorial the previous Friday; it was logical, wasn't it, that this would follow? A betting pool was started, various malcontents cited. Richard put three bucks on Lawrence Lattimer.

"Lawrence?" his co-workers cried.

"It's always the mild-mannered ones," Richard said. "Always the last guy you'd ever guess." By noon, the building had been declared safe, the threat empty. That wouldn't be like Lawrence Lattimer, though, Richard decided, trudging up the stairs to his department. Lawrence would have followed through, blown an emphatic hole in the place that had betrayed him. No, an empty threat would be from someone like Jill King, the flighty intern who flirted outrageously and then later claimed sexual harassment. Her gestures were inflammatory yet random. She'd probably phoned in the threat and then gone online to stalk a former boyfriend. Later she'd hit the mall and successfully shoplift a complete outfit, feeling it was owed to her. Or something like that. She wasn't serious enough to stick to her word.

He was on his office line explaining Isaac and Danny's absence from morning classes when his cell went off, the special home ringtone that he never ignored. "Hang on a sec," he said to the school secretary.

"They go out!" Bonita said without preamble. "No here!"

"Are the boys at school?" he asked the secretary.

"No, sir."

For an hour, Bonita guessed, when he asked how long they'd been gone. As was always the case when he and Bonita spoke to each other—neither remotely fluent in the other's language—the information exchange was crude yet functional. It was she who'd phoned Richard to tell him of his wife's car crash, she who'd fielded the notification from the highway patrol. She who'd had only to say *"La señora"* and then wail to let him know. What Richard understood today was that the boys were on a collecting mission, in search of some necessary prop for the shared narrative developing on the living room rug. There were cars, stores, blocks; they had made a town and filled it with houses and businesses, tracks and roads and paths. On occasion, they left their indoor game to fetch a pile of twigs or sand or stones. Once, they found a turtle and built an elaborate habitat for it in their little city. Somewhere beyond the back door there must have been a critical piece, a shared imperative driving the boys out together.

He wasn't going to get any work done today, after all, Richard thought, clattering down the stairs.

He and Bonita divided the neighborhood in half and began walking. It reminded him of searching for the family dog, an irritating terrier that would never stay penned. Except that he wasn't calling or whistling, just speed-walking with the familiar hopelessness of dread, the urge and need to *do* something. He was trying to think like Danny and Isaac. Would they have walked to the comic shop? It was a couple of miles away, but it was the only place that Richard could imagine them going on foot—and their bikes were still in the garage. Same with their skateboards and scooters and trikes, two of each of the wheeled toys they'd grown up learning to master together. Richard had already envisioned teaching them to drive, taking them to the parking lots and cemeteries where he'd taken Suzanne when she was learning, last year. Bonita did not drive; she was, after nearly three decades in Houston, still afraid to navigate its streets and highways. She and Isaac rode the bus; it took them an hour to get to Richard's home.

"His place," Richard said aloud and abruptly turned around, convinced suddenly that the boys had gone to Isaac's. Just the week before, Danny had said, out of the blue, "It's weird I've never seen inside their apartment." Plenty of times he'd come along when Richard dropped off or picked up Bonita and Isaac. But the pair were always waiting in the murky ground-floor vestibule or rushing through it, on their way to their two-bedroom unit on the third floor, which was far too small for their large family. One of Isaac's chief complaints was that he never knew who would be asleep beside him when he woke in the morning: brother, sister, nephew, niece.

"Jessss," Bonita agreed, nodding thoughtfully, drawing out the word, when Richard found her and asked if it was possible the boys had needed something of Isaac's to complete their game. As usual, Bonita failed to buckle her seat belt, and Richard didn't correct her. The pinging alarm would soon silence itself. This vehicle was a replacement for the one that had been totaled three years earlier; his wife had not been buckled in either. "*Lo siento*," Bonita said for the hundredth time, shaking her head in self-chastisement.

"It's OK," Richard assured her. "They know better. *Está bien.*" Sitting close to each other in the car made them both nervous, Richard supposed; they hadn't ridden together minus the children before. Her distinct smell, the fact of her vanities—the orange-tinted streaks in her hair, the powdery makeup, the bra strap cutting into her shoulder, her impractical high-heeled shoes—strikingly present. Female and male, close to the same age, arranged together in their traditional spots. Other drivers on the freeway could have plausibly assumed that Richard and his passenger were a couple. When Richard exited near Bonita's neighborhood, he felt the observations of others would be less benign. These were people on foot, lounging on porches, leaning against poles, gathering at curbs, and then sauntering slowly into the street, forcing cars to give way, throwing Richard direct and challenging glares. It felt a bit like crossing the border, the convenience stores and groceries and taco trucks all offering their wares in Spanish, the smell in the air of Mexican food, a wariness in both the visitor and the visited. Bonita had come to Texas long ago; Richard had no idea whether her status was legal, knew only that her children had all been born here.

At her building, she was out of the car before he'd turned off the engine, running awkwardly, her purse forgotten on the seat. Anyone watching might reasonably have guessed that Richard had done something terrible to her, that she was fleeing. His habit in the past had been to wait until the light came on in her apartment upstairs, until Bonita showed herself on the balcony and waved to him. How foolish he felt now, following her, carrying her large pink leopard-spotted purse. On the walkway was a trail of trash—a diaper, a Frenchy's bag, a smear of food that someone had walked through. The pack of dogs that usually lay panting in the vacant lot next door were howling in the distance.

The building's door was open, for which Richard was grateful—the men and the dogs outside made him uneasy. Up the stained stairs he climbed to the third floor. Like much of Houston, this habitat had had its brief heyday, maybe fifty years before; it had been a fashionable singles' complex, built well enough to survive only its first set of tenants intact. Now it was a shoddy ruin, a place with broken balcony railings, pocked with a hundred ugly satellite dishes, a dry swimming pool filled with forsaken furniture and fenced off with concertina wire. Bonita's apartment was both too high for the rickety balcony to seem safe and too low to keep out a persistent climber. A breeding ground of anxiety and temptation.

A silver-haired man in coveralls stood on a step stool in the hall, repairing or disabling the sprinkler head on the ceiling.

"Excuse me," Richard said to him, "do you know which is Gutierrez?"

"*Cómo?*" asked the man, stepping down with difficulty, in his hand a tool Richard thought belonged in the garden or perhaps the kitchen, a small rake-like thing. Eye to eye, he realized that the guy was close to his own age, that his white hair was premature, and that the man was as confused by what Richard held as Richard was by the little rake.

"Bonita," Richard explained, gesturing at the purse. "Isaac and Bonita *y mi hermano*. No, *mi* hijo. *Aquí?*" He indicated a door that might match the balcony he knew was hers. The man was frowning at Bonita's belongings. "*Soy Richard,*" Richard added lamely. "*Trabajo?*" he said, hoping the word would inspire some kind of sensible cognition. Richard's wife had spoken Spanish, so she had done all the talking. She and Bonita had often had lengthy conversations that left Richard with only the scantest broad understanding, through the few words he recognized, all subtleties lost. Had he pointed this out, his wife would have told him that it was a fair representation of men's general understanding of the world: they grasped its fundamentals but not its tricky minutiae. "Gross motor skills," she would have said. "As opposed to fine."

The man in the coveralls put himself between Richard and the door to apartment 3C, rapping briskly on it, the clawed tool in his other hand. Richard was glad that the building had a handyman who wished to protect its tenants; Bonita and Isaac occasionally spent nights alone here, when the older brothers were not around. From Richard's wife, Bonita had learned how to have the locks changed so that her husband could not reenter the place. Richard's wife had also helped Bonita get divorced, and had insisted on restraining orders when neither a locked door nor a legal document convinced the ex-husband that he wasn't wanted.

"And sometimes?" Richard's wife was forced to concede. "Bonita actually *does* want him." That was the tricky part the law couldn't touch.

"*Gracias,*" Richard said to the man in the coveralls, who nodded, still skeptical of the hapless Anglo with the woman's handbag. "Isaac?" Richard called out. "Bonita? Danny? Open up, guys."

When Isaac finally cracked the door, the handyman stepped inside. Just before the door closed in Richard's face, he saw the raw panic in Isaac's eyes and understood that this character in the hall was Bonita's ex-husband.

"Fuck!" Richard banged on the door now himself. "I'm calling the police," he threatened. A door down the hall opened and a head leaned out, then popped back in like a turtle's. "I'm calling right now unless you open this fucking door! Danny!" he yelled. "Danny, Bonita! Open the door!" He was ransacking Bonita's purse in search of her phone, tissue and candies and a tiny Bible spilling onto the floor. Just as he found it, the door flew open.

"Dad," said Danny, pressing into his father's ribcage. "I'm sorry."

"It's OK. Where's Isaac?"

"He locked himself in his room."

"You go get in there with him, OK?"

From the kitchen came an animated exchange of Spanish. Not angry, Richard thought, but opinionated, people in passionate relation to each other, Bonita's voice the more strident, the ex-husband's explanatory, if not apologetic, pleading. Richard listened for some sign that he should intervene, follow through on the threat of phoning the authorities. He stepped around a plastic-covered dining table to wait outside the kitchen doorway. The buffet against the wall was stacked with canned goods, which reminded him of Bonita's first day working for his family, a decade or so ago. She had retrieved from their trash the unopened yet expired boxes and cans of food that his wife had thrown away in preparation for a housekeeper. An embarrassing moment, not unlike this one, in which Richard had not known how to properly explain why Bonita shouldn't consume the outdated food, or shouldn't accede to her criminal ex-husband's wishes. Above the buffet hung pictures of Isaac's siblings and nieces and nephews and sisters- and brothers-in-law, each and every one a school or studio portrait, groups in matched attire grinning at the photographer. A few included the father, who, on occasion, made his way into the annual photo, as he made his way into his ex-wife's home and maybe sometimes into her bed. Perhaps that would be today's story, Bonita being a naturally forgiving woman, weak in the face of some lingering, nostalgic bad habit of love. Love for that man in coveralls, that figure who came to Isaac in nightmares and made him scream, who might or might not have been responsible for knocking out Isaac's front tooth—a story Richard's wife would have gotten to the bottom of.

Richard left his listening post and joined the boys in Isaac's room. It was protected by a dead bolt. This despite the fact that the walls and door themselves would have easily shattered or splintered at the mildest use of force. The room, like the rest of the apartment, was very tidy and held a few familiar touches: a cast-off desk and chair from Richard's home, gifts the two boys had gotten in common—a lighted globe, a poster of SpongeBob. "We just needed this guy," Danny was explaining, in his palm a drunk-looking Duplo clown, while Isaac sat trembling on the bed with his hands over his ears. "We were making an amusement park in the town, and this is literally the only guy who fits in the cannon. Nobody else has the right feet." Richard sat beside Isaac and gently took the boy's hands into his own, explaining the problem with what the boys had done, the worry they'd caused, riding the buses alone, the risk of accident and mishap, the menace of malign strangers, adding that he and Bonita hadn't been angry so much as scared. Isaac burst into tears, and Danny just looked perplexed.

"If it's so dangerous, how come we let Bonita and Isaac do it?" he asked. "They do it every day, twice. And also, I think, statistically buses crash a lot less often than cars." Danny would be a lawyer, Richard thought, not for the first time. He was logical, and passionate about fairness, fearless in an interesting way. Right after Danny had spoken, however, he seemed to realize precisely what he'd said, and then he too was sniffling, burrowing into Richard from the other side. A time would come, Richard thought, when he and his children wouldn't think of that terrible car crash and death every day, when they would no longer be ambushed by missing her.

Through the thin walls, they could hear the voices carrying on in the kitchen, his and hers, cajoling, laughing, then the embarrassing noise of nothing. Intimacy. And then the sound of his being sent away, a quiet, reluctant goodbye.

"*Is OK*," Bonita eventually called at the locked door. "Is OK, *se fue*. Isaac?" Simultaneously, the boys pulled away from Richard, wiped their eyes, put on their game faces. Richard unlocked the door. "Is OK now," Bonita told him, her eyes also tearful. "He go." It was hard to say who initiated their embrace, only the second in their long association. It seemed a mutual impulse, sadness, need—the same feelings they'd shared at the funeral, three years ago. Bonita's shoulders heaved. Tears: they did not require translation. How convenient it would be, Richard thought, Bonita's wiry hair against his neck, her face on his shoulder, how terribly *useful* if they could simply wed, he minus a wife, she with her problematic ex-husband, and regroup together like in a sitcom scenario in the fortified comfort of Richard's house across town, an arrangement that would be possible if they could just ignore that troubling enigma of love.

"Oh no," she cried, smiling, when they separated, wiping at the mascara on his shirt. "How you say?" she said to the boys, wiggling her fingers.

"Spiders," they replied together.


"Dad?" Danny said from the backseat. Richard checked the rearview; his son's tone was hesitant. "Dad, inside your head, do you hear conversations?"

"Like memories? Like of disagreements?"

"No, like . . ." He tipped his chin to look skyward. "Like instructions," he finally settled on.

Richard considered this. "Not exactly," he said. "I mean, I think in words, and the words are about making decisions, sometimes, although sometimes I also just—"

"No, not like that," his son interrupted. "Like some other voice not your own."

"Sure. I hear people I know, or knew, when they said impor—"

"No, no, no. Nobody you know, not you or a friend or a relative."

"What are you talking about?"

"Isaac said not to tell anyone this."

"But you're worried."

"Don't tell Bonita."

Richard checked his blind spot and merged onto the 59. Rush hour was just about to kick in; the exchange from downtown was already filling, an army of headlights in the oncoming dusk. "Whatever you tell me, son, nobody will ever know I got it from you. OK?"

"OK. So Isaac says that inside his head people are talking."

"He hears voices?"

"I guess so."

"And what do they say?"

"How would I know?"

Fair enough, Richard thought. Was eleven the right age for schizophrenia to set in? His wife, master of all matters psychological, could have confirmed this. And more imme-diately relevant: was eleven the right age to scare his son with the idea of his best friend being schizophrenic? The problem with telling somebody something was that he wouldn't later be able to unhear it.

"Bonita and I will take Isaac to the doctor," Richard promised. His wife had done this in the past, when the mysterious nervous stomach had first flared up; it was she who'd insisted to Bonita that the condition was serious. In Isaac, she had, perhaps, seen some of her own anxiousness, an insidious presence that Bonita did not recognize.

"We should have never left the house," Danny said, shaking his head.

"If I had a nickel for every day I thought that," Richard agreed.

Suzanne was home when they arrived, filling the house with the sweet chemical smell of soft-serve. She often brought home "mistakes"—confections lacking the trademark swirl, or misunderstood orders, edible but wrong. Danny especially appreciated the Peanut Buster Parfait mistakes, his favorite. But Suzanne wasn't due back until midnight tonight; Richard sighed, assuming she'd been fired. This day—would it never stop sending up trouble? But no, she hadn't been fired. She was tearing up the house in search of her cell phone.

"The last time I know I saw it was like two in the morning last night!" she shrieked from her bedroom. She'd thought it was in her backpack, she reported. Then she'd figured it had fallen out in the car. After an anxious hour at the Dairy Queen counter, she hadn't been able to stand it any longer.

"And it's *nowhere!*" she wailed. Like Isaac, Suzanne panicked at problems that others might approach more casually. She had always been high-strung, particular about details, a self-critical perfectionist like her mother, unconvinced of her beauty, easily flustered. On her forehead a crease from premature concern; a skeptical tuck of her lip when she deflected a compliment.

"She ruined our town," Danny complained. "She kicked everything over."

"Have you called it?" Richard asked Suzanne, and received only a withering glance. The three of them spent the next half hour ransacking the place, reminding one another to try to think like Bonita, who might have found the phone earlier in the day and put it somewhere she thought logical. Long ago, Richard's wife's missing diaphragm had finally been located in a basket of bath toys; the parts of the food processor tucked away in the tools drawer. She was sometimes too thorough, Bonita; once she had rearranged all of the books in the house, after dusting the shelves, restoring them not in alphabetical order but by color and size: short red books all together, tall yellow ones side by side. Richard's wife had pulled him into the study just to marvel—at the sight, and at the labor it would take to undo.

So Danny checked the bowl of remote controls on the coffee table, and Richard crawled around the kitchen floor reaching under the counters and between the appliances. Suzanne kept up a continuous chant of "God damn it"s.

"We'll get you another," Richard called out to her. "Really, sweetheart, it's probably time for an upgrade anyway."

"Mom's messages are on it," Danny said quietly when they met up outside Suzanne's bedroom door to watch her heave her mattress and its bedding to the floor.

"Oh shit," Richard said. Just the week before, he'd opened a cookbook and found not only his wife's handwritten notes in the recipes, but a few of her fingernails between the pages. She had been a lifelong biter. In a flash he'd seen her leaning over the book, chin in palm, pinkie between her teeth, humming while waiting for something to boil or reduce on the stovetop.

"We can get them back," Richard said, of the messages. "Probably," he added, because he wasn't positive.

"This has been a terrible day," Danny said. "Even though nothing exactly bad happened."

"Agreed," Richard said. Naturally, they were now both thinking about the worst day, the one on which Danny and Suzanne's mother had been killed after driving into the path of an eighteen-wheeler. For an instant a wave of rage filled Richard, a plosive pure fury at his wife for not being here where she was needed.

On days like these, terrible but not exactly bad, he could entertain the dismal possibility that her accident hadn't been an accident. "Before you ask me," Eve had said when Richard began to propose marriage twenty-five years ago, "I have to tell you a secret."

"I'm listening." He'd smiled indulgently.

"No, seriously. It's bad. As a teenager, I used to play this dangerous game when I was driving. Closing my eyes. Turning off the lights. Speeding. It was pretty out of control. I was that unhappy. I really didn't care if I lived or died." She'd closed her eyes to recall it there at the restaurant, their table abruptly an island in a sea of surrounding meaningless chatter. Red splotches had appeared on her cheeks, beads of sweat on her upper lip. That worried crease on her brow, which she would share with her future daughter, and her young voice, forever thereafter in Richard's head. "Just so you know," she'd told him. "You can change your mind about me. Just forget marrying me and move on."

But that turned out not to be true. He couldn't.

# SOLDIER'S JOY

IN HER DREAM, HER husband had written her a love letter. It closed with the following sentence: *I've looked at myself in the mirror—an admittedly warped and unreliable facade—and been keenly aware of how lucky I am that you want to live with me.*

"Humble bugger, aren't I?" her husband said when she told him about her dream letter penned by him.

"But what about me?" Nana answered. "So self-aggrandizing! So passive-aggressive!"

He rose up on an elbow to blink down at her, his large head and leonine hair eclipsing all else. "*I* dreamed that some friend of ours, some preposterously impossible person, was pregnant."

"Someone like Helen?"

He agreed: Helen. "I was very impressed, in the dream. It seemed so goddamned optimistic."

"What was I doing, in your dream?"

"You weren't there." He fell back upon his pillow. Mention of Helen, who had been their hostess the previous evening, reminded Nana that she had a phone call to make. It was not an uncommon call; it might not even be necessary with this particular hostess. Yet perhaps that was what Nana's dream had been trying to tell her, that her husband *was* lucky to have her. Drunk last night, he'd made a pass at Helen and Edward Nolan's nineteen-year-old daughter. Even *his* dream was telling her to make the call, Helen's out-of-the-question pregnancy some kind of counterweight to her lovely grown daughter.

"I hope Rebecca wasn't alarmed," Nana said to Helen on the phone.

"Please. She was flattered, just like anybody." Nana heard the faint sniff of competition, the knotted business between mother and daughter, crone and princess. This vexed tolerance wouldn't be the response if one of Helen's sons had been kissed on the ear or patted on the fanny by a family friend. "No worries," Helen said. Nana made out the cigarette lighter flick, the deep, first-of-the-day inhalation. Helen's bad habit made her less likely to judge others'. She and Nana had met in graduate school and only coincidentally landed in the same city a dozen years later. Nana wasn't sure she would have agreed to moving to Houston, minus Helen's presence.

Helen was her best friend, although she knew she was not Helen's best friend.

"I was thinking of wearing the poppy dress tonight," Nana said, "unless you were?"

"We should match on purpose. Just to make Libby less bitchy. She'd love to be able to ridicule us. What a generous hostess gift that would be, us in our matching dresses, sizes S and L. She couldn't keep hating us, if we gave her that." Nana was the S—in every way less than Helen, not only physically smaller but with fewer attachments, no children, less money, renter rather than owner.

"I'll wear the poppy dress, and you can decide whether we'll match or not. Will you apologize to Rebecca?"

"She isn't so innocent as you think, Nana. I'm sure she was flirting. Just spreading her wings, testing the water. Et cetera."

Nana closed her eyes, visited the scene, her husband with his arm around Rebecca's bare shoulders, his mouth at her ear, his diving glance into the décolletage, solicitous, drunk, benevolent, happy. He could not resist beautiful women. "Sometimes he sort of oversteps the avuncular role," she said.

"Teenage girls are teases. You and I were, right? It was *us* flirting with Dr. Shock, once upon a time."

They were a generation younger than Nana's husband, their former professor; back then, it hadn't been clear which of them he favored, brash Helen or tagalong side-kick Nana. Nana hung up thinking about those flirtatious days, knowing that the circumstances hadn't been the same. She and Helen had met Dr. Shock at an apex, his as a certified celebrity, theirs as nubile acolytes. He had then been a casual tenant of his attractive still-young body, but now was a fearfully vain and anxious one of the older model. For two recent consecutive years he had gone about claiming to be sixty-nine, not even consciously, so averse was he to the number seventy. Now he was seventy-one. Before climbing into bed at night, while still in his cups, he would perform his exercises, the chin-ups, sit-ups, push-ups. "And sometimes throw-ups," he would always cheerfully conclude the list. Of Nana he had the expectation, never put into words yet understood nonetheless, that she would keep herself fit and trim and youthful, and that the effort, like the expectation, would be invisible. To that end, she now fixed herself a viscous muddy sludge in the blender, consumed it, and then pulled on gear, gathered the dogs and their leashes, and took herself for the morning run, all before Dr. Shock, her husband, the emeritus, rolled from bed.

"Your mother called," he said without looking up from the *Chronicle*, when she returned. "Hello, fellows," he said to the corgis, who dropped themselves panting at his feet, back legs splayed like chicken drumsticks. He'd sat there and not answered the phone. On the machine was her mother's tentative inquiry into Nana's distant, minorly exotic life. Her parents had not known what to make of her marriage to a man their age; they were still, many years later, perplexed, treating Nana as if she'd suddenly transformed from the young girl they'd known into the adult they couldn't fathom. Which was, essentially, the truth. She was an only child, the first on either side of her family to go to college; they could not debate what she'd learned there, nor what she'd acquired: a husband who was not only old enough to be her father, but divorced besides, with two estranged sons who were Nana's age. Never mind the degrees, undergraduate and graduate, a redundant pedigree that appeared to have led her no further than to housewifery, in the end. When they visited, her parents tried not to bother anybody, inhabiting the guest room like ghosts, treading lightly, making an occasional sound, leaving a slight impression. They brought her news of the neighborhood and their ailing siblings, and a box of waxy chocolates from the local candy maker. They sat working not to wince as they sipped at the wine Nana's husband insisted on serving them, an expensive bottle, always perfect with whatever meal they would politely eat but not enjoy, a meal Nana would have made from a gourmet magazine, something she'd imagined, in her parents' absence, that they would love, and then would realize, in their presence, was an offering far removed from their modest tastes. They wanted sweet tea and cream gravy. They wanted grandchildren.

Her husband, the professor, had assumed he could expand his in-laws' horizons. He had been confident he would seduce them, as he was famous for doing with students and colleagues by means of generosity, immodesty, flamboyant declarations, sodden affection. But although they were nothing but gracious around him, they were never going to fall under his spell. He could not make up for in charm what they withheld in mannerly disinterest.

"Daddy's had an accident," Nana's mother told her. Nana herself had taken a spill while running, twisting an ankle, falling hard on a hand, the fault of live oak roots, rumpling up the sidewalk, and of the dogs, each weaving in front of the other, trying to claim the lead. Her father had lost control of the car, driven onto a curb and into an outdoor café. Nana didn't even know Wichita had such things as outdoor cafés, and fortunately, the place wasn't popular enough for there to have been anyone sitting at the tables he'd crashed through. Her father had been injured, and then cited, requiring, first, surgery and, next, perhaps, a lawyer.

He came onto the phone now, clearing his throat, speaking weakly from his hospital bed. "Nana, honey, could you come help Mom?" And within the hour, Nana was behind the wheel of her car, headed from Houston to Kansas, Dr. Shock left behind to hold down the fort: care for the dogs and make an appearance at Libby's dinner party.

When she spoke with her husband, the next day, he dismissed her question about the party. "Dull," he declared, which closed the subject; he never tolerated dullness. This meant one of several things. Least likely was that the evening had actually been dull; next most plausible was that he'd gotten too drunk to fully recall events in a narrative worth retelling; most probable was that he'd done something he could very well remember and did not wish to discuss. Nana sighed, wondering if she should phone Libby to give a generic apology, then telling herself she'd consult with Helen first, discover what it was her husband wasn't saying.

"Was Helen wearing her poppy dress?" Nana asked.

He paused before responding. "I don't recall." And this was a lie, Nana could tell. But why lie over something so trivial as that?

"Was Rebecca there?"

"Yes," he said. "Her dress was black, in case you're wondering. A little black dress." The dogs began to bark then; Nana wondered if her husband had incited their racket, just to give himself a good reason to hang up. When Rebecca had been a young girl, she'd been overweight and overly furred, a mustache, thick arm hair, large brows; children had called her Ape Face. The transformation into confident womanhood had been impressive. Her parents weren't native Texans, but lately they'd been participating in their own version of unveiling the debutante, buying the new wardrobe and bringing her to parties. Dr. Shock had been exceedingly complimentary: "My god, you're gorgeous!" he'd declared one evening, genuinely astonished. "Look, everyone, isn't she spectacular?" And there Rebecca had stood, turning red in her tight-fitting green dress.

"The lads are protesting," her husband now said faintly into the phone. "I'll call you back." Nana could hear the dogs, those fat foxy creatures, yelping gloriously. It was easy to work them into such a state. You had merely to lead them to the plate glass porch door and point out the squirrel or cat running on the railing, or the automatic pool vacuum flipping its tail in the water as it carried on, side to side, end to end, tormenting mechanical scorpion. They were brothers, two and a half years in age. Lacking children, Nana and her husband had settled for dogs; their friends no doubt pitied their misplaced affection. This was the third pair of siblings they'd owned, first black Labs, next cocker spaniels, now the corgis—each set a slightly smaller breed. "We'll die with Chihuahuas," Nana had once told her husband.

"You'll die with Chihuahuas," he'd corrected her. "I'll die during the dachshunds." In the past, he had enjoyed pointing at the discrepancy in their ages, his future ghostliness that would haunt her. He didn't do that, anymore.

Nana's mother had asked about the dogs before she did her son-in-law. And how she struggled to call a man her own age her "son-in-law." The title begged to be inflected with irony, and her mother wasn't capable of irony.

"All well?" she said now, disallowing any answer other than an affirmative. She was rooting in her purse for lipstick, preparing herself for the morning's trip to the hospital. Nana had gotten in too late to visit her father the night before.

"Whose shoes are those?" Nana asked as they headed out, noticing for the first time several pairs of children's shoes by her parents' back door.

"Didn't I tell you who moved into the Dixons' old place?"

"Remind me," Nana said.

Peter Hinshaw. Nana's first boyfriend. Who now had a wife, and two children. He'd come to the open house only because he'd mistaken the address, thought it was Nana's home on the market. On a bored Sunday whim, he'd brought his wife and son and daughter, expecting to revisit the rooms where he had first had sex, first gotten drunk, first dropped acid, but instead, had found himself in the house next door, and his wife, untutored on any kind of context, had fallen in love.

Pete's wife adored her new neighbors, Nana's parents, as well. Her children had become their surrogate grandkids, running through the drive and yard that connected the properties, charging up the back steps and entering Nana's kitchen as if it were their own. They habitually removed their shoes, as was customary in their own home. They called Nana's parents by their first names, Bud and Lil. They had favorite places around the house, stations that they visited: the piano with its glass dish of meltaway mints, the base of the dining room table, where a town of blocks and thimbles was set up, a giant jar of change in the sewing room, too heavy to lift but lovely to study, and the aquarium into which they took turns dropping the minutest bits of food on the fishes' gawping mouths. Her mother's joy in these children, her father's reputed amused lenience, stung Nana. Nothing she herself could do would transport her parents in quite the same way. Indulging these two small people, ages three and five, a boy, his older sister, was as much as they could ever wish for.

After the visit to the hospital, Nana and her mother came home to find the children waiting on the back steps, pink chins in hands, two blond mops. They did not look like their father. Pete's skin had been sallow, his hair a dark, kinky, too-long mess, his eyes sunk in gloomy sockets. These drug-addict, rock-star features had attracted Nana, in high school. She was not immune to the appeal now. Pete had broken up with her to date a college girl, trading up. Nana couldn't even truly be surprised or personally wounded, although for a long while she had suffered—suffered as if kicked in the ribs by a horse, in tremendous pain but with no real hostility toward the animal itself. It might have been that college girl, all those years ago, whose allure had convinced Nana that she absolutely had to attend college herself. And a better one than the local U. She would be a coed from a school with a national reputation. She would show Pete Hinshaw.

In fact, her eventual marriage to her professor, from the next rung on her academic ladder, could very well have been the fruition of a seed sown when Pete Hinshaw had confessed to her that he was sorry, but he had met a college girl. *Say no more*, Nana had thought, sad but resigned.

"Hey, Pete," she greeted him at her mother's house, when he slouched in to retrieve his children. She wished he had lost hair and gained weight; instead, he looked as she remembered him, which was to say that she felt herself attuned to him, to everything about him, once more. She knew what those lips felt like, that coiled hair; she remembered the odor around his face of breath mint, smoke, beer. Still indulging and hiding his vices. The badly shaved rough neck.

"Ba-nana," he said drolly. He didn't disguise his lazy leering scan, dragged from foot to head like a reckless blade, like the amplified snarl of a guitar riff. From the hallway came the commotion of his children, the little boy and girl running headlong into the room then and suddenly silenced—brought up short, as if with reins—by his presence.

It was as if he beat them. Except he wouldn't beat them. He would embarrass them. He would make them self-conscious. He would not laugh at what wasn't amusing, nor praise indiscriminately, just from politeness. He was finicky, and frank, and relentless. "Intense," everyone had agreed uneasily, in high school; it had been a coup to be his girlfriend, to pass his peculiar muster.

"What are you no-necks up to?" he asked the girl, turning in her direction without releasing Nana from his glance.

"Playing," she said shyly, edging behind Nana's mother's knees.

"Playing," her brother echoed, a plea. In his hand he held an unraveling cardboard tube from wrapping paper; they'd been sword fighting, charging around the house's bottom floor.

"Peter," said Lil, flushed ecstatic as hostess, mother, ersatz grandmother. Queen of the castle, bestower of cardboard swords. "Sit down. Say hello to Nana, she's come to help." Her mother had no idea what had happened in her house, all those years ago. The blowouts in the basement, the escapades in Nana's bedroom, the hidden niches where the bottles and pills and baggies had been stashed—her own little stations, Nana thought. Her parents had been notoriously oblivious; it was her house that everybody had named as the location where they'd be spending the night.

The woman's innocence, compounded by the children's, had returned them to high school, Pete and Nana staring at each other beneath the whir of sweetness that ensued: bright pink juice being drunk and spilled, cookies offered and crumbled, sugar suffusing the atmosphere like pollen or perfume, while across the table, across years and other partners, a snaking heat coalesced between them, something engineered out of naughtiness and nostalgia, the knowledge of a shared naked history, wavering there like a faint layer of pollution.

Which would be thoroughly whisked away by the arrival of the wife. She wasn't the cool coed from back when. He'd married a physical therapist, an upbeat, wide-faced young woman, a leader of cheers. She, like her children, entered Nana's old home as if its inhabitants were her close relations, a confidence having to do with good intentions, purity. "Honey, I'm so sorry about Bud" were her first words to Nana's mother. "I took him a can of cashews and a puzzle book. Peter, you know you have messages on the machine?"

"Unemployed," Pete explained to Nana. "Downsized."

"Taking stock, sweetheart," scolded the wife. "Weighing some other options."

"That's right," Nana's mother concurred.

Pete's wife held out her hand to shake Nana's. "I would recognize you anywhere! All those pictures in the albums." Her smile made her eyes wrinkle up atop her apple round cheeks. She seemed so unlikely, Nana thought, though maybe Pete needed such a girl to keep him in line. To provide cover, to make small talk and utter pleasantries. A person person, as opposed to a misanthrope. To her every address she appended a term of endearment: *sweetness, monkey, pie-pie.* Her children scooted onto chairs beside her when she sat at the table, each leaning close to her radiant goodwill.

But what did he offer her? Martyrdom?

"Come see my tree house?" Pete said to Nana.

"It was our tree house," the little girl said, "but Daddy took it."

"Our tree house," the boy repeated sadly.

Pete stood, patting the shirt pocket over his heart, where a hard-pack of Camels showed itself now. "I'll check the messages," he told his wife. "Bye Lil. Coming?" he asked Nana.

Dr. Shock wanted to hear all about her ex-boyfriend.

"Why didn't you answer, before?" Nana asked. She imagined him ignoring the ringing phone, humming right beside the machine, bored, as she left her messages. It was nearly midnight, and she was up on the roof of the porch at her parents' home, there beneath the tree limbs, looking down at the Dixons' old house. Pete's house. Faint pink night-lights lit the upstairs hall; in the basement, where Mr. Dixon used to hole up with his nasty habits, another light was on, this of the bare-bulb variety. Nana guessed Pete would be under that bulb, playing the phantom of Mr. Dixon. Either there or in his tree house, designed for the children, co-opted by him. He'd led her up its metal circular-stairway treads, into its boys' club confines. First he'd gotten her stoned (hookah: who'd seen its Ganesha self, its burbling trunks, since high school?), then he'd leaned over to put his lips on hers.

The night had turned brisk, as it always did just before Halloween, a wind had whipped up, and what few leaves were left in the trees slapped against the porch roof, switched at Nana's legs. Her mother would have been horrified to find her here, this same place Nana came in the old days, imperiling herself on the roof. Would she never cease scaring that poor woman?

Meanwhile, Nana's husband was drinking. "The old soldier's joy," he informed her jauntily. He would be snug in his reading chair in their Houston study, paging through weighty art books. He couldn't concentrate on words, in this state, but enjoyed falling into the massive color plates of these expensive texts. His Rauschenbergs, his de Koonings, his Twomblys, and, saddest of all, his Rothkos. In this abstract mood ("This is when I relish visions of suicide," he'd told her once), he tonight discerned something about her commentary concerning Kansas, peeled back her father's (stable) condition, her mother's (chatty) busyness, to inquire into the neighbor, the former boyfriend, the surprise, the narrative aside. Underpainting, Nana thought, the hidden figures beneath the public subject. He could perceive it everywhere. At the hospital a nurse had frowned at Nana's swollen purple hand, diagnosing sprain in the index finger and wrist, swaddling her in a bright white bandage right there over her father's body in bed. The nurse had used her teeth to tear the tape, tidy as a beaver. Nana had been only dimly aware of an ache, the aftereffects of her fall in Houston, pain she'd been able to neglect during her tranced 600-mile drive. In the tree house with Pete, loopy on hashish, she had tucked in her pinky and ring finger, raised the expertly made package to his face near hers as if pointing a gun.

"Tell me about the reunion with the boyfriend," said her husband. "Spare no detail. A hug?"

"Uh-huh."

"Peck on the cheek? Kiss? Lingering glance?"

Nana heard his longing to have her say that they had fooled around. He wanted to be titillated by the situation, turned on by the scenario, have a little phone sex intermission before returning to his heavy art books. He liked it when men flirted with Nana, when they stood too close or stared overlong, tucked in her dress tag or brushed against her. And in the past, Nana had exaggerated, especially while making love with her husband, so that he could feel like the winner, so that she could feel like the prize. He made use of it as foreplay, stimulation; also, he seemed to think that it would excuse his own lecherous tendencies. But now that his inquiry might lead to something true, Nana found it difficult to remember how she usually played the game. "You sound like you want me to sleep with him," she eventually said.

"Do I?"

"You do."

"Maybe I do. If you did, would you tell me about it?"

"I don't want to sleep with him," she lied. "We already did that, a long time ago."

"Therefore, if you slept with him again, your overall stats wouldn't change." This number was known to Dr. Shock. A mere handful. Nana had been timid. His number of partners was much higher, higher even than might be expected given his twenty-plus-year head start. He couldn't remember all their names, those many women with whom he'd had sex.

"The stats would change." She had never been unfaithful; she had never wanted to be unfaithful. The stats had already changed.

"Nana," he laughed. He was so confident, she thought, so sure that she still felt herself the lucky object of the professor's esteemed attention. In her mind, she opened the drawer of his night table, just to be appalled by the number of pill bottles there, the dirty secret of his decline. At that moment, the side door at the Dixons' clattered open, the familiar metal racket from long ago, of Mr. Dixon's angry predawn departures to the newspaper stand—the boy on the bike couldn't get to their block early enough for Mr. Dixon. Except now it was Pete emerging, and he didn't let the storm door rattle shut but held it on its wheezing hydraulic arm, then simply knelt on his side steps and lit a cigarette. Nana watched him from her perch.

"Shhh," she whispered to her husband, without thinking.

They made love in her bedroom, on the bed where they'd first made love, when they were sixteen years old. Could these be the same sheets? Quite possibly. Their bodies loved each other, she thought, they remembered, they knew what to do when put together. Outside, the sky was tin-can gray, a depressing light that helpfully softened Nana's embarrassment. Yet, naked, there was no longer awkwardness between them; his suit of flesh, unlike her husband's, did not hang loose upon a discernible skeleton. His mouth tasted of marijuana, his body temperature seemed to be precisely the same as hers, his arrangement of limbs designed to perfectly match with hers, so that embracing him was like entering a dream, like falling under a spell. They moved with the familiarity of instinct, and when they rolled over, still wholly attached, it reminded Nana of her dogs at play, harmonious intimacy. Was she really comparing them to animals? Forsaking words, or even articulate thought? But was that a reason to disclaim the significance of what had passed between them? In fact, mightn't she find it all the more profound for that reason?

She wanted to say that she loved him—because she loved what had just happened, because she loved the strange intoxicant they had recovered and shared—but only a fool made that claim first. She knew enough to know that.

"Last time we used a rubber," he eventually said, a half smile on his contemptuous lips. Nana hadn't even thought about protection, proof of her innocence, evidence of this third- and not first-degree crime.

"Last time it moved along a little faster." She was trying to match his nonchalance, but nothing could have been further from the truth of how she felt.

Downstairs they heard her mother come home. Nana had claimed a headache this morning, watching from her window as, first, her neighbors took themselves away, the mom in the car with the boy and the girl in the back, waving to Pete in his sweatpants on the porch. He'd raised his eyes from their car as it pulled down the drive, seeing Nana through the glass. When her mother also drove away, it wasn't long before he rapped on the back door. She opened it and then did not move out of the way, forcing him, if he planned to come in, to step up and into her arms. They hardly spoke as they wandered the familiar path from kitchen through dining room, then upstairs and down the hall to Nana's girlhood room. "Haven't been up here lately," he murmured as she shut the door, latched the hook and eye she'd screwed into the woodwork years ago.

Later, when they listened as her mother made her slow way along the same route, then heard her knock on the bedroom door, Nana finally registered something like what she'd expected: guilt, shame, delinquency. Till that moment, she'd been operating in some sort of performance or memory, some hazy excited intuition of what felt good, and of what came next, and of the merciful gift-like absence of her mind. Fantasy—the heady stuff that disassembled when she opened her eyes. She croaked out that she'd be right down

"Daddy's coming home this afternoon," her mother said through the door. "Maybe you could pick him up while I fix supper?"

Pete was sitting on the bed's edge by then, still naked, staring the way an athlete did on the bench after, revving, yet worn out. He turned then and gave her a devilish grin. "Sure," Nana called.

"*Daddy,*" he mouthed. "*Supper.*"

She laid her head on Pete's back, on the soft top knobs of his spinal column, where his hair reached her cheek, where a few loose coils drifted and fell onto her sheets. Again, she wished to say that she loved him—not because she was sure she loved him but because it was such a perfectly insular sentence. No one knew they were here, together. She wished never to leave this instant, its singularity and repleteness.

"Keep her in the kitchen," he said into Nana's ear. "I'll go out the front."

Her father reclined across the backseat, pain medication making his sentences syrupy, his bare toes at the end of a heavy full-leg cast resting on the door handle. Without meaning to, he'd let down the back window. The air was wet, cool, and when Nana accelerated, a wobble went up due to odd pressure. She cracked her own window. The chill felt good, was clearing the odor of antiseptic and plaster from the vehicle. Her husband was only four years younger than this man. Of course she had always known that. It was because her father was sedated, prostrate, because he'd not bothered to put on his eyeglasses, that his age and vulnerability, and by extension her husband's age and vulnerability, now suddenly upset Nana.

And also because of Pete, because making love with him had left her younger.

"Mom's fixing meat loaf," she announced, overloud.

"Mom," he said, the only word he'd ever need; it would be his last, she thought.

For the rest of the ride Nana let herself fall into a full flashback, sink into sex with Pete. In the windy car it warmed her like a glowing pilot light, steady, ready to flare to action.

On the phone with her husband she lied, claiming that her father was still not home yet. Her husband would never call her mother to find out otherwise, never contact that woman who was peer to his first wife, and yet also, paradoxically, a preposterous mate to him. Once more Nana sat on the roof, out of earshot, endangered; a cold dusk was settling, the sky was tinged green. "They're worried about infection," she told him. "He still has a fever. And diarrhea," she added, for the verity that only a non sequitur could provide.

"And how's the boyfriend? That good neighbor?"

"Pete?" She looked down automatically, to the places he might occupy, and felt a faint ignition in her chest.

"Peter, the boy next door, that one. How's the reunion shaping up? Nothing like a rekindled romance, in my experience."

"What do you mean?"

"I mean I fucked Deborah, a few years after the divorce, and it was terrific. Much better than when we were married, light-years better, like strangers, like Anaïs Nin characters. Ahh," he sighed happily, for a moment off in memory somewhere, then back: "And of course that was long before I met you. Now, tell me about Peter."

*Pete*, Nana corrected, as if cradling his warm head in her palm. "I don't like that word," she said.

"You use it all the time."

"Not as a verb." She'd not *fucked* anybody, ever. "He's fine," she said, of Pete, wondering what her husband really hoped to hear. They weren't often separated for more than an afternoon; conferences at one time had kept him away for a few days. They'd spoken on the phone frequently, then; now it bothered Nana to hear his self-assured voice, his confession about his ex that seemed to demand a reciprocal response, tit for tat. It was like a parent trying to coax a badly lying child into admitting an obvious truth. Or maybe it felt like that because that was what it so closely, factually, resembled. "He's pathetic," she plunged ahead. "Unemployed, hanging around like a sullen teenager. Even down to the tree house. He'll be lucky if his wife doesn't leave him."

Dr. Shock laughed. "Just like me! Isn't that what I wrote in your dream letter?" Then he told her he had been invited to the Merrills' for dinner, was leaving in just a little while. Their friends would take care of him, in Nana's absence, rally round to feed and entertain him.

"Stay away from the stemware," she warned. He'd broken many glasses, over time, at the Merrills'. They insisted on serving wine in extremely fine crystal; sometimes Dr. Shock demanded to use a jelly jar, prophylactically. It was a standing joke; their friends found him charming; he was famous for his passionate arguments, stormy exits, followed by exorbitant apologies, heartfelt embraces, exquisite handwritten notes. Beloved, he was, flaws and all. And Pete was . . .

As if sensing Nana's wobbling loyalty, Dr. Shock said one more thing before hanging up: "I don't care if you sleep with him, but you have to tell me. Agreed?"

"I'm not going to sleep with him," Nana said. She closed the cell phone and held it to her throat, shut her eyes and felt Pete all around her.

Now she debated phoning Helen. One wanted to tell, she realized. After the initial crucial privacy, one wished to speak aloud what had transpired, spread the incendiary heat. As an excuse, as an opening gambit, she could ask Helen to keep an eye on Dr. Shock's drinking at the Merrills'; also, she could thank Helen for the flowers, which had arrived that afternoon at her parents', lurid nonnative blossoms that had vaguely alarmed Lil. Nana could ask what Helen would be wearing tonight, what had transpired at Libby's, two evenings before. Rebecca answered at Helen's house.

"She's over at your place," the girl said.

"No, I'm in Kansas. My father was in an accident." She started to fill in with the information about his hospitalization, his (invented) fever, and so on, when Rebecca cut her off with an exasperated sigh.

"Come on, woman. Do you really not know what's going on with them? Is that really just how totally out of touch you are?"

"I'm sorry?" Nana's first thought was that Rebecca was drunk or high, that she had regressed to the terrifying adolescence her parents believed had, thank god, passed.

"It's been, like, *years*," Rebecca went on. "If *I* know, if my dipshit *brothers* know, it just seems impossible that you don't know. Doesn't it? Don't you?" The girl paused, her youthful impatience perceptibly demanding an answer. Nana had pushed herself back to the window that led onto the roof, was beginning to climb back inside. Fear had gripped her; she felt she might suddenly, after all these years, truly be at risk of falling from her perch. "OK, whatever," said Rebecca. "I'll tell her you called. *Bye now,*" this last a sardonic Texas Lady farewell.

Nana was out the front door before she realized she'd emerged from the guest room, passed through the hall, and gone down the stairs. They'd flown beneath her feet, as they always had, lightly, as if she were floating from second to first floor, noting on her way the purple and black flowers from Helen, obscene red stamen lingering on her retina as she left her parents' porch. She went immediately to the Dixons' house, stepping up Pete's walkway and to his front, rather than side, door. Her mother did not have a view of his front door from her kitchen window. Her father could not see it from where he was propped before the television in the den. Pete did not immediately ask her in, but stood on the other side of a torn black screen. She must have had a look about her, because his expression grew more guarded. And had she come here to test for that guardedness?

From the kitchen, in the back of the house that shared a similar floor plan with her parents', came the sound of singing, of children laughing. That was what he guarded.

"I came to say goodbye," Nana chose to say.

Now he unhooked the door, pushed it open. He hadn't shaved; she longed to bury her face in his rough warm throat. She wished to squeeze shut her eyes, banish both her husband and Helen, forget Rebecca's no-nonsense voice, and disappear in Pete's embrace. But he turned his back, picked up a beer from the end table next to a chair. Why was he in here, in the dark, instead of in the lighted kitchen? What had he been doing when she rang the bell? Back when he'd found the college girl, when he'd shrugged his helpless farewell to Nana, she'd taken her cue from him, too; she would not show her need.

"Daddy's home?" he asked.

"Daddy's home."

"No complications? Lawsuits? Sometimes I'm a lawyer."

She shook her head. "He's fully insured," she said. "Over-insured, maybe."

"Good to be insured," Pete said. That was what she'd hoped he would offer, Nana saw: insurance, a plan B. "And I'm not much of a lawyer," he added.

When her husband had been hosted by the department in Houston, they had taken him out to dinner with other endowed chairs in the liberal arts. Helen had been married to one. Dr. Shock had phoned Nana later, in California, to tell her the news: her old friend, now Mrs. Helen Nolan, ready to reenter her life, incentive, lucky happenstance, sign. Helen might have been standing beside him in the hotel room even then, pulling earrings out of her ears, or replacing them, running her hands through her hair, lighting a cigarette, pre- or postcoital.

Nana could not say which of those people, her husband or her best friend, was most responsible for the pain she now felt, that kicked-in-the-ribs sensation. She had no doubt that Rebecca had spoken the truth, that she knew better than Nana what was going on in her home when she wasn't there.

"Beer?" Pete finally said, glancing reluctantly toward the noisy kitchen, where the beer apparently was kept.

"Do you think I should stay here?" she asked, and, when he scowled, as if she'd meant his living room, added, "In Wichita, I mean? Should I stay with them for a while?"

"I don't know. They'd be happy." He fell back into his chair, looked at the ceiling. He could be cold, she remembered; it was all coming back to her. When she began crying, he jumped up and hustled her out the front door. "This way," he said, not waiting for her to agree, but leading her around the drive, to the back, to his tree house, where he lit the gas heater. "Don't tell the codes people," he said, "but this is an illegal appliance." The small space filled with the odor of both the gas and the struck match. They sat on the floor beside each other, knees touching. Nana put her hand on his, and he removed it. "No," he said. "That would be a mistake."

*Why?* she wanted to wail. He'd disallowed her asking him then, when they were sixteen, and he disallowed it now. And this precluded other questions she might want to have answered: Why aren't I *enough*? For anyone, it seemed?

Instead, he reached for the hookah.

"Mr. Dixon died in your basement," Nana told him. Mr. Dixon: the pharmacist dishonored by drug abuse, relegated to his dungeon, where he finally overdosed one long-ago day.

"Yeah," Pete said as he slowly exhaled, smoke making a thin trail overhead. "It's got that aura." From the tree house they could see both the kitchens below, his and hers, figures moving in the lighted windows. Nana took her turn with the hookah, inhaled, felt the blue glow enter her. She and Pete had first kissed at a party in the country, sitting around a fire, smoking pot. They'd not said much to each other, just leaned away from the group and into each other. They'd only paused from kissing to take their turns with the passed joint. Now Pete held a lighter to the bowl, circling it expertly with the flame.

"You'd rather get high than kiss," she said. "Or make love."

He looked up, his eyes reflecting the lighter's yellow. "Or anything," he said. The hashish had calmed him, made him the beautiful boy he'd been. She nodded, hoping she looked to him like that girl she'd been. They'd indulged her desire, this morning; now they would indulge his.

She came home red-eyed, her shoes filthy with mud from the yard between their houses. She slipped them off at the back door, left them with the other children's shoes there.

Her father had somehow ambulated in from the den, and was arranged sideways at the kitchen table, bright white cast propped on a second chair. Her mother fussed between stove and table, narrating happily, like a twittering bird. As usual, her parents were completely oblivious to the redness of Nana's eyes—product of misery plus drugs—and the odor she must surely have brought with her. On the table, meat loaf. Milk. Soft bread and margarine. Nana fell into her chair as if she'd been pushed.

It was so exhausting to consider, the whole past that she would now have to revisit and amend, unstitch and patch back together, her husband and her friend Helen, from graduate school days to the current moment. Right now: sitting under the twinkling lights and the elaborate bug zappers in the Merrills' courtyard sculpture garden, where they would be passing appetizers, discussing art and politics, staring at one another over the rims of fine stemware.

"Just in time!" her mother said, hovering above the food, filling three plates, then settling in her customary seat.

"Thanks, Mom," said Nana's father.

"We're so glad to have you here," Nana's mother said to her. "I was telling Dad, even in these crazy circumstances, it's awfully nice."

Concentrating hard atop the foggy effects of Pete's hash-ish, Nana picked up her fork using her uninjured, wrong hand and faced this simple meal. It was very difficult, as if she were starting all the way back at the beginning.

# IFF

"**F**AILURE TO YIELD," MY neighbor says knowingly, nodding at the crooked stop sign. The accident had not quite knocked it over, and the city has not quite made repairs. On the tilted sign today is a poster. It appeared the way all the posters of the lost beloveds do, taped fluttering in the wind, wrinkled with weather, cheaply produced and faithfully hung, flagging—nagging—every tree and pole.

"Weird," says his companion, squinting at the print. A gay couple, Dave and Raymond, past their scandalous prime, now just two elderly men trying not to trip on the broken sidewalks.

But the photo is not of a dog or cat, but of a teenage girl, and the description is far lengthier—typed font rather than Magic Markered scrawl—than the ones describing pets. Pets are so simple, by comparison. For starters, they want to be found.

"Does somebody have to die before they fix that sign?" Raymond himself is dying, his partner Dave now his nurse, holding an elbow, navigating the oxygen tank. In the old days, their roles were reversed; Dave was the needy one, an alcoholic loose cannon, likely to be rip-roaring down the street midmorning drunk as a skunk, accompanied by his dog, Plato the black Lab, also drunk. And Raymond, who sold cars, whose voice on the radio for years had promised Albuquerque listeners they'd be "Toyotally satisfied!," would be summoned home by one nosey parker or another to retrieve his errant boyfriend.

"This wasn't here yesterday," Raymond says angrily. "We'd have noticed." We study it the way we do the others, hoping to be the hero, to perform the neighborly deed, to sight the lost, notify the owner, reunite the duo. Never mind the reward; virtue is its own.

"A *mystery*," Dave savors, he who's never had a child, he who's lately been charged with finding fun wherever he can. He and Raymond routinely tour the blocks surrounding the park at dusk. The bicyclist who pulls over and uses his muscled leg as a kickstand is also a regular, as is the woman being dragged by her three riotous dogs—*working* dogs, she will proudly inform you—as are the recently arrived retirees from Minnesota, and the grumpy hermit watercolorist. An impromptu neighborhood meeting convenes beneath the sign; we begin discussing the missing girl. Her name is Ashley Elizabeth MacLean but she also answers to Madonna Rage.

"Madonna *Rage*?" says the young mother with the elaborate stroller. She and her husband divided local opinion several years ago when they demolished an ancient adobe home and built in its place a modern mansion. Our neighborhood has fallen on hard times; that a young couple wished to live here impressed us. That they also wished to rip out a historical structure sullied the matter. Addicts and pigeons had been holing up in the old house. Feral cats. The place didn't so much fall down as disintegrate when the wrecking ball swung, a drift of ashy pink sand. The couple's new baby has softened some hearts. Not all hearts. Dave and Raymond are not fond of the little family, although they were very kind to my family, when we were young and our son was a baby. Their dog Plato was a puppy then; in some square piece of wet concrete across the park both Plato and Liam left their youthful footprints.

The new mother furrows her brow as she reads the rest of the poster's description. Her expression says that the swaddled infant in her care will never run away. Never dye her hair blue or pierce her tongue. Never be identified for any passing stranger as someone with scars on her arms from having cut them. Her stroller's complicated wheels rotate smoothly into reverse, bumping over the curb without rousing the occupant. Her smugness sends up in me an urge for disaster—where's the driver who fails to yield when you need him?

"I wonder if she's one of those gangsters at the gazebo?"

"When I call the cops, they say to call the school. When I call the school, they say blame the parents. The parents throw up their hands." Mrs. Minnesota throws up hers. "Typical pass the buck."

"The noise!" says the watercolorist. He is grizzled and unpleasant, yet his paintings are sentimental landscapes: the Sandias, Santa Fe, Mexican fieldworkers in gold and periwinkle meadows. "Noise is pollution, too," he adds, as if expecting argument. There's always something to complain about, and these days it's the teenagers in the park. Like flocks of birds to certain trees, they've recently been mysteriously drawn here. We turn as a group to appraise the centerpiece gazebo, empty now, innocuous. Site of weddings, barbecues, quinceañera parties. Only an hour or so earlier, high school students were smoking and shrieking and stomping on the benches, music beating like jungle drums from their car stereos. From a distance—from my kitchen window, for instance—you can't tell if they're playing or fighting, celebrating or rebelling. They probably don't know, either. At Christmas they methodically broke every single tiny bulb in the strings woven through the trellising, a labor far more elaborate than the city's in hanging the lights.

"Seventeen," Mr. Minnesota says wistfully, concerning Madonna Rage. He and his wife are newest to the neighborhood, zealous busybodies, scrambling to catch up on decades of gossip. They exchange a look that maybe means that they had a teenage girl themselves, once upon a time in the Midwest, that this trouble isn't unfamiliar, and also that they are glad it is no longer theirs. Their troublemaker would maybe be a mother now, her offspring—their grandchildren—not yet old enough to raise this particular kind of hell. "Take care," they call as they resume their evening's power walk, hands cinching rubber weights, legs in military conjunction.

The working dogs are restless; off-duty, they have been known to urinate on people's feet; "OK, OK, OK," their owner scolds ineffectually, letting them drag her away. In her yard, she and her husband and father practice roping; more than once I've been startled by the steer-size sawhorse, that crazy creature fitted with longhorns. The woman was a rodeo queen back when, Miss Bernalillo County; her father occupies the attic, like a rumbling thought in the mind.

What do the neighbors know or think about me?

"Kids take their health for granted," the weathered cyclist says, refastening his helmet, straightening his blaze-orange safety vest. The poster's author has noted Ashley Elizabeth MacLean/Madonna Rage's pills, the appointments she must keep. She isn't stable.

"What does it mean, 'permanent retainer'?" asks Dave, stalling. I think it must be he who insists on these evening constitutionals, he who needs air, to escape the house and its smothering atmosphere of illness. When he was hauled away caterwauling in the street, all those years ago, he would berate Raymond, slapping at his arms, blithe and slippery, "I'm a kept man! I'm humiliating my meal ticket!" But he grew up, and then old. Plato the dog died long ago.

"I'm guessing for her teeth," I say, of the retainer. "My cousin had one. She used to pop it out to scare people." Like a mechanical drawer ejected from her face, two bright bits of porcelain on a tray.

"Excellent," he says, nodding. Raymond clutches his arm—those tusklike fingernails, the particular guilt-producing grip that signals the stalling is over, time to go home. Dave gives me a rueful smile over Raymond's head. "Gay *and* gay," I always said approvingly of Dave; my ex-husband dismissed both men. He eventually dismissed the whole shabby neighborhood, its hundred-year-old houses, its cranks and misfits, packed himself up and moved to a gated golf course community carved out just below the mountains. *Seemly*, I suppose you'd call his new place.

The men make for their house down the block—their forsaken garden where once there were roses, their smudgy convertible once waxed every weekend—oxygen machine trailing like an old pet.

The watercolorist's cell phone begins singing, although it's hard to imagine who would call him; he severed ties with his sister after a shouting match with both her and the fire department when she reported the amount of potential accelerant he kept in his garage studio. "For your own good!" she pleaded, weeping on the sidewalk. "Interfering *cunt!*" he shrieked in response, and then the uniforms restrained him.

The jogger restores his earbuds. "Bye," we say to one another. We all head toward our houses around the park, to the cloistered business that goes on inside them. Only occasionally is there evidence of a flaw, a public announcement of failure, rescue summoned in the wee hours, the open spectacle of something gone horrendously wrong. The drunk man singing in the street with his drunk dog. Maniac painter and frantic sister. Today, this poster.

The last part of the message is in italics, as if the author were whispering directly into the child's ear: there is still time for her to graduate from high school, this voice promises, all will be forgiven, her father loves her. The bald appeal, the father's pain, the girl's desperation seem to require shelter. Seeing their intimacy exposed makes my heart hurt, my face hot, as if there were something I ought to be doing for these strangers, some action I should have taken ages ago.

I was a difficult girl myself, growing up, causing my parents heart-hurting hardship. Also, my son is a teenager, so I feel for this parent, especially given the evident fact of his being the only parent. I imagine him tragically widowed, although I am that more pedestrian sort of single parent, divorced.

But maybe what interests me, what stopped me at this stop sign today, involves another teenage girl, my son's girlfriend.

I wish *that* girl would disappear.

*Do you go to school with the missing girl?* I text Liam. School ended hours ago, but he won't be home. He is with

The Girlfriend. When he is with me, he texts her; with her, he texts me. But he is always more with her than with me.

He responds immediately. *Used to. Now she's at the Bad Girl school.*

*Pregnant?*

*Druggy. Also knives. Armed and dangerous.* Before I can reply, he's sent another, speedy on the keypad. *You said pregnant girls weren't bad.* He's good at reminding me that my ideal self is better than my daily one. In the middle of my composition of a suitable response, another of his arrives. *Her dad's a tranny.*

*Really?* I have neither the manual dexterity nor sufficient patience to ask for clarification via text.

*Wouldst I lie to you?*

He wouldn't. I peer into the girl's eyes with new guesses about her trouble. Her father now seems more vividly defenseless. Albuquerque would not necessarily be friendly to a man like him. Its citizens might understand and sympathize with the child who wished to abandon such a parent. The girl's half smile possibly reflected her ambivalence toward everything and everybody. It might have held her own prospect of change, of the scissors and dye and razors and rings—*knives!*—she would use to transform herself, of the escape she would make from her home. Of the parent she would leave behind, who is now out hanging signs on signs, begging for mercy.

I glance around for witnesses, then snatch the poster.

"Looky here," I say to my mother-in-law. Gloria is startled, as always, by someone entering the house; pensive and elderly, she rarely steps outside, spending the day studying catalogs and the newspaper, adrift in her relationship with the world, first alarmed and then grateful when her grandson or I come home to interrupt her solitude.

"What's this?" She peers through cat-eye bifocals at the girl.

"Liam says she's at the Bad Girl school. He says her dad's a tranny." Though it is evening, Gloria still wears pajamas and a bed jacket; her life is convalescence. She presents a kind of nostalgic 1940s glamour-girl-in-the-boudoir fashion statement, face glossy with makeup, white hair teased in an updo. Vain, she keeps the lights low, and seems ever ready to drop supine and sultry on a chaise.

"What does that mean, 'tranny'?"

"Either he dresses like a woman, or he is a former woman. One of those, I think."

We settle into cocktails and speculation. For many years, Gloria ran a beauty school and hair salon in Ohio. She feels a lot of affection for young girls, and also a lot of impatience. Like me, she doesn't trust Liam's girlfriend. She stares at the missing-girl poster and hazards guesses both suspicious and bighearted: Spoiled child grabbing at attention! Poor confounded thing in need of a mother!

Gloria says she once knew a boy who dressed as a girl, back in Columbus. Also, she's wondered if our alternate mail lady might not once have been a man. She finds it sad that people cannot be happy with who they are. This overarching insight leads her, as most of our conversations do, to her stepson Nathan, my ex-husband. His real mother died while Nathan was in high school, and his father married Gloria a few years later. Because she had no children of her own, Gloria was eager to declare Nathan her son. But Nathan didn't feel he needed another mother; he vaguely resented his father's needing another wife. Since his father's death, he seems to have forgiven Gloria her blameless presence, her unrequited affection for him. But he can't muster a responding love. He tried to explain it to me once, shrugging helplessly, claiming that he shared no blood relation with the woman.

"Me, either," I said.

"So you shouldn't feel an obligation to her," he said, mistaking what I'd meant.

"No," I told him, "you and *I* don't share blood." And he went opaque, that therapist talent he has. It is as if he can fall into a detached trance, right before your eyes. Willfully decline to face facts.

"I hate Friday night," I pronounce. "It's by far the most anxious night of the week." The sirens have started up. There's a high school football rivalry to settle. A girl has gone missing. My son isn't home, and it's already dark, not even a moon this evening.

"Maybe that's why I miss cigarettes the most on Fridays," Gloria sighs. She'd still smoke if it weren't for Liam. "Shall I shampoo you?"

"That sounds wonderful." I smile at her effort to rally me; usually, it's the other way around. "Have you decided about tomorrow?"

"I haven't." Gloria is debating whether or not to attend Nathan's wedding. Her loyalty has shifted from him to me in the year and a half since she moved into our home. After his departure, Gloria stayed.

"I can't even bring myself to dislike that woman," I admit. "Don't not go on my account."

"Oh, I don't dislike her, either," says Gloria. "Just sorry for her. For that matter, I feel sorry for Nathan. He has no idea what he's getting himself into. But she's just pathetic."

The fiancée is a far needier person than I, an innocent. You can see it in the way she greets you, grabbing with two palms to shake your hand, to detain you in her clutch, the watchful face that wants to please, her childlike smallness, the frizzy hair that suggests frightened thoughts.

"When I used to see her playing piano, back before I knew about her and Nathan, I kept thinking of her as that busy little tyrannosaurus. The BLT." I make Gloria laugh by illustrating the fiancée's attack on the keyboard, her fierce concentration and her too-small, nail-bitten hands. Gloria has a great laugh. It's good to live with a laugh like that.

"Do they really want me there, Nathan and the BLT?" she asks.

"Go with Liam. I know they want Liam there." If Liam weren't around, we would all fly apart. What would be the point, without him? "You're hard," Nathan explained, when he left me. He couldn't meet my eyes, but what he said is true: I peer at the world through an ever-narrowing skeptical lens. I make no new friends, and I trust strangers less. Nathan and I are the same age, but I've had to deduce that women grow hard over time while men grow soft. He had lived with what I called *realism* and he named *cynicism* long enough; our marriage had accrued it, each year another layer of shell. Finally, he decided to climb out. I could sense what he'd shed, witness his heart's expansion—like something formerly root-bound, prepared to embrace the waiting pathos that was his next wife. "He needs a project," I told my mother-in-law, but understood, privately, that he merely needed to be able to smile.

Nathan will never acknowledge the true beginning of our demise as a couple. It was Gloria's coming to live with us. She moved in after a failed suicide attempt. Nathan and

I disagreed about it, me believing (believing yet) that the woman was entitled to determine her own fate, my husband the therapist doggedly taking another view.

"It wasn't a very good attempt," Gloria has admitted. "Maybe Nathan is right, I was crying for help." She downed a bottle of Xanax. The dose was too low to kill her. For a few weeks afterward she was incarcerated in a mental institution, finally phoning Nathan, here in New Mexico, to come spring her. She moved into our guest room; sixteen-year-old Liam was good for her. I like to think that I was also good for her, the two of us trading stories at the kitchen table at the end of every day. "What was there left for me?" she will ask rhetorically. Her husband died and her business went bankrupt. She was bored, tired, done. This was in Ohio; part of the trouble may have been the weather, that annual midwestern mourning damp and gray. Here in Albuquerque she marvels daily at the forecast: *mostly sun*. Here, *mourning* and *gray* describe the ubiquitous querying doves.

Nathan's new marriage might grieve my mother-in-law, yet it might also distract her, give her one more thing to live for, its uncertain but surely jagged plotline. Nathan has not stopped compelling her concern.

As Liam has not yet stopped compelling mine. He, too, is a conversation touchstone. Gloria retrieves the wine bottle from the refrigerator and refills our glasses. She drinks all day—mimosas in the morning, chardonnay after noon—yet never seems drunk. It pleases her to have company in it, and in the snacking that will become our evening meal, the two of us dining on little bites of cheese or meat on crackers, shrimp, baby carrots and tomatoes, chips and dips. We pass the hours this way, as if at a cocktail party for two.

"Is The Girlfriend going to the wedding?" Gloria asks.

"I don't know. It's an occasion to put on fancy clothes and be admired." If I insist, Liam will come home, will leave his loitering post at the coffee shop where The Girlfriend works on Friday nights to join me and his grandmother. He would be present yet texting her, politely ours, but not passionately. "I was thinking that I wished it was The Girlfriend who'd run away," I confess, "instead of poor Madonna Rage."

Gloria nods in understanding; as a suicidal person, she has an expansive empathy. "But then Liam would be crushed," she says. We both know that The Girlfriend's moods are like natural phenomena, rolling over the house and determining its atmosphere. "He loves her too much," Gloria says. "She has him wrapped around her little finger. It's not good."

"I know." I had that power over Nathan once, and for a long while. Gloria had had it, too, with Nathan's father.

"He's too nice to her. She's toying with him. She's waiting to do better."

I sigh unhappily. It is all true, a fact of femaleness that Liam could not know but that his grandmother and I understand with chilly certainty. Every few months The Girlfriend breaks up with Liam, sending him into a terrible despair. Its depths are frightening; I would rather suffer it myself than witness it in him. Already thin, he has to be forced to eat. At night, I have to sit beside him on his bed, stroke his forehead, hold him against me as he shudders in tears, waiting for sleep. "You have to learn to step away," I counsel. "Turn off your phone," I beg him. It seems terrible to have to advise indifference. But even if he'd take the advice, he can't turn off his feelings. He sleeps with one of

The Girlfriend's sweaters, a bundle of orange angora like a wadded blankie. For Christmas, he gave her a diamond ring. Both Gloria and I were horrified when he showed us, his face wounded when we didn't congratulate his thoughtfulness, his generosity, his large vulnerable heart. That diamond like an evil twinkle in a villain's eye.

He would want to kill himself if The Girlfriend left him for good. Neither of us mentions this, but the thought is with us in the room. It has been punctuated by the lost-girl poster, by her father's similar fear clearly lingering between the lines.

"Shampoo?" Gloria reminds me hopefully.

At the kitchen sink, she massages my wet scalp with her seasoned professional hands. I luxuriate in the intimacy, my mother-in-law's scrubbing nails vaguely erotic near my ears, the fragrant suds popping, warm water flowing over my head, a cool trickle leaking along my neck and down my shirt. At first, Gloria was suspicious of my requests for a cut, sensitive to being condescended to. But over time she's let herself enjoy her old talent. She cultivated a new hairstyle for me, something backward-looking, an asymmetrical bob from the sixties, dyed a purple brown named aubergine. She likes to say the word. Though shaky and tentative at other chores, her fingers move confidently when in possession of a pair of scissors and a comb. She does Liam's hair, too, finishing him with a burring electric trimmer around the neckline and sideburns that always causes a highly satisfying frisson to cross his face. "Too hot?" Gloria asks loudly.

"Just right," I reply. I could stay under the water, under these skillful fingers, for hours. At the beauty school in Ohio, when Nathan and I traveled there for his father's funeral, all the girls, employees and students and alumni alike, clucked protectively around Gloria, supernaturally teary for her loss. The group was exuberant and chatty, physically affectionate, brash and pretty. When they didn't have customers, they practiced on one another, grooming and debating all day. They'd treated Nathan's father, Woody, like a mascot. Apparently, he had taken to hanging out at the salon with them, sitting under a dryer hood reading the newspaper, making conversation, flirting. "Dotty old sot," Gloria said of him, fondly enough.

Gloria, Nathan said, was nothing like his mother, the only fact that made him curious about her, or maybe more curious about his father. The man who would spend his days in a beauty parlor wasn't the Woody whom Nathan had grown up with. He'd been a bastard dad, Nathan always claimed; but then Woody had grown old and sentimental, disarmed and harmless, a character in his second act. Nathan had finally chosen to see his father as reformed, penitent; his stepmother had some other thoughts on the matter. "Senile," she said, finger twirling at her ear. "Brain all turned to mush. He would have been horrified to see himself. I'd've left him if he wasn't so wretched. And if I wasn't already so old and lackadaisical," she acknowledged. "You know, you ought to have to renew your license to live. Some people are no longer qualified. Some people wouldn't pass the test."

Liam chimed in then, as he occasionally did when we didn't realize he was listening, when we sort of forgot he was in the room. "A liver's license," he said.

Gloria shuts off the faucet and squeezes water from my hair before performing a tidy upsweep with a towel, tucking the end into the bundle. "I'll get the dryer, you open a new bottle."

*

We discuss transvestites. We discuss transsexuals. Doesn't a sex change usually go the other way, from man to woman? Isn't it the boy who more often feels he's been wrongly assigned his gender? And would Madonna Rage's mother/father have had surgery? Aside from the obvious subtractions and additions, what small touches might be attended to? Adam's apple, for instance? The weathered flyer on the table serves as a coaster for Gloria's wineglass; the girl's color image is blurring.

We both look up at the sound of a car door slamming outside. A second slam follows. We straighten our spines, take girding sips of wine, and then Liam and The Girlfriend are in the kitchen, she with her haughty tossed head and aggressive ballet stances, the faint floating odor of coffee and coconut. "She got fired," Liam says. "Her boss is a sexist asshole," he adds, which explains The Girlfriend's quivering, righteously indignant expression. "Hi, Grandma," he says to Gloria, bending to put a kiss on her cheek. He has lavender circles under his eyes, my old-souled son.

"Oh honey," she says. The Girlfriend chooses to think this is directed toward her, while I know it's Liam for whom Gloria feels sorry. He will suffer The Girlfriend's bad news. Her business is the house's business, her tempers paramount.

A year ago, I would have challenged them, saying, "Define 'sexist asshole,'" because a year ago, it was The Girlfriend trying to earn *my* approval. Now that's changed. Back then, I was delighted by her, a smart and arrestingly striking child, one who had skipped ahead a grade, and whose poise and confident costumes were a pleasure to behold, a girl who was seemingly obedient to her parents, a teenager with a job, straight As, and who'd had the good taste to find Liam worthy, to become his first girlfriend. But as my marriage eroded, so did the enthusiasm and respect I was accorded by The Girlfriend, as if she found me guilty, even though it was Nathan who left. Her contempt feels specifically female, her judgment on my skills at old-fashioned womanhood: I failed to keep my man. Perhaps it seems I've traded him in for an old woman who drinks too much and never changes out of her pajamas. The Girlfriend sends an imperious, castigating gaze around the room, establishing a distance between herself and me as if fearful of contagion. So I say, "I'm sorry."

She blinks a slow, tortured expression of contempt. "That chick's a skank," she says, spotting the poster of Madonna Rage. "We were in sixth grade together. Before I got accelerated."

"Maybe she was kidnapped," Liam says.

And all three of us, in unison, tell him quite confidently, "She wasn't kidnapped."

"Unless she kidnapped herself," says The Girlfriend, voicing my thought precisely. Do I not like her because she reminds me of me? Maybe.

Then Gloria asks, "We've been wondering: Did her father used to be her mother, or does he just like to put on women's clothes?"

"Limited options," Liam notes.

The Girlfriend lifts her lip in disgust. "Gro*tesque*ness! All I know is, that girl wore the same pants every single day of sixth grade." Can I realistically wish that The Girlfriend were the missing girl without also dooming Liam to heartache? No, I cannot. I do what I always do: Invite her to Sunday dinner. Compliment her outfit. Ask if she and Liam have decided about attending Nathan's wedding, if they would like something to eat, something to take with them as she leads and he follows to his bedroom.

It's a room that shows two influences: the innocent accessories and pastel adornments of childhood, for which I am responsible, and the newer, brasher colors and business of adolescence, which accoutrements The Girlfriend supplied. Retro cowboy-and-bronc wallpaper now covered by sneering musicians. Finger-paint table suddenly groaning beneath a perilous stack of pachinko machine and television. Post-it notes of The Girlfriend's Red-She-Said lipsticked kisses on every toy and shelf and remaining childish object. And, finally, snapshots of her face, like that lost girl's face on the street, everywhere. During the times when she breaks up with him, he lies immobilized and surrounded, four walls' worth of mocking, taunting images.

When his door slams behind them, Gloria leans across the table and confides, "What do you want to bet that boss is not so much a sexist asshole as that girl is a royal pain in his behind?" Like me, Gloria is relieved when Liam's relationship is going well and distressed when it is going badly. His unhappiness brings up her own, reminds her that joy can not be trusted. It is understood that Gloria will decide one day to die. She will commit suicide in such a way that Liam will be spared. He doesn't know about the overdose. He will be told that she died of old age; to a seventeen-year-old, the whole household could believably perish of this affliction. Nathan will know the truth; he will accuse me of being an accomplice. What did he expect me to do? Abandon Gloria, as he had? "She should be in therapy," he said, stubbornly defending his profession, and also, maybe, defending his lack of interest. He does not want to think about the ways in which living no longer appeals. To him, she is another woman grown cold.

"Sometimes it seems like I'm inside a room with a too-tiny door," Gloria once told me, her pale blue eyes dilating as she tried to capture the feeling, to put it into words, "and the room is shrinking. As is the door . . ."

"That sounds *awful*," I said, shivering.

Out of nowhere, Liam chimed in. "That's why cats have whiskers, so they won't get into a space they're too big to escape. That's why it's cruel to trim their whiskers." He was fiddling with his movie camera on the floor. Gloria and I had yet again forgotten he was with us.

"I did something naughty," I confess to Gloria now.

"What'd you do?"

My bit of sabotage was forwarding The Girlfriend's mail. On a sudden whim, I filled out the form while at the post office forwarding Nathan's, forging his signature, then pulling another card from the stack and checking the box for individual (as opposed to family—what have I got against them?) forwarding, so that The Girlfriend's mail would be sent to Montana. This is the season of college applications; she scored nearly perfect on her SATs. Now, all of her acceptance letters will be winging their way to Anaconda.

"I *love* it!" Gloria declares, smiling hugely. "That child needs to be taken down a peg or two."

"Maybe getting fired will improve her."

"Ha!"

Gloria falls asleep on the couch. "Passed out," Nathan would say, superior to such an impulse himself. She prefers sleeping here, on the couch in the living room in the middle of a cinematic drama, to spending the night in the small dark guest room and daybed. She prefers for sleep to take her unaware. She lay down holding the television remote in one hand, her wineglass cupped by the bell in the other. I remove each from the grip of her elegant, manicured fingertips. Her hands fold automatically into one another at her throat. It's the position of the dead. It's the position of the fetal.

"It's the only saving grace of not being a mother," she said to me once. "I have permission to kill myself. You don't."

When the house phone rings, its shrill jangle passes over her face like a burst of air on a still pond.

Nathan. He sighs when I answer, his usual disappointed salutation. "Checking in," he says. "Hoping to speak with Liam. He's not picking up his cell." Usually I let the machine answer the land line. I like to treat Nathan to Liam's ten-year-old chiming voice requesting that the caller leave a message for the members of our former nuclear family. The injury of that gone-forever time.

"Not here," I lie. "Off with The Girlfriend." At the kitchen table I pick at the wine-stuck corner of the rippled poster. Madonna Rage is streaked blue, her father's pleas draining away. It's quite possible Nathan knows them; the man's eloquent way with words and his complicated situation suggest that he is not a stranger to therapy, to seeking help. But I would learn nothing by asking. For years I've carried on a taunting imaginary conversation with Nathan's professional self and his rigid code, me playing the brat against his steadfast droning advice, in my head alternately resorting to tears or telling him to go fuck himself.

"You want me to encourage or discourage Gloria about your wedding?" I ask. Time teaches this, that you are astonished at what winds up coming out of your mouth.

"It's a little bit of a hike," he says. The aspen trees. The wilderness forest just above his manicured new home. He will never say that he wants nothing of his former life except his son, that singular, culled, impeccable emblem of the future. For this reason alone, I will insist on sending both Gloria and Liam tomorrow; The Girlfriend can make her own decisions. In the midst of his lengthy explanation about the rutted parking lot, the exorbitant BLM fees, the unknown quantity of the weather, I reach for my cell phone and text Liam.

*It is almost midnight.* Liam always makes fun of my inability to operate the keypad's apostrophe.

*She's upset.*

*Take her home.*

*I don't want to.*

*She will get in trouble.* Before I can add, *She will get you in trouble*, Liam's message comes flying back.

*To me it seems like everybody's in trouble all the time anyway.*

"Goodbye, Nathan," I say to his final breathing ponderousness. He prefers having the last word.

"Don't let her drink," he chooses to say.

Liam's bedroom door remains resolutely closed. I debate knocking, nagging. I worry that The Girlfriend's parents are going to blame Liam for her being out beyond curfew. For her getting fired. For having a mother who plays juvenile pranks like forwarding mail. For the other juvenile prank of having put Liam's old baby monitor beneath his bed, the receiving end in my own bedroom. I can tune in, listen to what they say or do. Once, I heard them talking about calculus, The Girlfriend teasing while Liam struggled to finish his homework; she didn't mind being coy and ditzy, wasting time, idling and flirting and distracting, making him prove over and over his extravagant affection. "I remember 'If, and only if'!" she squealed. "I always thought that sounded like *wed*ding vows!" Liam gave a grudging laugh. Another time he told me the names he and The Girlfriend had picked for a boy baby, for a girl baby, including me in an improbable fantasy future that made my chest ache.

I listen to the monitor only occasionally, only in quick bursts, his privacy something I invade like a wasp sent whizzing through a small gap into the room, then swiftly out, frightened of what might happen.

I move through the house switching off lights, extinguishing the television. With every muted room comes another sensation of opening vastness, as if I were carrying a candle, bearer of the last small illumination. On the bed I shared for nineteen years with my husband and now occupy alone I find the cat. "Hello, cat," I say as she, sleek and impassive, pours herself to the floor and slides away toward the cat door, toward the night. If she is ever lost, if ever I find myself tempted to make a poster, I will be reminded of this evening. "Do not get run over," I order her vanishing tail in vain.

For that wasp's flight's worth of time, I switch on the monitor. On it, The Girlfriend cries. My son consoles, more like a song than words proper, a murmuring litany of steady care. My ex-husband would offer the curt opinion that I'd dislike any girl Liam chose, and perhaps that's true. But I can't hate her, crying. She sounds too much like the child she was, too much like somebody so well loved that losing her could not be survived. In the summer Liam will go to Europe—the Grand Tour, Gloria's exorbitant graduation gift—without The Girlfriend. Maybe the time zones, and the technology, or its absence, will divide him and her. Maybe he'll meet someone else. I might even have the heart to feel bad for The Girlfriend, if that's what happens.

Because, of course, he will be leaving me, too. He has already left me.

Around the bed the room expands exponentially, not like Gloria's shrinking coffin but like space. It will be during this summer, I think, while Liam is gone, that Gloria will end her life. Or she might postpone until fall, when he's away at college. Then what? I ask myself, beginning to slip away into sleep. What then?

Hours later, I am brought upright and alarmed by a car outside. It screeches hideously at the tilted stop sign, slides screaming over the pavement for an unthinkable length of time. I brace to absorb the impending certain crash; surely all my neighbors do the same—lonely Dave as he cruises the Internet, Miss Bernalillo County's father-in-law the insomniac, Madonna Rage's vigilant parent—our breath collectively held. But it does not come and does not come. We blink in the black, waiting.

# FIRST HUSBAND

"Lovey," her husband said gently, which was his way, "it's for you." The velvet blackness of two a.m., of nearly death-deep sleep, the ringing had been a fire alarm in her dream; reluctantly she'd exited that make-believe building yet not wakened, hovering in some liminal space. The building was filled with naked bodies, she wished to return to them, their naughty party, and instead this dull insistence. "Lovey," said her husband's voice again, and she was livid with him, with his presence here so close to her dream, his forcing her to attend to him when she wanted to retreat back inside the burning building . . . "Lovey," he said, and then the light snapped on.

On the phone was her stepdaughter. Her ex-husband's youngest, most difficult girl, Bernadette, who was busy apologizing, as usual, for she was always sorry to bother her former stepmother.

*Ex. Former. Step.* As if there was some remove in the relationship. As if there ever had been.

"I'm so sorry, but he's been drinking," Bernadette was

saying of her delinquent spouse. "I need to find him before something happens. I mean, he can't afford to get arrested again."

"I can be there in twenty minutes."

"Actually? I'm sorry, but could I bring the kids to you? If he comes home, I don't want them to see him. You know, it's just so hard to have a conversation with kids around. Or a fight, either, for that matter, which is probably what's going to happen. God, I'm really so fucking sorry, Lovey . . ."

"Bring them, please, it's fine, you should never worry about that." Sleep and dreams and the velvet black had all fallen away. She was restored to the razor-sharp real world, having left behind, she suddenly realized, her first husband, whose hand she'd been holding in her sleeping mind. Had he been nude, too? That wasn't like him, naked in public.

"I'm already in the car with them, I was thinking I could start on Central and just see if he's parked on some barstool or other. Please don't tell Dad, okay, I mean, he already thinks I'm a total fuckup and he hates Aaron enough, plus he'll tell my sisters." And then she was crying. Poor Bernadette; had the girl ever not been miserable? Even as a child, she cultivated hurtful friendships, was forever suffering slights and neglect and flat-out cruelty, this girl like a loyal beaten dog.

"Honey, I would never tell your dad, we're not exactly on speaking terms. Bring the kids, I'm up, don't worry." Her ex would visit only in dreams. That was how a belief in ghosts must have begun, Lovey thought, when the dead or gone came briefly, searingly, back.

"Actually?" Bernadette said. "I'm in your driveway, God, Lovey, I'm really really sorry!"

*

The seven-year-old carried the diaper bag and a backpack, tilted sideways bearing the load, while his mother brought in the two car seats holding his sisters, who slept. "God, it smells like snow out there, how often does that happen at this time of year? I pumped," Bernadette was explaining in a whisper. "Give Lovey the breast milk," she told Caleb. The boy produced a pair of tepid yellowish Baggies. There was always something a little unsavory about dealing with breast milk. Maybe if she'd had her own babies, Lovey wouldn't feel this way . . .

The two sleeping children were left in their car seats on the living room rug, which seemed wrong somehow, people lashed into chairs, especially the three-year-old, whose big head looked unnaturally perpendicular and like it would lead to a terrific neck ache. On the other hand, it was also true that the two girls were sure to scream if wakened; there was no happy solution to the problem of these quarrelsome girls.

Bernadette was squinting at her cell phone, lips moving as she read something there. "Shit, he's with Lance, that can't end well. So you could just nuke a bottle for her, I think she'll be good till maybe like four?" She pressed her hand into each breast, checking. "And Caleb. Well, he could watch Loony Tunes maybe? With no sound? Will you watch Loony Tunes on mute so Lovey can go back to bed, honey?"

"Don't worry about us, we'll play Monotony." Lovey had been studying the boy, this child who had been her first grandchild, born the year she divorced his grandfather, the year she was a mere thirty-seven, far too young to be a grandmother, or to be called "Grandma"! In public she was still mistaken for his mother, and it was he for whom she'd come up with an acceptable name, Lovey, to take the place of Evelyn. A serious boy, a boy who had not spoken until he could do so in complete sentences, who had said, quite frankly, at the birth of each of his sisters, that he did not like her. "How's your new sister?" somebody would ask. "Terrible," he would reply. Nor did he laugh easily, yet his feelings could be hurt so simply. He was like his mother that way, a child too tender, who bruised. Nobody but Lovey would indulge his fondness for Monopoly. He was always the hat.

"Please don't think I'm a fuckup," Bernadette pleaded as she whirled her way toward the door again. "And tell William I'm sorry I woke him. Be good, Caleb, I love you." But Caleb was laying out the game board, counting money and stacking up the Chance cards. He had the thick copper hair of his grandfather, Lovey's first husband, as well as the large brown eyes and plush lips, a beauty. When she married him, he was at the tail end of his fruitful handsomeness, its fulmination, at forty-five, still moving in the world with the confidence of a man who'd bedded a lot of women, all of them except the first few—when he was a beginner, when he was on the receiving end of a romantic education—younger than himself; he was a serial seducer. "Handsome men are dangerous," Lovey's mother had warned her. Lovey had been his third wife; perhaps she could have predicted that she would not succeed where those others had failed, but that was the nature of love, and of youth, and the combination, youthful love, to make one arrogant, or stubborn, impervious to the lessons of others.

If you took all the lessons of others, you might never do anything.

Caleb handed Lovey the dog. "I want to be banker."

"Fine," she said. Now it would be more difficult to make sure he won. But that was the challenge in raising children, wasn't it? Ensuring that your lies grew in tandem with their ability to believe them. At some point you might be able to come completely clean. Mightn't she one day, for example, confess to her stepdaughters that parents did not, actually, love their children equally? Her ex-husband had preferred his eldest, the prettiest, the strongest. And Lovey? She'd always been partial to needy Bernadette. Bernadette's sisters had found their stepmother lacking—she was so young, surely they'd forgive her eventually, now that they had reached and passed the age she'd then been? For a while it was fun to be mistaken for their older sister, or, alternatively, to be the extremely young mother, the one who shared clothing with them, who knew and liked their music, the four of them ganging up against her husband, their father, who was old, so old! So old-fashioned! So out of date! So shockable! But he wasn't, not really, and at some point his indulgence began to falter, his paternal tolerance turned tense, at least as it regarded Lovey, because eventually she was no longer his lovely young wife, she was, instead, somehow familiar, too known and knowing, too something he could not even particularly put his finger on, but he no longer wished to have sex with her, no longer found her desirable enough to be *able* to have sex with her. It wasn't willed, he assured her, it wasn't his fault, he could cry if she insisted, he could medicate himself into readiness, but did she really want that? Did she, he asked earnestly, want him to fake what he could not naturally desire? Was that the kind of love she wanted?

Yes, she confessed to herself yet not to him. Yes, that was what she would take, if it was all he could offer.

"You told me to be honest," he said. "So this is me being honest."

The first stage of the game was the best, all the acquisition and possibility, the tidy array of money, the fairness. Caleb sat on his knees in his chair, poised over the colorful board like a squirrel with a nut, rolling for Lovey when she needed to check on his sisters, moving her Scottie dog forward, providing her two hundred dollars when Go came around again. In order not to land on Boardwalk first, Lovey allowed one of the dice to fall to the floor, citing a number that left her on Luxury Tax, whatever that was, instead. At last, Caleb finally acquired his beloved cobalt blue plot. Later, when it was expensively developed, Lovey would land there an inordinate number of times so that he could fleece her.

Why was it so satisfying to see him win?

It was nice, this strange intimacy in the kitchen at three in the morning, no other light in the house—or in any of the houses. They were outside of time, Lovey thought, waiting for when the rules kicked in again. If it did indeed snow, schools might be closed. Albuquerque was not accustomed to weather; Lovey had grown up in the Midwest, where snow days meant an actual blizzard instead of mere flurries or patches of ice. Her first husband had brought her to the desert; she could thank him, she supposed, for that gift. When he left, he'd not wanted much of what they'd collected together in their twelve years. Was it generosity? Guilt? Or simple indifference?

Caleb heard the baby first, his head tipped toward the living room with his hand halted over the board in mid-count. "Forty-five seconds," he told Lovey, concerning the breast milk and the microwave. "I can do it." Lovey took the opportunity while the boy was at the refrigerator to put a five-hundred-dollar bill from her stack of cash back into the bank.

She could not figure out the car seat's elaborate buckle, so the child's crying became hysterical. Caleb silently undid the clasp, next finding the three-year-old's pacifier and stoppering her with it before she fully woke as well. "You're a good boy," Lovey told him repeatedly. In the kitchen the warm bottle waited. Lovey had only to sit down and assume the position, the girl's face at her own breast. While she fed the baby, Caleb played both sides of the game, counting aloud, asking if Lovey wanted to buy the electric company or not. "Not," she said. Her pickiness about property he never questioned, seeming to think he alone knew that buying everything was the secret to success.

Caleb's sisters were utterly unlike their brother. They demanded what they wanted. They entered a room and began immediately competing to be its center of attention, the baby now knocking her head into Lovey's sternum, making fists with her hands and banging at her bottle; if her nails weren't clipped she'd rake her own face until it bled. If you asked the boy how he liked his sisters now, his answer wouldn't be much different than it had been before. He was only being honest. He was simply telling you what you claimed you wanted to hear. But he did not like them. They required a lot of attention. They made a great deal of noise. They could not be reasoned with—it was useless to try—they could not understand taking turns or sharing and resorted to crude shortcutting cheating substitutions like grabbing and screaming. "If they were dogs," he had told Lovey, "you could put them in a cage."

"If they were dogs," Lovey said, "you could take them to the pound."

When the baby began gagging, Caleb informed Lovey that the bottle was to blame, that the milk came out faster than it did from his mother's breast, that the baby was used to sucking harder. So she choked herself. "Greedy girl," Lovey murmured. "I wonder where your daddy is?"

"I don't know," Caleb said. "But he rode his bike and he forgot his helmet."

"Dangerous." Although safer, by far, than driving. Aaron's sobriety was tenuous, court-ordered, the elephant in the room at any family get-together. He would sit meekly at the table studying his sparkling water while others pretended not to be aware of his every sip. There were times he simply stayed home rather than suffer his in-laws' worry, those two sisters-in-law and their upstanding moderate husbands. Months would pass—a new child would be born, a better job would come along, things were looking up—and then the phone call in the middle of the night. Bernadette had always loved this kind of boy, the bad one, the attractive nuisance. Her first boyfriend had drowned in a lake after having driven a car into it. Some other night and Bernadette would have been in that same car with him. Aaron had probably been friends with that boy, it would make sense. Bernadette had not really had a chance to get much past high school. She'd wound up pregnant with Caleb her first semester at the U. The child had been responsible for her cleaning up and completing that year, her only college experience. In fact, this little boy's arrival gave everyone some distraction. His grandfather might have gone away—not only left Lovey but left his daughters, moved a thousand miles north and started anew—but in his place was this beautiful easy boy.

Without Aaron, there would be no Caleb. Lovey had to remind herself of this sad fact. Her ex-stepson-in-law was a lot of trouble, but here before her was a boy for her to love, who loved her. He would grow up and perhaps grow away from her—there was no shared blood, and someday he would understand that, he would untie the knots of those prefixes that labeled this woman Lovey, ex and step. He would turn into a teenager and disappear like his father into the night. Lovey had lived through those adolescent years with her ex-husband's three daughters, each more harrowing than the one before, as if they were competing, culminating with the spectacular miscreance of Bernadette, who apparently had no kernel of self-control or will or restraint at her center, who ran away, who totaled vehicles, who got arrested, who inhaled or smoked or drank whatever substance anyone handed her, who landed in jail, who disappeared, who perhaps could not find a way to make herself care to continue living.

Until Caleb. She'd made her own little kernel, it seemed. The boy had saved her, as well.

The baby was still fussy after her bottle, agitated and thrashing. This one didn't want a pacifier, she didn't want to be left kicking on the floor under the spell of a musical mobile, didn't need a new diaper, couldn't be made contented, it was as if she wished to break out of her own skin. Lovey sat her upon her lap and the child grabbed up the tokens, stuffing one in her mouth before either Caleb or Lovey could stop her.

"If she swallows it we have to wait for it to come out in her poop," Caleb said. "Which is gross."

"Jesus Christ." Lovey hooked her index finger into the child's mouth, removing the little metal dog. "Maybe she's still hungry," she said over the renewed red outrage.

The noise woke the three-year-old, who began wailing from the living room, "Ma ma ma ma ma ma!" Her brother went to fetch her, having first pushed the game to the center of the table, out of reach. Lovey put several of her yellow and blue hundred- and fifty-dollar bills back in the bank. She also removed a few houses from the long crowded row of red and yellow properties where she'd become an inadvertent real estate mogul.

In came sad Celia, not as lovely as her older brother or her little sister, the child who'd lost in the looks lottery, big-featured and -boned, and immoderately loud. She also seemed developmentally behind—still wearing diapers, still chewing on a pacifier, still sobbing inarticulately. It felt bad to dislike her, and if asked Lovey would never confess it, but the child oppressed her. She sat now on the kitchen floor and started babbling around what they called her "plug," mostly just wanting her mother. Over and over the plea, a great mass of green mucus beneath her nose and chin. Lovey had closed the kitchen door so as to keep William from waking. He had hospital rounds in the morning, in a mere four hours, he needed his sleep. These children could not compel his specific interest, coming as they had into his life, two or three times removed, these ex-step-in-laws-by-marriage. He had his own children to fret over; their hardships were a whole other scenario, ongoing on the other side of town, in his former house, with his ex-wife and her new husband.

Lovey got out the chocolate candy, the surefire solution, a small pile of M&M's for Celia to take solace in. "Is there enough for me?" Caleb asked.

"Not really," Lovey said. "Just the one snack bag. I have raisins."

"No thanks," he sighed. Raisins: that was his lot in life.

Even after her second bottle, the baby was not satisfied. Bernadette had predicted four A.M., and here it was. Lovey texted her and got no reply.

"There's formula in the bag," Caleb told her, and then proceeded to fix a bottle of it, studying the ounces on the measuring cup, leveling the powder with a knife on the scoop. It made Lovey sad to see him shake up the concoction before microwaving it, and sadder still to watch him test its temperature on his wrist.

A text arrived from Bernadette: *Found him, heading home!*

*Everybody fine here*, Lovey wrote back. The beauty of texting: no telltale soundtrack. For the kitchen was loud, both girls miserable, the chocolate gone, the formula apparently not to the baby's taste. She wanted the real thing, from the real source.

"Hey there," William announced himself, hair mashed flat against his cheek, shirtless and in P.E. shorts, which always reminded Lovey that her first husband would never appear in public without a shirt, or wearing shorts, without his hair combed, he was vain about his body, his age, his aging body. In her dream, had he been nude like the others in the burning building? At night he took to bed with him an apple, so that he could freshen his breath with a bite first thing in the morning. William gave Lovey a perfunctory stale-smelling peck on the cheek, "What's all the hubbub, bub?" he asked the three-year-old as he stepped over her to get to the coffeemaker.

The child swung her arm out to hit his shin.

"I'm sorry," Lovey said.

"Mercy," said William. "That kid packs a wallop. And you appear to be getting your ass kicked," he said, regarding the game. "I've arrived here not a moment too soon." All of Lovey's friends preferred William. They approved of his jocularity, his slow-moving steady ways. He'd been an E.R. doc; it had given him perspective. There was, in this dawn kitchen, to his practiced eyes, no real trouble. Her first husband had been known to storm out of dinner parties, to take offense and cut off friendships—"Dead To Me!" he would declare—to behave like a child always on the verge of tantrum. With him, Lovey had had to be careful, to tread lightly, to pay her full attention.

"Give me that," William said, taking the baby from Lovey. "Let's try some shock therapy, shall we?" He opened the back door and stepped out into the cold air, which silenced the baby instantaneously. When he brought her back inside and she began to start another wail, he did the same thing.

Caleb said, "Maybe you should leave her out there?"

"It'd be tempting if there weren't snow. And then there's *that* one," William said, "sitting in her own filth." This made Caleb laugh, a bright burst of surprised happiness that rarely came upon him. He would repeat this expression for days, amusing himself with its perfectly droll un-profaneness.

William took over the Monopoly game while Lovey attended to diapers. "What is that pile of cash doing there?" he asked of the Free Parking money. It wasn't in the rules, but it was tradition. William's children were teenage boys who played football in high school. That was the sort of father he'd been, one who enjoyed a team and rules. If Caleb were his son, he'd have a bristly haircut and would never be allowed to stay up all night playing Monopoly.

And if there were to be a board game, it would be something dignified, like chess. By the time Lovey got back with the freshly clothed girls, Caleb's lip was trembling, something William wouldn't necessarily notice, since he was playing along just to be a good sport, placeholder. He hadn't even finished his first cup of coffee. The Free Parking money was gone, she noted.

Lovey let Celia knock the whole enterprise to the floor, a glorious clattering spill of cards and tokens and fluttering cash. Caleb would recall where everything went. He would know whose turn it was and what was mortgaged and which property had hotels.

"An act of god," William declared. He stretched his fists over his head and flexed open his mouth in a mighty yawn, finished his coffee, gave Lovey a knowing lift of his brow and Caleb a ruffling of his hair, then disappeared into the shower. By the time he returned, the game was underway again and Lovey was nearly destitute.

"You're hopeless, honey," William said, settling at his computer for the news. "Hey look," he said, swinging the screen around for Lovey to see. For a few seconds Lovey studied the Facebook photograph, Bernadette in a short dress, holding a cigarette and a beer bottle, on either side of her Aaron and another man, the two of them equally in possession of her in this flagrantly drugged and drunken state. *Freak blizzard in Duke City!* the comment read, the time imprint only thirty minutes earlier. She had come to Lovey many an occasion, when a teen, wasted and weeping, afraid of her mercurial father, repentant, apologetic and grateful, claiming again and again that only Lovey understood her. That same girl still before Lovey, her loose sedated face, the same idle boys whose reckless seduction she could not resist. And then suddenly the photograph was gone. As if it had been the product of Lovey's imagination, something she had dreamed. "She took it down," William said. "Of course. She knows you'd see it, of course she took it down."

"What?" asked Caleb, monitoring what was transpiring.

"Let's check with your mom about school," Lovey said. "Maybe you can take the day off."

"I don't want to miss school."

"Maybe it'll be a snow day."

When Bernadette didn't answer, Caleb suggested calling his father's mobile number. Before Lovey could find it, Bernadette rang back.

Lovey understood immediately that she was still drunk. "Lovey," she said. "I'm sorry, the good news is I found him, he's fine, but the bad news is we have to talk, it's time to come to Jesus, again."

Her first husband had stolen from Lovey her best years, keeping her captive during the time that she would have, in some other circumstance, delivered children. He'd fooled her, she thought, he'd held her hostage and then released her when it was too late.

That was the story she told herself and mostly believed. And Bernadette alone of the three girls subscribed to it as well. The others split their loyalty equally, judging nobody, visiting their father, accepting their new same-age-as-they stepmother. Only impulsive Bernadette had severed ties. Only loyal Bernadette had stood by Lovey.

"Let her sober up before they go home," William advised. "Let them both sober up. How about you guys go watch TV?" he asked the children. "How's about I set up some

*Tom and Jerry?*" Lovey had met William through friends, a match everyone approved of, "age appropriate," her friends and family agreed, pleased to have Lovey squarely tucked away again, married. Her parents had never been happy about her first marriage, never visited without awkwardness and sad sighs, the tragic absence of true grandchildren, these three half-time stepdaughters who did not particularly respond to them. In the story everyone else believed of Lovey's first marriage, she was lucky to have gotten out before her older husband became a patient, a third aging parent, before the inevitable illness and decline. Those eventualities were still ahead, she supposed, they hadn't yet come to pass. He was sixty-four, his new wife in her thirties, her picture was also online, available, an undeniably pretty woman. Young. Fresh.

And William? Lovey loved him well enough, in the way of adulthood, she thought, not in the feverish former manner of witless drowning immersion, that love she'd fallen into heedlessly as if into a body of water, with no idea of what such a thing could cost her, it had nearly killed her when all was said and done. Meaning, she'd felt like dying. She would never be that kind of lover again, never endanger herself that way again. And she understood that William, too, had been disposed of, that his ex-wife had had a similar nuclear potency, and that he loved Lovey with the same conscious intensity of somebody exacting a kind of revenge, or, perhaps, simply forever behaving with the belief that his ex was paying attention, that he had need to prove he'd survive and thrive, the victor. *A* victor, anyway.

"I feel like an idiot," she told William. "How could I let her do this to me?"

"What has she done, really?" he said. "I mean, she could have gotten you to babysit, if she'd wanted, she could have asked you to stay over at her house with them, and you would have. Or she could have told you they were going on a date night or something, either way you would have hung out with the kids overnight, so it's really not so different. When you think about it."

"I guess I thought she trusted me."

"She left her children with you. She called you when she felt like getting trashed. How much more trust do you want?"

"I still feel like a fool."

"Don't be so hard on yourself. Everything's fine. See you tonight." And he provided another peck on the cheek, this time of the minty variety. And once again Lovey thought of her first husband, his apple-flavored mouth, his kisses that could paralyze her with brutal desire, still, still, even in absentia. That's what she would have been waiting for, in her dream, his incendiary kiss.

Caleb came back from the television to put in a request of the three-year-old. "She wants Cheerios. I told her no milk in the living room, then she threw the remote at me." He touched his forehead. He was too thin, and this morning he had dark circles under his eyes. Lovey should have made him go to bed, put him in the girls' old room with their dolls and posters and trophies. From the living room came the ruckus of cartoon violence, the three-year-old liked to turn up the volume, maybe she was loud because she was a little deaf, Lovey would have to mention that possibility to Bernadette. When she next saw Bernadette.

Meanwhile, Caleb was checking the game board. "Lovey," he said, "what happened to all your money?"

"What do you mean?" There was surely an explanation he would believe.

His face was suddenly furious, his rage as rare as his laughter, and this time aimed at her. "Don't let me win," he demanded. "Don't you dare let me win!"

# THE VILLAGE

S HE HAD ONLY HAD her driver's license two weeks
when she totaled the family car. Darcy's father had to
rouse a neighbor in order to borrow a vehicle to come
retrieve her from the scene of the accident. Her best friend,
Lydia, had been taken away by ambulance.

"I love you, Papa!" Darcy cried, before anything else
could be said. Preemptive strike. She was still drunk, so that
her voice seemed to be produced by a slightly other person
than herself, as if she were both ventriloquist and dummy.
Crashing into the stone entryway of the cemetery had
added adrenaline to the mix, puppet and puppeteer equally
manic. Twenty-five years later she recalled her intense urge
to run, run, run through the gravestones, to discharge that
amazing crazy energy before it did some additional harm.

"I love you, too," her father had told her. He didn't mind
her blood on his shirt. A blanket was provided by the cops
to protect the neighbor's car's interior, and Darcy was driven
home, the long way, by her father at four in the morning,
down Lake Shore, skirting the far edge of Cabrini-Green

and roaming the inner tunnels of the empty Loop, steam rising from the street grates, shaggy figures leaning on their shopping carts moving like benign monsters. Drunk still, Darcy viewed this the way she had illustrations in picture books, her father reading aloud, she safely on his lap.

But that night, twenty-five years ago, he ended up telling her a story about himself. A confession, really, intended to defuse the horror of what she'd just done, of the mistake she'd made, of the terrible consequences she expected. "First," he said, "nobody is dead." Drunkenness and trespassing were her public crimes; for them she would be penalized in a completely quantifiable way. That punishment would have an end point. "But your mother is going to be very . . ."

"Mad?" Darcy said, choking up again. "Mad" was a mild description of what her mother would be. She was going to be apoplectic with rage, anxiety, disappointment, frustration—what a *waste* such an accident represented! Not to mention the ancillary trouble—the station wagon was the only family vehicle. People had to go to work, to school, to the store. And who would be left to solve this series of extremely tedious and costly problems? Who would be charged with filing insurance claims, shopping for another secondhand car, enduring the judgment of neighbors and co-workers and extended family? Her mother prided herself on being a superior parent, the kind of parent other parents called in order to ask advice, display their own ignorance and need; Darcy was the second youngest of six children, five of whom were exemplary citizens. Now look who'd gone and tarnished her mother's stellar reputation.

Vindication—that, too, would come with the rest. Her mother had always insinuated that this was exactly where

Darcy was headed. "I wish I *was* dead!" she declared to her father.

"Darcy, you don't!" he said.

"Yes, I do!"

"No!" He stopped the car, pulling abruptly to a curb. "People make mistakes," her father pleaded. He amended his platitude: "People do things that other people might call mistakes." And then he told Darcy about his friend Lois. Darcy leaned against the cool glass of the passenger window, miserable, wrapped in a blanket that smelled of tire rubber, aware of Chicago's shadowy homeless population—also in blankets—as they sought shelter in an icy Saturday's most severe hour while her worried father confessed his own shame, that thing that other people might call infidelity.

There had been two Loises at the nursing home where Darcy's father spent the last years of his life. This had been convenient; his Lewy body delusions featured several characters whom most of the family did not recognize. The Sergeant, for instance, who was always ordering Darcy's father to do outlandish things like take off his clothes in the lounge or crawl into closets or shout obscenities; the Little Girl, who simply rocked in a rocking chair beside his bed, comforting him; and Lois, who made him laugh.

Darcy never told her siblings or her mother that she thought all of these invisible visitors were more real than they knew. She was 90 percent sure that the Sergeant was her mother, that bossy, imperious person, that leader of a small army. Lois, of course, was her father's long-ago mistress. And even though it felt uncomfortably like bragging, Darcy believed that she herself was the Little Girl, an idle innocent rocking happily nearby, keeping him company, making no demands.

Community service had been part of Darcy's punishment after her car accident. Her father had arranged for her to serve it in a soup kitchen downtown. Overseeing the Friday-night meal was his friend Lois Mercer. She was a tiny woman with the flashy smile and careful coiffure and costume of the saucy female lead in a movie musical, ready at a moment's notice to leap on the kitchen counter in her heels and unleash a song. The disheveled men who came there did not frighten her. When one of them placed his hand on Darcy's ass, Lois quickly seized the guy's other hand and put it on her own, asking him to compare. Joking, she turned him into a jokester. Darcy hardly had time to be scandalized before she was amused. It was just her ass. It was just a hand. And so what if he chose to give her a bruising pinch before he removed it?

In the kitchen, Lois shared her flask of amaretto. Darcy had never tasted liquor like it. Everything about Lois seemed perfumed, decorative, feminine. Over her pretty dress she wore a floral apron, different from others because of its sleeves, which had elasticized wristbands. She pulled up the sleeves and offered her scarred inner arms for Darcy's inspection. "Bakery burns," she explained of the faint purple cross-hatchings. She'd grown up cooking; her family owned a restaurant still, on Chicago's South Side. But her husband was a surgeon; he didn't think his wife should work. Instead, she named it philanthropy, and performed it here, for vagrants.

Darcy's mother wouldn't have gone to the trouble of making sourdough bread for anyone, let alone men who spent their days on the street begging from strangers, drinking from bags, talking to statues. She would have declared store-bought day-old dinner rolls more than sufficient. Darcy's mother wouldn't have weekly transported fancy knives or marble rolling pins or unsalted butter or pearl onions or any other exotic object in her car trunk from her kitchen to a homeless shelter. Darcy's mother was practical, sensible, down-to-earth; in fact, her shoes were called Earth Shoes. She did not pluck her eyebrows; she did not watch her weight. In conversation she cut people off because she knew exactly what they were going to say next and she wished to save time.

Lois Mercer taught Darcy to knead, to fillet, to debone, to zest. To crush garlic cloves with the flat of a chef's knife. To hold matchsticks between her teeth when mincing onions. To love capers and asparagus and lox and acorn squash. To tug the leaf from an ugly artichoke and then gently savor its tiny butter-soaked morsel of flavor after scraping the flesh with her teeth. To relish the action of the meat mallet, the dough hook, the melon baller.

"Do not serve them if they are inebriated," ordered the black pastor who ran the kitchen. He was very stern.

"Of course!" Lois would agree, then serve everybody, regardless.

"Which of the ladies do you like best?" one of Darcy's siblings would shout at their ailing father in the nursing home.

"Lois," he would say, his expression briefly undone, sincere. And they would laugh indulgently, because there were two Loises, because they thought he was guessing or improvising. Darcy was married now, so it made her heart hurt a little, to know that he preferred his old friend to his wife. It hurt especially because Darcy preferred her, too.

Lois had been her friend, her only friend, it seemed, in that terrible time after the car accident, since Lydia Lydegan's family had prohibited Lydia from seeing Darcy—bad influence, drunk minor—anymore. Lydia had been thrown teeth-first into the dash and had had her beaky nose fixed as a result. Then she was transferred to the private school her parents had been threatening her with for years, and Darcy never saw her again.

Her own face had also been banged up, but nobody had offered her cosmetic surgery. She'd gotten Lois, instead, given to her by her father when he'd wished to lessen her despair. It was a secret gift, although he'd never told her not to tell. How had he been sure she wouldn't?

For a future reporter, she had very poor investigative skills.

But she *did* know that her father loved Lois. She knew he'd provided his indiscretion to Darcy in order to mitigate the lonesome horror of her own. She continued not to tell anybody. Over time, she wished she *could*, but none of her known associates—mother, siblings, friends, husband—seemed the proper audience. Who, then?

At the nursing home, when her father requested a drink, only Darcy understood it wasn't water but alcohol he wanted, not simple thirst he wished to quench but something else.

Only coincidentally did she hear about Lois's death. It was her day to visit her mother at the old family home, and Darcy had rolled her eyes when she'd seen the blinking light on the answering machine. Her mother refused to figure out technology, even of the simplest sort. Technology was for spendthrifts.

"Um," said the man on the machine. "I'm the son of Lois Mercer? And I'm calling to notify the friends in her address book of her passing. This message is for a James somebody. Or a somebody James. And I apologize if I've reached the wrong person." He hesitated for a moment, then left a phone number. The area code was for Florida.

"Who were you talking to?" her mother demanded, stumping into the pantry with her four-pronged cane.

"The library," Darcy said. "Your books are overdue."

"They are not," her mother said confidently. "Their computers are always getting it wrong."

From her own home, Darcy phoned Florida. A woman answered, Lois Mercer's daughter. "Mom died a few days ago. My brother and I have been calling people. She had Alzheimer's, so it's been hard to figure out who's who. Who mattered, I mean. To her."

"She knew my father," Darcy said. "When she lived in Chicago, a long time ago. James." Only his first name, in Lois's address book, his beloved first name.

"I grew up in Chicago. My dad still lives there, up in Evanston. But when I moved to Florida, I brought Mom with me. She was already having trouble taking care of herself."

"When was that?"

"Nineteen ninety-six, I think. No, ninety-seven. Tell me who your father is?"

"Actually," Darcy said, unwilling still to unleash her father's secret, "your mom was important to me, too. I mean, you said that about who mattered to her, and I don't know whether I mattered, but she definitely mattered to me. When I was a teenager, after a car wreck."

The daughter had no answer to this. Eventually she said, "The service is next month, when everybody can get away.

In New Smyrna. We're going to scatter her ashes at this place on the beach."

Since Darcy had been laid off at the newspaper, her husband expected her to be both demoralized and casting about for the next thing she would do. A trip to Orlando for a cooking class didn't seem outrageous, to him; the expense could be justified, if she thought it might lead to her new career. The sunshine would do her good, March being the hardest of all the hard months to endure in Chicago. "My mom won't even know I'm gone," she told her husband a few weeks later as she packed. Her siblings would visit, fill prescriptions, shop, take her to appointments, wait and wait and wait in those waiting rooms. They'd always been far better at fulfilling duties. Darcy was best at being fallback, the one to call as a last resort.

Even her little brother, family baby, obvious accident, still known as Teddy, had been known to pat her on the head like a pet.

Her husband hugged her goodbye, smiling tolerantly. At the paper, Darcy had been a member of Lifestyle, early deemed expendable, while her husband was in News and therefore still necessary, employed. This fact had put a certain eye-averting, throat-clearing strain on their marriage, the embarrassment of acknowledging that they'd been in a competition, and that she'd lost, and that he was married to a loser. All very awkward.

The airplane was full of people riding for either their first or their last time. Disney World! Or the old folks' home. Next to her sat a woman with a pretzel of oxygen tubing at her nose, small tank on her lap. "Hey, Dad! We're going! Hey, Dad! We're going!" crowed the child behind Darcy, son to a handsome man who wore headphones and was riffling through a golf magazine, indifferent.

"I'll give you this lizard if you quit kicking my seat," she turned around to tell the little boy later. She held up a rubbery toy that had been in her purse since she'd packed up her cubicle clutter at the paper.

"OK," he agreed. His father observed the transaction apathetically, thumb rising to his tongue for his next round of page-turning. A tinny noise emerged from his headphones.

"What's your name?" she asked, when the boy's kicking resumed.

"Gavin," he said promptly, a little defiantly, as if people were always challenging him. He had torn all four rubber limbs and the tail off the lizard and was now twisting its head. Of course he had to kick her seat.

"Gavin," she repeated, nodding. As usual, she would fail to achieve rapport. Children, like dogs, like horses, could sense fear and incompetence. With each of Darcy's little nieces and nephews she had tried, thinking that some-where, somehow, there'd be a kindred spirit. But nope. She just kept being Aunt Darcy, the black sheep bad example dragged up to illustrate wicked wasteful adolescence. Even this little strapped, bored stranger could find nothing better to do with Darcy than kick her in the kidneys.

Without taking off his headphones, Gavin's father suddenly reached over and delivered a loud whack to the boy's legs. "Cut it out!" he bellowed. Angry tears sprang to the child's eyes and the lizard's head popped off.

She would never have recognized Lois's son if he hadn't been holding up a piece of cardboard with her name on it. Darcy always wanted to ask people how old they were; in

93

the newspaper, it was the first piece of information you got; when you were a child, everyone asked it all the time. And then suddenly, at some point, it wasn't polite. You had to go at it sneakily—"What bad band did you once love?" "What president did you first vote for?"

"When did you leave Chicago?" she asked Jules Mercer. He probably hated his name. He'd probably been tortured for it all of his life. He told her he'd left as soon as he could, had gone to college in Miami, now lived in Orlando, and planned never to spend more than ten minutes ever again anywhere with a windchill factor.

"It was zero degrees when I left today," she said.

"Exactly." He led without letting her walk beside him, his posture unpleasantly strict.

Outside, the air was precisely the same as inside, perfect. This made Darcy remember something. She text-messaged her husband: *Please don't forget to feed the sponge.* On the kitchen counter between the flour canister and the paper towel dispenser lived the sourdough starter in its giant jar. It predated every other thing in the house, older by far than Darcy's relationship with her husband. It had been a gift from Lois Mercer when Darcy had left Chicago to go to college in Urbana. There, it had sat on top of her roommate's little refrigerator, jar of sludge and stench, heaving up, sliding down. Darcy had frightened an RA on the hall by threatening suicide, and so was given access to the dorm kitchen, where she now and then made bread. For this talent she earned a reputation unlike anyone else's in the dorm. Respect? Puzzlement? Hard to say, but she enjoyed appearing with a crusty domed loaf and a stick of butter to supplement the late-night television sessions. Even if some of the girls went to purge immediately after, it still seemed nicely homey to cook for them.

"Here we are," said Jules Mercer in short-term parking. His car was an old station wagon.

"I totaled a car almost exactly like this," Darcy told him. "That's how I met your mother, doing community service at the soup kitchen."

"What?" He'd never heard of his mother's evenings with the panhandlers. Darcy spent the hour-long ride to New Smyrna describing Lois to her son. He was one of those drivers who didn't look away from the highway, but she could still sense incredulity in his wrinkled brow and slightly parted lips. *Huh?* Clearly this wasn't the woman he remembered.

"I think of her often," Darcy said, "especially when I'm cooking. I'll be shaking fennel seed into the spaghetti sauce, or pouring amaretto over some brie, and there's Lois, and it makes me smile."

"I always just wished she'd serve us something *normal*," he said.

"Why?"

"It was so embarrassing to open our sack lunches at school. All I wanted was Wonder Bread or a freaking Twinkie. I mean, really, what's so hard to understand about that?" He shook his head, still bewildered by his mother's obtuseness. "Although, she *did* have Alzheimer's, and I've noticed that Alzheimer's afflicts people who are naturally scatterbrained. She was extremely illogical." Saying this, his voice broke, a sob there behind the steering wheel, as if he'd surprised himself with his harsh words. Darcy was about to start liking him when he said, "Seasonal allergies," and pulled a wrinkled hankie from the car console, mashing it against his face and making an awful noise. Allergies might have explained his bright red nose. Or maybe he was under the influence of grief; Darcy remembered how it sabotaged at such inconvenient times. Tears weeks after her father's funeral, pouring down her face not at a therapist's office or in conversation with a sympathetic beloved, but at the grocery store, there in the aisle with the baking goods, specifically before the molasses.

"The bunny or the granny?" she could hear her father ask, weighing the choices in his hands, smiling. He had enjoyed his whimsy. She had been his best audience. *Lollygaggers*, the family had called them both, sometimes sort of fondly.

Darcy said to Jules Mercer, "I didn't really think of your mom as scatterbrained. But I was a teenager when I knew her. I was probably the scatterbrained one." True, Lois had not finished sentences so much as strung together associative ideas, plucked them from her mind and trilled them out. Her son seemed gloomy, too daintily made, and resentful as a result. The fey little heterosexual man. Poor Jules. Darcy hoped the sister was grateful for her mother's gifts.

Alas, no. They were fraternal twins, and Jillian Mercer was the same as her brother, their mother's quick happiness nowhere in evidence. Lois's children seemed so perfunctory: one boy, one girl, unadorned as drones, heads capped with hair the exact color and function of rodent fur. They weren't light and spry. Their smallness seemed more like incompleteness. They did not smile, they did not flirt, they appeared to have been middle-aged and moderate all their lives. They must have been (*had* they been?) disappointments to their mother. Darcy's heart lurched: Family! How it never let loose of you.

Or maybe that impression, like others, came from their grief. They were not themselves just now. Dour, Darcy thought, and then could not unthink it. Moreover, there were only the two of them to bear the burden of their loss. How much luckier her family had been, six children to share their father's death, each confident of the others' load. They'd taken turns being overwhelmed, falling to pieces in shifts, the same way they'd divided time spent at his deathbed, spelling one another.

Her father's last words had been not to her, but about her: "Where's the Little Girl?" he'd asked her oldest brother. A day later he was gone.

Jillian said, "It took us forever to figure out she had Alzheimer's, she was always such a ditz anyway."

"Extremely illogical," repeated her brother. He had brought Darcy to Jillian's home, a condominium a few blocks from the beach, and now sat at a glass kitchen table drinking iced tea.

"She always just talked word salad anyway, such a chatterbox, so for a while nothing seemed weird."

"My dad had dementia, too," Darcy offered. "He kept insisting there was a sergeant in the nursing home basement, staging a coup." *Lois*, he said, when asked who he liked best. "But I don't think he was particularly scatterbrained before." Fanciful, silly, kind, forgiving, and sentimental. But not ditzy. Weak, perhaps. Too weak to leave his wife. Or perhaps too selfish: He wanted it all. Wife and family—hearth and home—plus the mistress, clandestine, giddy.

"Then she started mixing up ingredients when she cooked," said Jules. The two twins looked at each other: "The shampoo banana custard," they said together, shaking their heads morosely.

"She taught me to cook," Darcy told them. "She was great."

"We had to ban her from the kitchen," said one of them. "She would have killed us all," said the other. Darcy could not recall which later, as if they'd spoken those words in tandem, too.

"Great instructor," Darcy said later to her husband from her hotel room. It was far more pleasurable to invent a cooking class adventure and the environs of a rackety industrial kitchen than to give him the dreary news of Lois Mercer's mopey offspring. Twins: maybe they were two hopeless halves of some potential one person. "Chef's teeny-tiny, sort of like Rita Moreno, and totally enthusiastic, like Carmen Miranda, all bubbly and feisty. It's going to be great."

"Good," he said. Like her blood relatives, he enjoyed encouraging Darcy. Her family had been pleased when he'd showed up to take responsibility for her. Her mother had once predicted that Darcy wouldn't live to see twenty, she was so reckless and dumb.

"She wears spike heels—to cook! And you know what? She has an apron just like mine." Her apron with the long sleeves and elasticized wristbands, hanging at home in the corner. She'd found it at a thrift store many years ago, one almost exactly like the one Lois had worn, periwinkle flowers, ties long enough to wrap around the front, a useful pocket over which you knotted those strings. So unsexy as to be sexy, her husband had told her. Her siblings teased her when she forgot to take it off at the table. "You'll be buried wearing that thing," her oldest sister once commented. Now Darcy wondered if Lois still had her apron. If her children had dressed her in it before they fed her to the flames.

No. They would have put her in something black and decorous, something sober and presentable, even though she wasn't going to be presented. She'd lived with her daughter, occupying the guest room, expelled from the kitchen, tolerated but not beloved.

"If there's one thing worse than Alzheimer's, it's *alcoholic* Alzheimer's," Jules had said.

"A*men*," said his sister.

"My dad liked a little nip now and then," Darcy told them. "Sometimes I sneaked him a snort." Hip flask at the senior citizens' center, his breath sweet with brandy.

"*She* couldn't remember where she hid the bottles."

"She couldn't remember which bottles were *booze*."

"We don't drink," the twins said together. Of course not. "Did you ever have your mom or dad live with you?" Jillian then demanded of Darcy. And Jules said, "Did *you* ever take care of a crazy person who went around drinking Drano?" Well, no.

"Your mother called," reported Darcy's husband. He played the recorded message over the phone. "This is your mother," said her mother, as if otherwise Darcy wouldn't have known.

Of course the twins loved their mother. They just didn't love her properly, for the right things. They loved her generically, helplessly. She hadn't rescued them.

"She rescued me," Darcy practiced saying to them, hoping she might convince them. "Your mother played a vital part in my troubled adolescence. She actually saved me, once upon a time." Would they appreciate hearing that from a stranger at their mother's memorial? Probably not. It might seem sly, upstaging, proprietary. Yet maybe they would want to know the small but essential kindness the woman had performed, that inadvertent help she'd given. Darcy couldn't say that Lois had also, more profoundly, rescued her father. There was no one left to ask how long the affair had lasted, whether Lois's divorce had created a problem.

Lois had eventually left her surgeon husband. One spring Friday she'd come to the soup kitchen and flashed her bare left hand for all the bums to admire; she'd encouraged their leering observations and chivalric offers. Darcy didn't know if Lois had expected her father to do the same and leave his wife, but even then, sixteen years old, Darcy could have guaranteed her that he wouldn't. She'd known that without having to have it spelled out.

Say they'd run off together. Say they'd come here to sunny Florida. Here they'd have been, two addled old folks, one with invisible friends, one ingesting poison.

Darcy sighed, turning over in her hotel room bed. Together, would he have needed invisible friends? Together, would she have felt like drinking poison? There simply wasn't any way of knowing. Or anybody to ask.

There weren't many people at the service on the beach. The ex-husband came. That's who the twins had accommodated by delaying the event for a month, their doctor father who still saw patients, who was vital in the world. He in no way reminded Darcy of her own father, but why would he? Hadn't the whole appeal of Lois been the difference between her and Darcy's mother? This man was clear-eyed and dapper, trim and much younger-seeming than his years.

He gave a tight-lipped confident smile to everyone standing in the breeze, squinting at the gorgeous day. He was a cardiologist, still living in Chicago; his children approved of his second wife, who stood at a respectful distance, wearing a modest dress, smiling gently. They'd told Darcy that their mother had been a fool to divorce him. They'd never understood what had gotten into her, to do such a foolish thing. They would never understand her, period. The heart doctor put an arm around each of them and squeezed their shoulders so that they leaned in toward him. Like Darcy, they felt kinship with their dad.

Poor Lois, she thought, turning to the teapot-like urn that held her ashes. Lois, whom everyone seemed to believe was very impractical, an exasperating dingbat, a menace to herself. At best, decorative. A luxury, nonessential. Except, maybe she *was* essential. Maybe that's what Darcy wished to be able to tell somebody, somebody who would agree rather than argue. Who would applaud rather than be appalled. When the refrigerator at the homeless shelter had gone rogue and frozen a dozen whole chickens solid, Lois had smiled naughtily. Before the hungry vagrant men arrived, before the thawing and cooking began, she and Darcy took the frozen birds out into the dining hall. It was a long room with a polished linoleum floor, empty now of folding chairs. Lois had a terrific throwing arm for somebody as slight as she was. Away the rock-hard chickens slid, across that long slippery space. Sent often enough over the floor, some of the packaging came undone, some of the legs splayed open, the bodies spun, thin blood and innards spilled out. It was like bowling, it was like bocce ball, the game pieces sort of like infants, the same sort of flesh-toned wrongly proportioned parts. To prove that she believed a little time on the floor wouldn't hurt a chicken, Lois later ate a bowl of the coq au vin she and Darcy made. In Darcy's recollection, it was delicious.

This was the story she tried to tell when it was her turn to take a handful of ash and bone, to toss it toward the waves. Only one person—an older, friendly-looking woman wearing six different shades of turquoise clothing and scarves—bothered to make eye contact while Darcy was speaking. The ashes all blew back into Darcy's face, onto her black sweater. Leaving the beach, she noticed that everyone had worn sensible shoes, even Darcy herself. The woman in billowing turquoise, who'd listened and smiled during Darcy's anecdote, was headed in the opposite direction. She wore no shoes at all. Small waves washed over her feet.

"The Blue Lady," said Jillian. "She's always out here rambling around, giving shells to strangers."

"Did you notice her skin?" said Jules. "*That* is some terminal sun damage!"

The twins had probably not planned to invite everybody back to the condominium after the service, but the whole group came anyway. A dozen people. The cardiologist was more astute than his children, more curious about others. "And you are . . . ?" he asked.

Darcy felt herself blush. Had he known? Was he aware of why he'd been left, long ago? "Darcy Mortland," she said, adopting her husband's last name for the occasion. "I was a wayward girl that Lois helped out back in the old days. She saved my life."

"She was a giver," he conceded. "Big heart." But the way he said it made it sound as if there were a second unspoken part: Big heart, small brain. Or something similar.

"She helped when nobody else really could," Darcy said. "Everyone was really upset with me. I needed a friend." That had been the first, but not the last, time she'd felt like killing herself.

The doctor smiled sagely. "It takes a village, they say."

"Yeah," she agreed, because it was easy. But she thought that maybe it took less than that. One person, perhaps. Yet it had to be the right person. And that actually might be not less but more than a village. Harder to find on a map, for instance.

He leaned closer to her, squinting, lifting his aquiline nose. "Lois wore that same perfume," he noted.

"Yes, that's right," Darcy nodded. She'd been wearing it for years. Her family recognized it, too, as hers; every year, it made a very easy and reliable Christmas gift. Perhaps its scent had been a trigger for her father, when he'd lived at the nursing home without his familiar surroundings, without his coherent memories. He might have enjoyed Darcy's visits because she smelled like Lois, his old flame.

She had to spend a few more days in Florida, attending her make-believe cooking class. Around the kitchen supply store she wandered, looking for a gadget she didn't already own. She loved these items, the dangerous razor-sharp zester, the oversize electric juicer, the comical onion goggles, the squeaky pastry bag, the flexible measuring bowls, the clever degreaser, the perforated baking sheet, the tiny lemon shower caps. She could be pleased for hours, touching these silly perfect inventions, admiring their discrete, specific purposes.

# WINTER IN YALTA

"LIFE: A SERIES OF lessons you don't want to learn."
Cara said this to the girl beside her on the plane while everyone wasn't listening to the seat belt lecture. The brown man across the aisle holding the Koran had been told a half dozen times to turn off his cell phone. His beard reached his sternum although he wore not a turban but a hoodie; Cara's seatmate, who was feverishly writing things in a small book with the word *Diary* fancily scrolled on its cover, had asked if they should be nervous.

"Not about him," Cara assured her.

"We're flying to New York," the girl pointed out. "*City.*"

"Yes," Cara said. "See, that's why we are absolutely the safest people in the air today. Because it already happened, what you're thinking of. It won't be that again. What you need to worry about is going to Navy Pier. Or a Cubs game." Back to scribbling went the girl, turning the book so that Cara couldn't read what she was writing. She now disliked Cara, which was not an uncommon thing to happen after Cara opened her mouth. And that was the exact opposite of why she was today flying from Chicago to New York. *City*.

She had received a miraculous summons from her old best friend Rochelle two days earlier. After months of both making halfhearted gestures—brief emails that promised, always, "more later" and then failed to deliver, or missed calls minus messages, each perhaps having had the most fleeting impulse but insufficient time or energy to follow through—Cara was literally poking at Rochelle's area code when the text from the same number appeared on her little screen. Synchronicity! Fate!

*Funkytown*, it said. And Cara burst into grateful tears. It was time. They were newly fifty years old. Apparently that meant something. They would meet, as usual, in the city, where everything between them had begun more than thirty years earlier.

"Rochelle's been dumped again," Cara told her husband. He rolled his eyes. He'd met Rochelle, but only in the second stage of her adult life, the defused one. He understood what led men to unload her, but was baffled as to why they'd take her up to begin with. "You and Emmett will have to batch it for the weekend," Cara told him. The story at her house in Evanston was that Rochelle was needy, lonely, likely to throw herself under a train if not for Cara's ministering aid. At Rochelle's house, which was a romantically run-down apartment in Key West, there would be no story. She lived alone. At most, she would have to hire a dog sitter. To whom no story would be owed. To whom any story would be just fine.

"OK, Florence Nightingale, have fun." As a physician, as a card-carrying member of Doctors Without Borders, he could not argue with Cara's purported agenda. She had Hippocrates on her side.

Their destinations—high and low, be they Met or Barney's, be they bookstore or thrift store, Shakespeare or stand-up—were all merely incidental, stage sets utterly secondary to the *talking*, and in order to truly talk, they would have to drink, so that while their meals would be inarguably sumptuous, they, too, would be simple props, obvious excuses to order liquor, and lots of it. Also: a few helpful pills, cigarettes. The women would share their stashes, as they had always shared, since first meeting in college. Under the influence of a few drinks, it was those young women they beheld: two doughy midwesterners woefully misplaced in New York City, frightened silent, pretending and defended by reflex, throwing their hands into the air on busy corners as if snatching at flying objects, frantically adapting, scrambling to shroud themselves in black, instantly setting about to starve and smolder, walking awed endless blocks with their heads tilted back like baby birds, helpless and hungry.

So hungry.

At LaGuardia, Cara didn't recognize Rochelle. On first sight, there was nothing special about either of them, Cara thought, two women who blended, camouflaged, dull as everybody else, each in an outfit best described as modified sleepwear: Cara an obvious runner in a velour sweat suit, Rochelle a middle-aged matron wearing blowsy linen, ingeniously disguised as a harmless grandmother. This miracle—hiding in plain sight, sizzling sensibility bedecked in two different yet ubiquitous uniforms—thrilled Cara. No one (no one!) knew what she was thinking. Neither would anybody believe what her friend Rochelle was conceiving, right before their eyes! The scathing commentary that went on without relent, you had only to hit a particular button, she would open her mouth and scandalize you, it was incredible. Everyone was not like this, adamantly not, and how had Cara, anyway, ever located this rare gift? How, in all the world of billions who did not, did not, *get* her, had she found this essential inimitable friend?

By being assigned the bed across from Rochelle, a million hours in the past, that little dorm cubicle that some random Powers That Be At Barnard had furnished with two girls whose hastily tossed-off written inventories in the application packet had somehow led to their being deemed roommate material.

It was harder to find a true friend than it was to find a spouse, Cara had discovered. For she'd found three of those, and only one of these. And always she had run to Rochelle when it was time to abandon that marriage, and maybe? Maybe it was coming again, although this time would be different, what with the child. What with the fifty years she suddenly had to admit was her age, although people always guessed she was younger. Always.

As usual, they were shy at first, each with a tucked smile, a slightly averted gaze.

"Why Funkytown?" Cara finally asked in the cab. "I mean, I'm there too, it's that time again." She was falling out of love, had already fallen. It had taken longer, and it would be harder to extricate herself, but there was no denying the signs. Yet mightn't she, because of twelve-year-old Emmett, have to stay? Her online dating profile made no mention of a husband, yet confirmed the boy. And an age of forty-two. Divorcée. Maybe she should claim widowhood? Nobody could blame a widow.

"Oh, you know," Rochelle said vaguely of her own blue season, a fleeting sad flinch crossing her forehead. "The vapors." With her she had a new dog, this one wearing a service animal badge. "Why not?" she'd said at baggage. "As soon as they see the word *Psychiatric* I am in like Flynn." Until she'd become a world traveler, Rochelle's love life had indeed been what brought her down, sent her to Funkytown. But vacationing abroad had taught her about all the fish in the sea, and the seeming infinite variety, the nature of love having released her from its former fixated grip. "European men," she would sigh in wonder. "They have no interest in the twenty-two-year-old. And why should they? Those vapid brats. And Mediterranean men, oh my god? Please." She was forever urging Cara to follow her lead, to forget the dooming relentless striving to be ever-young, to instead resign, *recline*, in*dulge*, let loose of vanity's tedious toil.

"Hold this?" she said now, handing over her wallet to Cara. "Sylvia Plath eats money, don't you, you little shit?" The dog blinked blankly away from the open zippered compartment. "No comment, *bien sur*."

"Where?" demanded their driver, who was from where? Rochelle would know.

"Times Square," Rochelle answered. "Times Square," she murmured to Cara, as it was she who'd made the reservation. "I dunno, I felt like being in the thick of things, like any other little old lady from Florida. Do you mind?"

"I would go anywhere." Which was true. Where Rochelle said to go, she would go.

"Read this label," Rochelle said, twisting her blouse collar tag toward Cara. "This line is all about fortunes. Execrable dreck. I edit them."

To *Inner beauty* had been appended *Outer yech*. She rose on her massive hip to give Cara access to her waistband, her pale dimpled skin crazy with tiny red spots and wormy purple veins, a shimmering river of stretch marks, this brief reveal suggesting that beneath the garments it could only be so much more of the same or worse. Cara could not imagine allowing such ruin to fall upon her own flesh. Their twenty-year-old selves would have been appalled at the sight. Rochelle had so grandly done that thing they'd promised themselves they'd never do: let themselves go. And how far Rochelle had gone! How extravagantly! The cabbie did a double take in the rearview. *I am great, people are terrific, life is wonderfull* had become *I am greasy, people are terrible, life is mispelled.*

"Remember that taxi last year with the urine?" said Cara. "Oh my *god* were we hungover."

"I'm just glad I got in first. I pride myself on never landing in the wet spot."

"So. Gross!" Cara had returned home last year ill and listless, blaming it on Rochelle's exhausting saga, never confessing to how fully fun it had been, how the sadness was in being back, home to Ordinary Life.

It wasn't always mostly fun. It wasn't always New York, either. There'd been Greencastle, Indiana, when Rochelle's mother had had to be moved. There'd been drunk camp in the Utah canyonlands, which Rochelle had required and which Cara had attended in sober solidarity. Miami, when Rochelle had undergone uncertain surgery and subsequent chemo. There'd been the deaths of parents, all four of them, each of a radically different tenor, these only-children left finally orphaned, and there'd been Cara's deep postpartum depression, Rochelle swaying sleepily on her feet with tiny Emmett in her arms, Cara a fetal ball in the rocking chair. There'd also been her decisions to leave her husbands, Rochelle knowing before those innocent men, helping plot the exit strategy, script the kindest, gentlest scenario. Between the women there'd been so much. They'd become adults, helped raise each other, moved away, yet never lost touch.

Last year it had been the death of Bad Samson, Rochelle's beloved wretched dog—which, maybe because Cara had grown up on a farm, a place overfilled with animals and death, they died and became dinner, even if they had names and personalities in advance, she'd learned to behead chickens, *somebody* had to—and still, even if Cara couldn't quite muster true grief, it was a point of pride to pretend such compassion and concern for Rochelle's rescued Pomeranian.

And now a new one, Sylvia Plath in her purse. Cara could certainly understand how Sylvia Plath, like Bad Samson, had come to be discarded the first time around, and thereby in need of rescue. Without children, without spouse, here was where Rochelle's love was poured—because love had volume, and needed a container, a way not to be wasted.

Early on, there'd been a low moment between them. For one long hard school year they had loved the same man, and they might have parted ways forever as a result. But after? They'd shared the deepening kinship of caring beyond that same man, and where was he now, anyway? He'd been everything, once upon a time, Louis White from across the way, and now was nothing.

They'd met him their third year of college, he and his roommate in the building across the street from Cara and Rochelle's apartment, acquaintance made on an angry sweating summer night while audience to an altercation from balconies above it. A highly amusing distracting drunk fight between four fat marrieds, shoving and punching and

ANTONYA NELSON

stumbling and shouting. Louis and his roommate were commentating.

"As a betting man, I'd put money on the ladies," the roommate said into his fist, leaning over the iron railing.

"We're gonna have to agree to disagree on that one," Louis said into his. "I'm going with the guys here, not to be sexist, but let's not forget our friend testosterone."

"Lou, that's just where they'll fool you, wait and see." Sure enough, it was the pudgy husbands who eventually sat defeated in the street, one with his head in his hands, the other searching for his shoe, wives stalking away huffily pulling garments back into order, all angry elbows and head-butting, victors, Louis calling lazily across the way, "You guys got anything to drink? That whole debate brought up a powerful thirst." From the first it was clear that Louis was the one to desire. His roommate, James Huckabee, Chuckles, laughed too eagerly, had settled already into his role as wholesome bewildered sidekick, not intense enough, his glance clear, his motives pure, he played the banjo and wore wire-rim glasses and would marry young, have more than the national average number of children, love the same woman in the way of the parishioner for decades and decades. Louis, however, was a Bad Boy, and would never wed. No girl could resist trying to win and rescue him. And better if there were two of them, to compete for the position. Slippery, elusive, sultry-eyed Louis.

Cara lost her virginity to him. Rochelle had already had a half dozen lovers, her current one her econ professor, several of them one-night stands taking place mere feet from Cara's bed back in that little dorm room. Poor Chuckles, who spent that first evening gamely trying, falling flat, and Rochelle and Cara nearly at each other's throats by its end, trading the snidely betraying information they possessed of one another, exposing weakness after weakness, Louis the listener, Louis the judge, Louis the point on which they'd risk their friendship. She could still see him, leaning back on their futon couch that night, chin tilted toward the ceiling as his beautiful throat swallowed their liquor, his rangy easy-limbed self soaking up also the palpable pleasure of being desired, a boy filled with heady intoxicants.

He'd graduated from Columbia. He worked as a bike messenger, he wrote songs for a band, he dealt weed. He'd grown up in the city. His pet name became, for Cara, Manhattan, since his, for her, was Buckeye.

But first he chose Rochelle, and broke Cara's heart. Then next he chose Cara, for longer, for better, she the ultimate winner. He wouldn't have sex with her for nearly a month, despite having fucked Rochelle the first night out. This respect, this care, this difference between the girls that he recognized and honored became part of his complicated appeal to Cara. Never again in her life did she ever have a lover half as well tuned to her. She'd never have known it was possible if not for Louis. Three husbands later, she could say so with confidence. It was rare to be so thoroughly, bodily, suited.

The cost of that first love, that first real love, was the friendship with Rochelle, who did not like to lose, yet whose tragedy that continued to be. No matter Cara's pleading, no matter the evidence that Rochelle could *always* find men, and Cara could *never*, or hardly ever, or with such monumental difficulty, no argument would budge her. Rochelle seemed bent on an ultimatum: either him or me. For the remainder of that year they lived as enemies, occupying their tenancy as if on shifts at a plant, guards of the same inmate, Rochelle camping out at the econ prof's office, Cara across the street at Louis's, occasionally glimpsing from his apartment window the shadow of lean and miserable Rochelle in theirs.

Cara pretended to have given him up when in fact it was he who left Cara, he who began sleeping with the ballerina in her thirties, the sophisticated beauty who'd also grown up in the city, who had a life history he more readily recognized and esteemed. He would have continued to sleep with Cara, but it wouldn't have been the same. She was somebody, she learned, who had to be the only one.

To explain her heartache she ran back to Rochelle, spinning the tale of having chosen their friendship over Louis White. Her sobbing grief was real, a useful side effect, a purported sacrifice, tribute to their friendship. She was practical, that way; hadn't farm life taught her to improvise, to make the most out of what otherwise could not be controlled, weather and animal plague and government fickleness?

They swore then that they would never say goodbye to each other. Never.

"April doesn't *look* so terribly cruel, does it?" Rochelle said of the sunny day outside the cab.

"There's studies that say April is when last summer's vitamin D runs out. That's why people get saddest then."

"Let's blame April."

"Yes. The month of April: Discuss."

Their trouble was joined together now instead of being borne separately, en route to sturdy, busy Manhattan. Suddenly Cara's issues felt more thrilling than frightening.

It was the possibility of impending freedom, a promising new love. She had already been chatting online with potential future mates. The world was opening again, as if once more in bloom, she could embrace it, April was also spring! Yet a small part of her trouble panicked her, the damage she would cause her boy. The hurt she would be responsible for in her boy's father, whose feelings mattered to gentle Emmett. She'd kept this husband longer than the others, and had brought something substantial into the world with him.

A bad dream had provoked her reaching out to Rochelle. A dream in which her punishment had been Emmett's death. In the dream, she had already made a choice, a dooming one, and she had woken profoundly shaken, Emmett dead and buried. She had reached out because it had seemed a portent.

And there was Rochelle, reaching back. Now here they were in this too-warm cab, the city skyline from the bridge a nostalgic sight, the stiff creak of the seat and the exhausted suspension of an overdriven vehicle familiar and real, hair oil smudging the windows. Cara was feeling immeasurably reassured already. Divorcing her husband did not mean killing her child. That was nonsense. She had Rochelle as well, this steady witness and friend, this presence beyond all others. Rochelle reminded her that she, Cara, did not discard all intimacies, was capable of loyalty and love.

"You're from Russia," Rochelle now said to the driver, gargling something along the lines of "I visited recently" in his native tongue. The man flicked his gaze to the rearview, then shrugged. *So what?*

"Yalta wasn't at all what I thought it would be," she said to Cara. "I mean, true, it was winter instead of summer. I went right to the cliffs and looked down at the waves. Big deal."

"I have no idea what you're talking about," Cara answered, "but keep going."

"On the other hand, I guess I was actually warned of the same . . ." She stroked her dog, in her bag, mindlessly. "If I willed you Sylvia Plath, would you not be mean to her?"

"I would. Would not," Cara corrected. "I mean, I'll do what you want."

Rochelle reached across to lay her other plump freckled hand on Cara's knee, which gave Cara a place to look, to realize that she would recognize that hand anywhere, that she'd been familiar with it for longer than any other hand in her life besides her own.

"Is it back?" she asked the hand.

"No, no, that's not it," Rochelle said, checking around for something wooden to knock, settling on the scarred plastic divider between them and the Russian. "I'm clear, there."

"Then what?"

"No, you first. I want to hear about you first, and only after we've had a few." Cara began putting together the story she'd not been able to frame aloud for anyone else. The story of the perhaps end of her current marriage, the conceivable explosion of her life. Emmett was what gave it extra gravitas, that dear twelve-year-old boy, he who'd only in the last year quit requiring Cara to tuck him in at night. In one way, it was easier to think of leaving, since she would still have Emmett. And in another way, it was considerably harder.

"Why did I bring so many books?" Rochelle said of her heavy suitcase at the hotel curbside.

"Mine's full of shoes."

"There's us in a nutshell, all right." Rochelle had retired from the law nearly a decade earlier, choosing to travel and read books. Combining the two, in fact, taking literary tours of England, Mexico, Ireland, France. "All I want to do is read," she'd confessed in her thirties. "I'd rather read than anything else, even sex. Even eating. Is that terrible?" This was rhetorical; Rochelle had already made peace with loving literature. It was her religious practice. She'd pilgrimaged on its behalf, this past year to Russia; Cara had the postcards to prove it, her son the pretty stamps.

Her son, whose godmother was Rochelle; Cara had had to argue with her husband about it. He'd wanted his brother and his brother's loathsome wife to be assigned. Cara, however, had prevailed. The fact that Rochelle had started Emmett's college fund had been helpful.

"It's not terrible," Cara had said, of Rochelle's passion for reading. "I wish I could be that satisfied with a book." She would read what Rochelle recommended, always with the dim suspicion that she was being scolded or diagnosed, certainly cared for in a unique way, and shy about being grateful for the lesson, even if it stung. Some of the books in that suitcase were surely destined for her.

But Cara admired Rochelle's love of literature the way she did Rochelle's approach to men, envious of what she could not truly understand. This was, in fact, only half a lie. Over time, many things about Rochelle had become curious to Cara. Why didn't she want the trophy, the husband, for instance? The proof that she was uniquely desirable? In the beginning, Rochelle had been a kind of sick collector of men, torturing herself with one obsessive inappropriate object of affection after another—those men who were either married or in some lethal position of power in the same law office, or were vastly younger, or, once, horrify-ingly older, not to mention married, another time ludicrously famous, a sickening, hopeless pursuit, but what they shared, time and again, was unavailability. They would not choose her, when the time came to choose.

"Why don't you want to be chosen?" Cara had pleaded. It was only Louis White who'd turned her away, long ago, only Louis who had been the one to break her heart, instead of the reverse. Had he taught her how not to thoroughly risk her heart? Perhaps. Rochelle's aching romances gone wrong had led, in the old days, to skeletal thinness and tragic dark circles and cigarettes being lit off the burning embers of other cigarettes. Cara had been jealous. No healthy habit or athletic regimen had ever driven her to such desperately tawdry loveliness. "Why do you keep opening the same wound?"

"I don't *know*," Rochelle had wailed, miserable, the beau-tiful blue veins in her temple pulsing. "I don't think it's on purpose?"

Hardly anything on purpose was interesting, Cara had told her, not knowing if that was true or not, but feeling it was right to say. Now it was difficult to recall that version of Rochelle, that fragile unconfident woman with the straggly black-dyed hair, that open book of need splayed on the barroom table or hotel bed. This new version, which had grown—literally!—over time, did not recall or suggest that girl; this woman seemed the mother of her, *grand*mother, even, patiently knowing, padded, calm, gently dismissive. Her hair white, her clothing like the sheets or tarps thrown over furniture or cars, coverage against the elements, noth-ing more, her shoes those of the service industry, nurse or chef or custodian, she was at least double the weight she'd once been, twice the size. "I am vast," she would say. "I contain multitudes."

Before she quit dyeing her hair, people sometimes asked when was her due date.

"You haven't changed a bit," Rochelle always said, and Cara never once thought it could be anything but a compliment. Unlike Rochelle, Cara was terrified of letting herself go, and so remained ever alert and loyal to the self-conscious fear she'd found at age fifteen, under the gaze of boys and men, what they reflected back to her paramount. Without a mirror, she panicked. In the photographs from thirty years ago she and Rochelle looked so alike as to be mistaken for sisters, not quite twins, but nearly so. They had tended, each of them, to adopt the accents and attitudes of those they were near, the Midwest being a state of mind eagerly abandoned. Ohio, Indiana: Ohoosia, they named their commingled states of origin. And soon they squawked like New Yorkers, their parents horrified that first Thanksgiving, the two of them on the telephone disparaging the fat content of the meal, the dull dullness of dullsville. Cara's grandmother hadn't recognized her when she came through the mudroom.

"Oh my lord," she said, clutching her bodice.

"Your hair," lamented her father.

"Don't lose any more weight," warned her mother.

Cara could still summon up the picture she'd made of Rochelle's home in her mind, replaced eventually by the reality, an enormous tall-windowed house in the college town where her parents were professors, and where Rochelle had, in high school, had all manner of promiscuous misadventures with both the town *and* gown elements. Cara had gone to that home to help Rochelle remove her mother from it. Professor Emeritus Carmichael had opened the doors to the animals and weather; she appeared to be subsisting on kibble herself.

"I think it was the coyote that was the last straw," Rochelle had said. She had taken Cara on a tour of the bars that had hosted her misspent youth. "I mean, you would not really guess this, to see her now, but my mom really had a stick up her ass about housekeeping, once upon a time. I mean, she used to make us leave our shoes on the porch." The neighbors had complained to the city. Cats were one thing, and owls another, and raccoons and opossums and squirrels and the occasional wild dog, and deer, well, deer, but coyotes? Somehow the upper echelon of the food chain . . .

"I look like my mother, don't I?" Rochelle said now at reception, her mind having gone, as it often did, to the same place Cara's had, perhaps not by the same route, but arriving there regardless. Maybe the man checking them in had mentioned AARP? "Don't worry, I could not care less. I am ridiculously smitten with my own mind, so who gives a flying fuck what I look like?"

"That's so enlightened," Cara said carefully.

But Rochelle just laughed. "You are so full of shit. Gimme my wallet, will you?"

Rochelle rode the elevator up; Cara took the stairs, working her biceps with her suitcase. The hotel was extravagant, dark, filled with the possibility of rock stars and famous athletes, because that was a luxury Rochelle still indulged in, most others necessarily abandoned. Her father's death had led to her early retirement, the large inheritance having bankrolled her jobless life for a while. Later, she'd sold the art and antiques that he'd left, an Indiana house's worth of items in her family for generations, and she indifferent toward them. Only more recently had she had more difficulty affording her languor, yet never agreeing to Cara's offer of a loan. A gift, it would have been. Cara would, could afford to, give it, but Rochelle was fierce in declining. It was part of who she was.

They settled at the seventh-floor bar before taking their luggage to their room, eager to begin their Lost Weekend, aided by the pulsing drumbeat and no-clocks-or-judgment atmosphere. Rochelle ordered wine and shrimp cocktail and crab cakes, Cara vodka neat. The dog was brought a saucer of water, which it turned its nose up at.

"How often have you been in love?" Cara had asked Rochelle once. "Truly in love?"

"Dozens of times!" Rochelle had said. "Or maybe never? Once? And I already know how many times you think you've 'been in love, truly in love.' Three."

"Wrong," Cara lied. "It's four. And don't think I didn't notice that totally unnecessary 'you think,' because I did." That she'd not been in love with two of her three husbands was understood; the ring on her finger reminded her, mostly, that she could always get divorced and take it off.

Upon hearing Cara's dilemma, a not unfamiliar one, Rochelle nodded atop her loose and fleshy neck, offering the opinion that unhappy married parents were worse than divorced happy ones. Further, Rochelle believed that Cara's husband was entitled to know the truth, however painful. Would Cara, Rochelle inquired, want *him* to keep such news from *her*? Adults, to Rochelle's way of thinking, ought to be accorded respect from one another. Rochelle, Cara was kind of puzzled and hurt to behold, was not very interested in this problem of Cara's, sort of phoning in the advice, her estimable mind quite clearly elsewhere. Here at the bar with the ubiquitous television playing behind them, it seemed not very exciting or worth discussing, unsexy even, vaguely maybe juvenile? Perhaps they hadn't had enough to drink yet?

"This show is so boring," Cara said suddenly, attempting to jolly up and jump-start their conversation. Rochelle joined her in watching the live feed from Times Square. "Elmo is morose, and Hello Kitty just seems tired."

"Captain Jack Sparrow's on Adderall," Rochelle added after a minute.

"You'd have to be. Wait here." Cara took the stairs to the first floor and hustled up the block. The scene was far less subdued in the light of day, with a lusty soundtrack, ticket sellers hawking shows, car horns, tourists gaping and holding up their cell phones, stunned and amazed, and the shrill alarm of sirens, more than one, coming and going, the relentless signal to somebody else's disaster. Cara found and faced the camera and began waving, mouthing *Hello, Rochelle! I love you!* and madly blowing kisses.

Back at the bar Rochelle had ordered another round. "That was awfully sweet," she said, smiling forlornly.

Cara was pleased with herself, breathless from the run up seven flights.

"Listen," Rochelle said, a catch in her voice, "I have to tell you something." Were these the worst words in the world? Yes, they were.

"The cancer's back! I knew it." No wonder Cara's story had seemed paltry and selfish. Rochelle was dying!

"No. No, that's not it. Not cancer, OK? I promise." The two of them made fists and knocked wood on the tabletop, which made Sylvia Plath suddenly burst out barking.

Nobody even looked their way, this hip bar with its unflappable occupants. "But remember Louis White?"

"Louis?"

"We got back in touch a while back. I mean, I found him, I don't know, a while ago, ages ago, just suddenly I was thinking about him. Maybe I had a dream? Anyway, it took a little work, he's not exactly on the radar out there. But then I found him. And it was like, I *found* him. Do you know what I mean?"

Her eyes were tearing up, small there in her fleshy florid face. Yes, Cara knew exactly what she meant. She had lost that foundness herself, so long ago now. And yet the feeling for his perfection, or theirs, at least from Cara's perspective, had never left her. She'd never been as fully in love with another, never been as good in bed, at love, with any body, anybody else. So yes, she knew what Rochelle meant. "He moved to Tucson, to live with his father. He had this arthritic father, and they shared a double-wide. Trailer," she added. Cara's breathing was growing heavier, she realized, her heart was pumping as if for a fight, in fear, rage, outrage. In this state she heard the tale of bewildering decades-long correspondence, nearly daily phone calls. "And he came with me, sometimes, abroad."

"What?" Cara was gathering information the way one might in a car accident or tornado, pieces of import flying randomly around her, what might she need to grab on to?

"Not all the time, just when he could afford it. When he could leave his dad. That's why he moved to Arizona back when, his family ended up there. It was his idea to go to Ireland, I've never thought much of Joyce."

"Joyce who?"

"Who Joyce, you mean." Through her tears, Rochelle offered up a small smile. "He's a very good drinker. You probably remember that." On the Internet they got drunk together late at night and said or wrote things neither recalled the next day. Or one recalled what the other couldn't, and there was the record, if they wished to consult it, a long record of their thoughts. Also letters. Books they read and sent to one another, notes in the margins.

"What does he look like now?"

Rochelle considered this, stroking Sylvia Plath in the bag on her lap, sighing. "Like me, I guess," she finally said. "Out of shape, a little bald, with a few missing teeth. I tried for a while to pay for replacements, but you know Louis."

"No," Cara said stiffly, "I don't know Louis." That was the whole point: she had. Once upon a time she'd won, and then renounced her prize. Or so Rochelle believed. In the version of the story that Rochelle possessed, Cara had taken a sacred vow. Except maybe Rochelle knew that wasn't true. Embarrassment swelled in Cara, shame to now join nerves and that initial ongoing outrage.

"We look like every other lazy middle-aged American," Rochelle went on. "We live in the two places where people go to take it easy, to ease out in easy chairs. We are Winter Visitors. Snowbirds. Who don't migrate come summer."

Cara now featured herself and her husband at the gym on a grim sleety morning, feverishly pedaling and lifting, hanging on to—running after—an impressive image that was reflected back to them from a thousand mirrors, the walls being made of those, those and a few windows, through which you could view grey and despicable weather. They were often named a Handsome Couple. Their kid was beautiful as well. All of which seemed, suddenly, very average and dumb, as if she'd invested heavily in faulty stock, been swindled by a cunning con man long ago, yet had only herself to blame.

"Are you OK?" Rochelle asked.

"I don't know."

"Mental pause," she said, sniffing, cocktail napkin to her nose. "I sometimes lose all track of everything, plus sweating. Do you hate it when people tell you it's better than the alternative? I want to say, just which alternative is it you are referring to, anyway, because obviously you are a person who believes there's only one alternative when there are *endless* ones, is it better than the alternative of being, say, thirty-*five* again, before there was ever a whiff of the possibility of something like a hot flash or a brain freeze or a whisker of a chance of a chance whisker—"

"I'll be right back." Cara's chair threatened to spill over, she stood so swiftly from it, and around her vision swam tiny flashing stars. In the restroom stall she wondered if she would weep. It appeared she would not, she was still too stunned, her heart banging in her neck. Did Rochelle truly not remember that Cara had loved Louis? That in the official record of their friendship she'd given him up for Rochelle's sake? That for years and years she had longed for him, that he was hers to long for? Could she be faulted for that, here? The humiliation of what she'd just learned wouldn't leave her alone, it rushed her like Mother Nature, in the way of illness or weather, relentless, and she powerless under its force, buffeted and dizzy. Cara was going to have a lot of thinking to do, she couldn't do it all right here and now, semi-crocked in a bathroom stall, in New York. *City*. So she flushed, and when she returned to the table she would blame the shellfish snacks, even after all this time she was, it turned out, still a simple farm girl from a land-locked state, and exotic cuisine turned her stomach. In the meantime, she stopped at the front desk to book another room, a single, terribly expensive, terribly necessary. Maybe she would never see Rochelle Carmichael ever again. Ever.

On the table lay a folded paper. Rochelle nodded at it, so Cara read it.

*I love you. Goodbye.* It was the old trouble: she'd been thrown under that train again.

"I get it," Cara said, "you two were in love, life mates, like penguins or something, and now it's over. Better than best friends. Better than being mar—"

"He shot himself in the head last weekend."

When Cara could not fashion anything more than a gulp in response to that information, Rochelle added, "Hello, Funkytown," and Cara realized at least one thing was certain: she wouldn't be staying in that expensive single she'd just booked at the front desk after all.

"Typed on a typewriter," she finally noted, having to note something. Only obvious things occurred to her, as she was having to remind herself to breathe.

"Yeah, just like back in college. He didn't answer his phone, no email, too many days had gone by, so I called his sister."

"I didn't know he had a sister."

"He has a sister," Rochelle sobbed. "He actually has *two* sisters." She had never looked worse, never more like her brain-addled ancient mother. Sylvia Plath was licking her hand as if to stop its frantic clutching. "That's the thing about a real live letter: it takes a few days for the news to arrive. There's no possibility of being talked or texted out of it."

"'It'? Oh, I see what you mean. That's true, there isn't."

"Apparently he didn't want to be."

She was supposed to say she was sorry, but Cara couldn't do it. Her sorrow was selfish, her own, and too sudden to extend elsewhere. Louis's father had died, Cara learned, and then Louis had been in a car crash. Despite its not being his fault—he was a very good drunk driver—he nonetheless was cited when revealed to be over the limit. He not only lost his license, but also suffered a serious shoulder injury, which led to a heavy regime of narcotics. And that to a singular kind of moroseness that would not lift. "I wish I'd been paying better attention," Rochelle said. "I feel like I could have saved him."

"That's the kind of guy he was," Cara said, thrown back abruptly to that intensely passionate past, lying alongside Louis, limbs entwined, she'd never forget because he was her first, her best. Into her ear he had sung a song, some silly thing he'd written, it was hers, from him.

"That's the kind of girls we were," Rochelle said. "Are, I guess. Still are."

They fell asleep in mid–drunk conversation, just the way they had in this city more than thirty years before, in twin beds then instead of queens, in a small room without air-conditioning, under a breeze from an oscillating fan that swiveled and blew, back and forth, all day and night, swinging between them, patient soldiering metronome, Cara could never encounter an oscillating fan, its faithful breathing whir, without thinking of Rochelle and talking in bed with her. Into the dark they had spoken, filling each other in on everything that mattered, and much that didn't.

Sylvia Plath lay on the pillow beside Rochelle. She'd snarled when Cara had reached for her water glass. "Little shit!" she'd hissed at her, afraid.

A strangely vital thing, love, a very invisible yet essential item, hidden as an illness, mortal that way as well. In her bed, listening finally to Rochelle's steady sleep nearby, Cara felt sure an answer would come to her regarding their friendship. It was not over. But where would it, where *could* it, go next? And whom could she tell how she now felt? Nobody, no body. Tomorrow she and Rochelle would visit the sites of their peculiar tastes, the Strand, the French dress shop, Little Italy, where they'd eaten so often back in their Barnard days, yet had never been able again to locate the restaurant they'd then adored, where the waiters had known them, brought them free desserts, flirted. Outside, the air was growing brisk, a last blast of winter. On Sunday, after they boarded their flights apart and home, they would each pass through those enduring clouds, that ongoing cold rain.

# THE THERE THERE

ONCE, WHEN THEY WERE still a family, and the boys were mostly grown yet still living at home, they were sitting, the four of them, at their customary seats at the kitchen table discussing the perfect crime. That is, the murder you would get away with. From his quadrant, Caroline Wright's husband radiated disapproval.

"Out on the ocean," said their eldest, Will. He had just returned from a college recruiting trip to UCSB, so the ocean would naturally come to mind. "You could rent a boat, get them a little tipsy, then dump them overboard. Later you would tell the cops you searched and searched."

"If it was a girl, she could be on her period," added his little brother, Drew. "To explain the sharks." Though he was the younger, he already had more experience with girls and their periods; he'd imagined, maybe, his difficult girlfriend on that boat, Caroline thought. "If she was on her period," he went on, "you could also go into the forest and wait for a bear ..."

"You'd have to do some weeping to the authorities," she added to Will's nautical fantasy, "but not too much. Shock tends to dry up the tear glands."

"Or," said Will, "I also like the idea of putting poison in a pill that's a prescription, so the victim will take it who-knows-when."

"You'd have to want to kill a pill taker," Caroline said. "A capsule-pill taker. And you'd have to find some poison that fit inside it."

"*My* perfect murder," said Drew, "would be where there are two people and each of them whacks the other one's enemy. Some strangers-on-the-plane kind of thing." He sat back to finish his pancakes, a diffuse expression clouding his eyes, the look he'd had since he was a toddler when overtaken by the land of make-believe.

"Train," corrected Will. "Not plane. Mom?"

"Up in the mountains," Caroline said. For many years she'd not really lived anywhere but Telluride; when she took her daily hike, she always half expected to find a body, an aspen-limb-like leg or arm amidst the blowdown. "Up somewhere high and remote, some slippery trail. Maybe after a wine-and-cheese picnic tryst situation, way above timberline, just when the trail starts to have frozen spots. One tiny misstep, and whoops, over they go."

"Like when people back up to get their picture taken at the Grand Canyon," Will added.

"It's weird when the pictures survive and the person doesn't," said Drew, apparently dreamily adding that factor into his own scenario with the strangers, the planes and trains, the bears and sharks, the hapless victims.

"If you knew somebody with a bunch of hogs . . ." Will was saying, and Drew was adding, "Yeah, yeah, yeah! I saw that show, too!," when Caroline's husband, Gerald, rose from the table and set his breakfast dishes gently in the sink, that condemning clink of porcelain on porcelain. He was saddened by the conversation, disappointed in his family, his closest associates. The weight of it caused him to stoop, and the boys hung their heads, regretful, silenced; they would later make it up to him and he would enjoy forgiving them, but how much more horrified her husband would have been to know that it was him Caroline was imagining, standing too close to the edge at the picnic tryst, next tumbling over a cliff.

Why, then, was she so distressed when he eventually left her? She felt like the victim of an elaborate con game or magic trick, some sleight of hand business during which she'd been looking over here when she should have been looking over there. And poof!

First it was Will who disappeared, to Santa Barbara, where he rented an apartment from a Peruvian woman named Adora Zabron. His parents heard about the land-lady frequently, her gift for all things domestic: gardening, cooking, kindness. Will changed his major to international studies (he'd intended to study philosophy) and then, after his first year (three classes in Spanish; maybe they should have seen it coming), he was suddenly more than merely her tenant and young hungry friend.

Her son was in love with a woman Caroline's age. His brother Drew, then sixteen, could not quite solve this confounding dilemma, no matter how many times he played with the pieces, no matter his angle of approach. A true conundrum. "When Will's thirty," Drew would say, "she will be fifty-six."

His father the romantic said, "Love is not logical."

"And when Will's *forty*—"

"Love is not about math."

Adora Zabron had two daughters who were older than Will who still lived with their mother. In his second year of college, he moved from the apartment into their home on the ocean. He returned to Telluride for holidays, and then Drew took his first trip alone to visit in California. This visit did nothing to solve the riddle of his brother's romance; he told Caroline, confidentially, that had he been in Will's shoes, he would have opted for one of the daughters, that they were both very pretty, but the mother was, "well, no offense, because you definitely don't, Mom, but Adora even *smells* old, like Granna, like that powder. Nothing like you. She's exactly opposite of you." Now who was the most perplexed? Her son had apparently chosen a woman who was not Caroline in every way except the most alarming one of her age. The two of them even shared a zodiac sign, born only days apart. Capricorn.

The Peruvian, Drew reported, was frequently overwhelmed by feelings that brought on tears. "Happy tears," he clarified. "She hugs everyone. She cried at the airport and gave me this necklace so the plane wouldn't crash."

When the family took their annual trip abroad that summer, Will for the first time declined to join them. Now it seemed he belonged to another family. And it wasn't the same, without both of the boys along. There was nobody to share the tiny backseat of the rental car with Drew. Nobody to race with around the ruins. Nobody to go adventuring with at night this summer, into Rome's or Florence's or Siena's streets. Drew simply had his placid parents, Caroline pondering the people, and her husband, an engineer by trade, marveling at ancient ingenuity. At the Colosseum, they had an unfortunate encounter. An overweight American couple was bickering bitterly in the shadow of the structure. "Where the hell *are* we?" the man shouted at his wife, who told him she didn't fucking *know*, hurling the guidebook in his direction, both of them sunburned in their too-tight red T-shirts. Caroline had begun laughing, her hand on Drew's shoulder as they both turned away tittering. But her husband had taken pity on the couple, offering a kind smile and a patient explanation of their map. He did not like to have fun at the expense of others.

"But Dad," Drew tried later, hoping to explain himself, "I mean, it was the *Colosseum*. That's like not seeing the Grand Canyon until you fell in it; like, it's the *there there*."

But Gerald refused to be amused. And then, by year's end, he had left Caroline for another woman. How alarming this was, to her; she had for years believed that it was she who had the choice, she who could claim the martyr's virtue of staying when she wished to go. Her pride injured, Caroline indulged in her old fantasy of Gerald's death; she would have far preferred widowhood to divorce, a sentiment that not one of her family members would understand and that she therefore kept to herself.

He was leaving her, he explained, because love had struck him, unexpectedly, without his asking for it, like lightning.

"Oh bullshit," Caroline said. "Even I know the function of the so-called lightning rod."

"You won't miss me," Gerald said. "You'll miss the idea of me, but not *me*." Which was, in fact, surprisingly true. Scorched by an idea, stung by a role suddenly undone, and, finally, zinged by her husband's smarts about the whole thing.

Next, when the time came, Drew graduated high school and packed for college. He should have gone to one of the coasts; he should have had the same kind of adventure as his brother (minus the aged Peruvian, Caroline mentally amended). But he couldn't bear to leave his mother and went in-state instead. That was her second boy, cursed with loyalty, and guilt, and softness. That dreamy look in his eyes. His brother, meanwhile, married Adora Zabron. His parents were not invited to the ceremony (civil; witnessed by his two new stepdaughters, those beauties, who were five and six years older than he), and were told, when they asked, that gifts were not necessary. Adora and he already possessed all the required gadgets and appliances and stemware. If they wished, his family could donate funds to rescue an endangered animal or build a sewage system for orphans somewhere in the third world.

It wasn't just his abandoned mother (his betraying father) who was responsible for Drew's choosing to study close to home. There was also his girlfriend, Crystal Hurd. Since they'd been children, she'd been his best friend. The nearby tomboy neighbor with her bully brothers and their de-scented pet skunk. For the whole of eighth grade she and Drew had feuded and not spoken; then they had sex in the ninth grade, and were once again inseparable, yet in a manner quite unlike their former inseparability. No longer did Crystal walk into Caroline's house without knocking. No more opening the cookie jar and helping herself to a treat. Instead of calling Caroline by her first name, she used no name at all to address her. In fact, when she spoke it was exclusively to Drew, as if she'd never had her bottom wiped by Caroline, or gum snipped very gently from her quite long and ratty hair. Crystal's parents worked at the same places Drew's did, but in completely other capacities. Her father served on the crew reclaiming the mine ruins, wearing a hard hat, while Gerald supervised from a trailer. Her mother was a lunch lady and custodian at the high school where Caroline had taught English before being promoted to vice principal. Management and labor, Drew would learn to label the difference. But it wasn't that simple, really; Telluride teenagers lived in a place perpetually in party mode, no matter who their parents were or why they lived there, and the ones who hadn't been sent to boarding school navigated it as a group, old-timers and newcomers alike, rich, working-class, white, brown.

Drew came home from college frequently, and Crystal joined him in his bedroom, yet when they emerged neither looked pleased. He missed Crystal, he told Caroline, when he was in Fort Collins, but at home he didn't wish to see her.

He wanted his old feelings, Caroline believed. They were gone and he resented Crystal's not being able to inspire them any longer. During his second semester, he only returned once, for spring break. By the time summer came around, he had met Elizabeth. Never Betsy, Liz, nor any other diminutive, always the full royal title. Drew kept his mother apprised of the marvelous and mysterious Elizabeth: Her father the Manhattan lawyer! Her penthouse childhood! Her current astonishing inability to operate a motor vehicle! For her part, Crystal seemed to have talked herself into thinking this rift was not unlike the eighth-grade one, a necessary separation that would yield, eventually, another reunion, an intimacy as yet unknown. Phoenixlike, their future would emerge reformed and pure, better and enduring.

Caroline didn't think it likely. Drew's Elizabeth was heading back to New York for the summer, and he planned to go with her. There would be no European vacation, this year, and when Caroline lay alone in the Telluride house where they'd all lived for so long, she imagined her former family members pinned on a U.S. map, each man with another woman, one on the West Coast, one on the East, and her ex-husband relocated two hours south. How had it turned out that she was the only one sleeping by herself?

A few years later, it was from Crystal Hurd that Caroline learned of her younger son's intention to marry. She learned it at three in the morning, Crystal slamming her palm on the fragile glass of Caroline's front door, simultaneously kicking with her steel-toed boot at the wooden base. The dogs were in such a barking frenzy that Caroline could not at first make out what she was yelling. "Why doesn't he want me?" Crystal was demanding drunkenly on Caroline's porch. "What did I do?" Her hair was wet with snow, her face smeared with eye makeup, her clothes muddy or bloody from a spill in the street on her way home after the bars had closed. "I can't be alone!" Crystal explained, falling into Caroline's living room, across a footstool. Then she abruptly righted herself and headed for the kitchen, where she lowered her pants and sat on a kitchen chair to pee.

"Oh, for god's sake," Caroline said, lifting her and leading her shuffling into the bathroom.

"Why?" Crystal kept inquiring, through the removal of her wretched clothing, during the hot shower, again and again while, afterward, being outfitted in Caroline's spare pajamas, which were startlingly too large, and over the scrambled eggs and toast she ate by using her fingers to load the fork. The girl, although twenty-six years old, had never really grown up. Her logic, to which Caroline was treated between bites, was a child's.

Crystal had been waiting, it seemed, hoping in the way of the faithful, in the way of the family pet, for Drew to graduate college, then graduate graduate school, then finally come back to his senses, come back home, come back to her. All that time, he'd been with Elizabeth. Elizabeth. Who'd been denied the Ivy League and sent far away to a state school in punishment for teenage rebellion. Who was disdainful of the West and frightened of nature. Who was allergic. Who, when she visited Telluride, had to stay in a condominium instead of at Drew's house with Drew's mother and Drew's old dogs. Elizabeth who had the power to keep Drew at that condominium with her; he returned home without Crystal Hurd's knowing he was there, approaching from a side street so as to avoid her front windows.

"He was gonna date in college and I was dating here, but we were gonna be together when we had some more experience," Crystal wailed. "He can't get motherfucking *married!*"

There wasn't any answer for this; Caroline's three men all either had gotten or apparently were going to get motherfucking married. She sympathized with Crystal. When Crystal had been in high school, when it had become clear that her family had no intention of even considering the possibility of college, Caroline had approached the girl with an offer of help. Help in finding scholarships, help in persuading her parents, help in the form of a modest stipend. "I can *help*," Caroline had said, the word there between them sounding suddenly utterly impotent, like a popped bubble. Crystal's face had clouded with a belligerent pride, the same expression her father had worn when laid off at the mine reclamation site, or her mother as she'd mopped the high school halls at the end of the day. The face of her brothers when cited for poaching or trespassing or trying to park a trailer home on their property. The delicate truce that existed in Telluride between its local classes was easily provoked. "You know, *Ms. Wright*, college isn't the only thing to do," Crystal had icily informed Caroline.

Now she was afraid to leave Crystal alone, and sat on the chair beside the couch to oversee the remainder of the dark hours. Clean-faced, sated, exhausted, and spent, the girl slept with her hands palm to palm beneath her cheek, like an angel. When she'd been little, she'd wanted to learn how to knit, and she and Caroline would sit on these same pieces of furniture, armed with their pointy sticks. She'd been wholly pleased with her lumpy doll's blanket. When Drew and Crystal had begun sleeping together, Caroline had provided condoms and promised not to tell Crystal's parents. Her husband hadn't liked that about Caroline, her willingness to conspire against others to serve what she believed was the greater good. He named it disrespectful. "You patronize," he said. "You think you know best."

Which was true: she thought she knew best.

The next morning, there was nothing of the angel left in Crystal. She rose furious with her hostess. "*You* wouldn't want him with me anyway!" she accused. "*You're* the one who made him go to college! *You're* the one who always thought I wasn't good enough!" She tore every single one of the buttons off the borrowed pajamas as she ripped them from her body. Caroline would find them for weeks afterward, while cleaning. The slamming door shook the house.

"Well, *that* didn't seem very fair, did it?" Caroline said aloud to the dogs.

A few nights later Crystal was back; once again it was three in the morning. Once again, she'd been at the bars. But this time when she banged on the glass and kicked at the frail wood below, she was yelling about all the pills she'd swallowed. She was having second thoughts, she shouted to Caroline, to the street at large.

Caroline pulled her, once again wet and muddy and freezing cold, into the house. "I don't want to die!" she screamed in Caroline's face. "He might divorce her later! *His* mom and dad got divorced, you guys, I mean! I don't want to die!" They rode together in the ambulance; it was Caroline who sat beside her at the clinic after her stomach had been pumped. And once again, Crystal was not happy to see her when she woke up.

"Should I come home?" Drew asked, sighing into the phone. He wanted to be told no; Caroline was tempted to say yes. If only she'd actually preferred Elizabeth to Crystal Hurd. If only Drew's desire to forget Crystal, his loving some other woman, hadn't conspired to make him less lovable to his mother. She'd thought it might be different with her second son than it had been with Will. But it seemed she'd lost them both.

"Don't come," she told him. "You can't do her any good. She has to get used to not having you."

The problem was, Crystal didn't have *anybody*. Her father had died (lung cancer), and her mother, although relocated nearby in Montrose, failed to comprehend a problem as puny as this; depression? "She needs to snap out of it," the woman told Caroline on the phone. "She has a house, free and clear, what more does she want?" If Caroline hadn't immediately said goodbye, Crystal's mother would have repeated the information that everybody knew: the land under that house was worth two million dollars. Two. Million. Dollars. *What more does she want?*

That was the problem: wanting more.

Crystal's brothers were also gone (prison, the army, Hawaii); the other nearby neighbors were not the old ones; their houses had been built in the former yards of the old places, giant homes that, despite filling the lots and resting nearer to each other, also managed to declare an aggressive architectural insistence on privacy. Young families with beautifully sporty mothers; second or third homes to skiers from California or Texas; one mansion halted midway, foreclosed and now occupied by a half dozen hippies squatting behind the plywood and Tyvek.

Caroline and Crystal were now equally alone in their homes half a block apart, newly aware of one another, both lonely for Drew. Caroline felt specifically responsible; when she walked to school in the morning, she'd check for signs that Crystal had come home the night before—boots left outside the door, overhead porch light extinguished. Some evenings she went to the Mexican restaurant where Crystal waited tables and sat in her section, drinking margaritas and talking. They had more to say to each other in public than they did in private. Or maybe it was the margaritas. Maybe one of them needed to be drunk before they could really converse.

Sometimes Caroline would see the girl bring home somebody from her nights out at the bars. Telluride was still and forever that same vacation destination; there was always a party to attend, people to meet and drink with, and Crystal was pretty, confident in the way of the insider, needy in the way of the lovelorn, and always familiar with someone on either side of the bar, tending *and* drinking. She could tell stories about the town's history; she knew who sold coke or pot, and which cop was the most lax if you happened to get caught. She had a within-walking-distance house where a drunk boy could crash; she was desperate to fall in love. But she didn't, or couldn't. Drew might have forever stunted her in that capacity.

As perhaps Caroline had been stunted, not so much by her marriage to Gerald as by his wishing to exit it, to undo it; she could not quite surmount the total surprise. He'd never surprised her before. If anything, it had been his predictability that had made her feel close to him: she'd known what he was thinking, what he wanted, what he would say. Some mornings, they'd woken having had the same dream—except that in Gerald's dream, his cohort was Caroline, and in Caroline's there was no cohort.

There was no man. In middle age, she had no patience for new intimacies; the groundwork was exhausting, all the accumulated details of some other person's life, the number of siblings, the catalog of troubles, and the high potential for some ludicrous deal-breaking belief in magic or miracles or money. Here was the consequence of having chosen to live in a tourist town, a place whose offerings had been, from the beginning, startlingly physical, if not gold and silver and lesser mining booty, then snowpack and tourist dollars, and forever a stunning beauty. Movie starlet gorgeous, and perhaps equally vacuous.

Caroline's sons would never mention her love life, or its lack; the idea would disgust Will and embarrass Drew. One morning, passing by Crystal Hurd's house, Caroline ran into the man who'd spent the night. A stranger, another in a long line of people who'd come to town for a wild weekend. Behind him, in the doorway, stood Crystal. The women appraised one another, Crystal still languid and unguarded, wrapped in a quilt, and Caroline bundled for the weather, waterproof, armed with trekking sticks. Crystal's expression said, *You envy me*, while Caroline worked to communicate *I disapprove!* Behind the girl, a dark room with a rumpled bed, the odor of sex and a stranger still pungent.

It was dizzyingly easy to imagine.

"I have to go to New York," Caroline told Crystal in May. "For the wedding." Ostensibly, she was asking the girl to take care of the two dogs for her, as she had a couple of times in the past. She fully expected to be punched.

Instead, Crystal's eyes filled and she dissolved into Caroline's embrace, a warm and pliant body that shook and sobbed for a good long while. Holding her, Caroline was struck by how long it had been since she'd been so passionately and physically near another person, how sticky and paralyzing a hug seemed.

Gerald came alone to the wedding, some concession to the truce he'd managed with his sons after the divorce. He'd grown stringy with age, and his smile seemed tentative; he'd become more vulnerable without somebody fearsome there to keep him defended. "I'm worried about Will," he confided to Caroline at the reception, after a few glasses of champagne. Alcohol had always gone straight to his head and made him sappy. "He's depressed."

"He's chafing," Caroline predicted. "He got married too young, to somebody too old. What was she, the first woman he ever slept with?" Will's wife, Adora, clapped merrily at the head of a spontaneous line she'd orchestrated on the dance floor, people running in a circle, partnering, creating a bower with their hands for the others to duck under, then reclaiming the circle, cheering maniacally. The antics beneath the bower got more outlandish with each pass through, a man now wielding his wife by the ankles like a wheelbarrow. Meanwhile, the bride, Elizabeth, looked on with a tight smile; sweaty people on their hands and knees wasn't what she'd had in mind.

"Some people don't have to have a raft of previous lovers," Gerald said primly.

"You should tell Will to have an affair," Caroline replied, leaning into her ex-husband's neck to make sure he could hear. "He hooked up too early, he hasn't had enough experience. Tell him to have a secret affair, and to let it inform the rest of his marriage."

Gerald pulled back as if singed. "I will not tell him that."

"Just because it's unconventional doesn't mean it isn't good advice."

Gerald squinted, sorting out the triple negatives. But then later it seemed her son had gotten the word anyway; Will made a point of keeping his distance the remainder of the weekend, not that he'd been especially enthusiastic about seeing Caroline before that. He was careful to prevent his wife and his mother from ever being in conversation together, as if he'd told Adora something scandalous or tragic that she would inquire into, given the chance. But what would it be, Caroline wondered?

She had been assigned no duty in this marriage ceremony, no part to play larger than placeholder. "Just show up," Drew had said. Elizabeth's mother and sisters had done the rest. Will had been best man; Gerald had written a toast and proposed it tearfully. Before Adora had hijacked the dance floor, Drew had taken his mother for a sort of waltz, holding her by the shoulders as if she were a large box.

"Mom," he said, "I know you wouldn't do anything like this, but please don't ever ask Elizabeth about grandchildren, OK?"

"I would never do that."

"I know, like I said, but she can't have any, so it's no good to bring it up."

He needn't have worried; Elizabeth brought it up herself, the day Caroline was scheduled to leave, during the delay at Newark. Drew had driven Will and Adora and Gerald to JFK; Elizabeth was stuck with Caroline. Whatever etiquette rulebook she'd been brought up with dictated she could not leave her mother-in-law at the curb. "Just so there's absolute clarity," she began outside security, "I want you to know that I'm sterile." So cold, Caroline thought, a trait she herself had occasionally been accused of. And also, as if Elizabeth assumed that her mother-in-law could only be interested in her as a vehicle toward grandchildren. Was she supposed to now offer sympathy? Suggest adoption? Pray for hypoallergenic pets? She could not tell; nothing in the girl's face gave her a clue.

Such a strange way to think of oneself, Caroline thought later, forehead pressed to the chilly oval window, eyes following the country passing below her. *Sterile.* It suited Elizabeth, that fickle aristocrat, she who'd placed a container of hand sanitizer beside the guest registry, who'd sulked when the wedding party had grown raucous, who'd disallowed children at the ceremony, who'd declined to invite Drew's friends' band to play in favor of a costly string quartet. Sterile, indeed; Caroline could almost prefer her other daughter-in-law, the plump postmenopausal weeping one she'd suggested her other son cheat on.

A For Sale sign had appeared in the Hurd front yard in her brief absence, and Crystal had her stubborn face back in place. "I'm not gonna turn thirty like *this*," she said to

Caroline as if Caroline was arguing with her about it. "I gotta go *do* something." She returned the dogs' leashes and mentioned that the terrier had escaped and been AWOL for a day and a half. "You're lucky the sheriff likes you," she said to Caroline.

"You're lucky the sheriff likes me," Caroline told the dog who'd strayed. Hugo.

There'd always been a couple of dogs in the house. The family had two types, the white terrier and the beagle. This had been the pattern from the beginning, a tradition Caroline had brought with her based on her parents' preferences. In fact, the first terrier in her life with her husband and children had been inherited from her parents when her father had died and her mother had been moved to a nursing home. The current pair were Caroline's companions as she hiked up and down her favorite trails around the town, two dogs who inspired other hikers to remark on their fortitude, the short legs of the terrier, the plaintive, straining expression of the bug-eyed beagle.

In July, Caroline's mother died in Denver; it was a mercy, her mind having slid far away from her long ago. Caroline's monthly visits to the old woman had passed without recognition or notice. "Why do I come here?" Caroline had asked aloud. "What is it I hope will happen?" "Granna?" Drew would shout over the telephone, and the woman would turn a terrified face to Caroline: why was this man yelling at her? Soon after the death, Caroline retired from the high school. There'd been a change of regime; she had not been promoted to principal, and that had seemed signal enough to step aside. Her farewell party was attended by a touchingly large crowd—graduates came from as far away as Grand Junction. Caroline found herself grateful for the ritual, willing to embrace her longtime enemies and antagonists along with the more benign of her colleagues. Defused, she could be approached with generosity, or indifference. Leaving the building she swore never to step through its doors again.

And for a few months, Caroline and the two dogs went through their days easily enough; she felt a kind of lightness that came from having no obligation, no to-do list, no reason to change out of her pajamas. No people in need of her. In September she traveled to Turkey and Greece with her friend the town librarian. They drank too much and made fun of the other tourists on the trip, elderly and frightened, overloud and incurious. Caroline revived the notorious Colosseum couple, and thereafter either she or the librarian would shout out, at each iconic landmark, "Where *are* we?" and the other would screech back, "I don't fucking *know!*"

Upon her return home, she discovered she could no longer summon up the password to her computer, as if a journey to the ancient world could have effectively supplanted the present one. She tried everything she could imagine—ihategerald!; Hugo8it; loveandsqualor—but none of her familiar whims would work. This forgetfulness, the swirling patch of miasma in her brain, frightened her. She could not move around it, nor could she ignore it; in the night, she woke with the sensation of having been sucked inside it, a personal black hole. She could have access to the computer restored, but to herself?

"If I get like Granna," she'd told her sons after a disastrous visit to the home, "somebody shoot me." Their grandmother had accused the boys of robbing and raping her; she'd butted at them with her skull, then raised her walker like a lion tamer; the home had learned never to send male personnel to tend to her.

"Everybody says that," Will informed her sniffily. "Everybody says, 'If I get like that, just shoot me,' like it would be easy for us to shoot you."

"Like we would have a gun," Drew added.

"Why don't you shoot Granna?" Will demanded. "Don't you think she'd have said that, back when?"

"I'd probably use a pillow," Caroline told her sons calmly.

"You're so cold," Will said, shaking his head. And Drew had begun to cry.

"He's the only guy I ever slept with when I wasn't drunk," Crystal confided to Caroline over margaritas. "I don't even feel like kissing anybody till I've had a few drinks. Except Drew. I always feel like kissing Drew." Present tense.

"You need to move on," Caroline said. She wouldn't have offered such pedestrian advice sober.

"Easy for you to say," said Crystal. She was supposed to be waiting tables; her boss, Steve-o, kept shouting out at her to look lively. It was off-season again; only locals. "I'm thinking of having a baby."

"By yourself?"

"Yes, that's actually possible, you know. Spendy, but possible."

"Why expensive?"

"Sperm donor. I've been online, you should see the sites. Fucking hell, it's something. Very different from dating sites, I might add. Night and day."

"I wish you could get Drew to make you pregnant," said Caroline, because she was tipsy, and because it was true. She wanted another chance at loving somebody. She wanted to be someone's beloved. *Nana*, she practiced.

"Really?" Crystal reached across the table and took Caroline's hand, because she was tipsy, too, and as in her relations with men other than Drew, this was when she could be tender with this woman, this difficult woman who'd known her for so long and in so many different ways: neighbor, teacher, nagger, savior. And Crystal's history with Drew made their sleeping together again something so habitual and native to them that it might as well be named another thing. It wouldn't be like the typical infidelity, would it? Not like cheating, exactly. When Caroline considered it, there seemed nothing more pure, yet also nothing more vaguely incestuous, these people who'd grown up together, sharing bath time, punching and screaming and spending the night, exhausted children sweating and sprawled at day's end, heads on one another's chest, sex not unlike any other game they'd played together as competitors, opponents. Or? As allies, teammates. "Make him come home," Crystal pleaded. "Let's make him come back here and knock me up!"

"It's so highly unethical," Caroline said, beginning to laugh, liking the idea precisely because her ex-husband would have been appalled. Utterly appalled. From the back came Steve-o's imploring bored voice reminding Crystal that, hello, she was at work, earning a paycheck, fucking up her tips. "I have to admit that I really like the idea."

"Make him come home," Crystal pleaded, this time with her wild eyes, with her scrawny starved body. She had not been well, since the wedding. She had what anyone in Telluride had as the weather closed in, as the social season faded, as the mountains' majesty occasionally appeared more menacing than beautiful, cruelly indifferent. It was a kind of personal off-season.

Sober, the women never mentioned their notion again.

Not long after, on a frozen January morning, a highway patrolman's car showed up in Crystal's gravel drive. Had the girl done what she'd always threatened to do? And how had Caroline not been roused, through her thin walls, her light sleep, her long-standing nearness to Crystal's life? She didn't bother to dress, found herself down the block and at the Hurd front door minus even socks or slippers, banging with her fist to accompany the banging of her heart.

Crystal answered, in her hastily drawn bathrobe, and Caroline saw her mistake. The highway patrolman was simply another in that line of men brought home on a drunken Friday night. "Are you OK?" Crystal asked, scowling, yawning widely. "What's wrong?"

"Nothing," Caroline said, turning angrily and taking herself home, one of her feet bleeding from a piece of broken glass in the street.

Thereafter, whenever Caroline saw the new man himself, a thick-necked figure bursting from his uniform, he never failed to touch his hat, a gesture of respect; or it was supposed to be, but Caroline was skeptical. She thought perhaps she was a fond mean joke between Crystal and the cop, the crazy neighbor who ran around in her pajamas. He wasn't from Telluride, he commuted from Montrose, he'd never been her student or a friend of her sons. Soon, she imagined, Crystal would be pregnant. The child would sleep in the room Crystal had grown up occupying. From some sentimental urge would come the idea of another pet skunk, that odd scurrying figure from the past. Caroline could not forget Crystal's confessing that she'd never had a first kiss with anybody except Drew when she was sober. "Not sex, either, except Drew. That's why I can't get anywhere," she'd said angrily, "that's how fucked up I am. If you want to know." She and the highway patrolman got drunk together, now. On occasion, Caroline could hear them. Their music. Sometimes something that rattled the house, its walls as thin as her own, its mining-times origins clearer with the overlarge presence of the patrolman contained therein. He roared up at odd hours; he slammed his official car door and puffed out his chest. He was coarse, crude, loud, proud; he was as different from her son Drew as a man could be. How had Crystal fallen for him?

When Drew phoned her for her birthday, Caroline mentioned Crystal's new beau. "That's good," he said. "She really, *really* needed somebody. I wondered why the drunk dialing went away."

"He's awful! He seems smug," Caroline told him. "And maybe not that bright?"

"Mom, you know sometimes you're a little hard on people."

"He's no you," she said. "That's all. I'd rather be alone than be with someone so inferior."

"Well, Dad always says you're the only person he knows who doesn't actually need other people." Drew was laughing, as if this were good news. Was it good news? It was news, anyway, news to Caroline.

"I wish I could clone you," she said to him, a compliment she'd paid him since he was young.

At the Mexican restaurant on a night when ski season was at full throttle—spring break, fresh powder, at capacity—Caroline found herself at the bar with the highway patrolman eating chips and sharing a pitcher of margaritas. On the house, Crystal's insistence. Crystal had put on some weight in recent months, was vaguely radiant, bustling among the tourists being sexy, stopping to check in on her new boyfriend and old neighbor now and then. "Hey, I have a question for you," Caroline said over the happy public ruckus to the cop. She was brave and buffered by the alcohol and high spirits.

"Shoot," he yelled back.

"What's your opinion on the subject of the perfect crime? I mean, how would somebody get away with murder? In your opinion?"

He looked at her glassy-eyed, the man who'd taken her son's place in Crystal's life. How she longed for Drew, looking into those impassive eyes, and how she missed Crystal's longing for him. This man was no replacement, not even close. "I tell you what," he said, leaning in, speaking into her ear so as to be heard. "I know for a fact you don't like me and think I'm a dumbass. I could care less, I don't give a shit. But what you're asking? Well, here's what I think: I think the way to get away with murder is to make them do it to themself." He leaned back and nodded at her. "If you see what I mean."

"I do," Caroline said. "I get it. Tell me your first name."

"I'm Johnny," he said, and held out his large rough hand to shake hers.

# CHAPTER TWO

Tired of telling her own story at AA, Hil was trying to tell the one of her neighbor. It had been a peculiar week. "So she comes to my house a few nights ago," Hil began, "like around nine, *bing-bong*, drunk as a skunk, as usual, right in the middle of this show my roommate and I are watching. I go to the door and there she is, fifty-something, a totally naked lady standing under the porch light." Even at the time, it had seemed designed to charm, her coy drunken neighbor sporting a plaid porkpie hat and holding a toothbrush like a flag or flower or torch. Choreographed, at least, and embarrassing to behold. Bergeron Love, grande dame in her own mind and all around the block.

"Looks like somebody's not getting enough attention," Hil had murmured as she unlocked the door. The night was soggy, Houston autumn, frogs like squeezeboxes wheezing in and out. Her neighbor's nakedness seemed sad and enervated, breasts flat on her chest, a kind of melted look to the rest of her flesh, ankles thick on splayed feet. Southern belle in decline, a dismal "after" picture.

What had "before" looked like?

"You gonna invite me in?" Bergeron Love demanded, raising her eyebrows flirtily in an attempt to rally her own outlandishness. She was known in the neighborhood for being a character—some composite of Miss Havisham, Norma Desmond, and Scarlett O'Hara—her ancient family manse with its aspect of ruined wedding cake, fenced as if to contain inmates, its fetid kidney-shaped pool where her multiple orange cats congregated. Sometimes Bergeron's antics were whimsical, like crashing a dinner or cocktail party, for example, or commissioning someone in a gorilla suit to deliver balloons, and sometimes they were a serious pain in the ass—reporting overgrown lawns or loose dogs or long-term parked cars, more than once phoning child protective services.

"You can't exactly say no to a naked lady on your doorstep, can you?" Hil asked rhetorically at the meeting. She made eye contact with the smiling older man holding the leash of his helper animal. There ought always to be a blind man grinning encouragingly, receptively, in the audience, wavy white hair like meringue. The dog lay panting at his feet, head grasped a little unnaturally high by the leash, by the man's inability to see. The man's genial countenance was generic—through every story, no matter how unpleasant, he smiled benignly beneath his lovely hair. He had, Hil thought, become like a dog himself, unable to judge.

"My roommate never met my neighbor before, so I introduce them." How strange to see a clothed person shake hands with a naked one, like the meeting of two utterly different tribes. *Bergeron Love, this is Janine.*

"Nice to meet you," said Janine, averting her eyes.

"Janine is getting her degree at the U," Hil offered. "In social work," she added, since Janine was shy.

"Ha!" said Bergeron Love, raising her toothbrush. "You can consider this visit a piece of immersion homework! What in the hell is that?" she asked, aiming the brush at the paused image on the television.

"A bullet puncturing somebody's heart in slow motion," Janine said. On the screen, a few perfect circles: bullet, organ, splatter. "Not *actually*," she added.

"Well obviously not actually," Bergeron said. "One of those true-crime shows? I love those, but my boyfriend Boyd can't take it. He literally can't watch gore. Isn't that just typical?" Boyfriend Boyd was a mousy man who donned an orange vest every school-day morning and stood blowing into a whistle on the corner of Westheimer and Taft, waving his arms to help the children across. He hid behind a pair of giant square glasses and a push-broom mustache. Only with his vivid vest and shrill whistle did he seem to have much confidence. Then, or after a few stiff drinks.

"You want a robe, Bergeron?" Hil asked. The woman was going to either sit or fall down, and the chair nearest was the one Hil's teenage son preferred.

"Why would I want a robe?" demanded Bergeron Love. "You got a problem with the human body? You're watching that shit on TV, and you can't look at *me*?"

"I just didn't want her naked butt on the chair where my son likes to sit," Hil explained to the AA meeting. "But she kind of collapses in his chair anyway, and starts to ramble about her fucked-up life. Sorry, Jim." The blind man had flinched; his single admission, in all the time he'd come and taken up his role as accepting group focal point, was that the word *fuck* still hurt his feelings. He nodded now, recovered, absolving.

"Friday night," Bergeron Love was saying, "I'm walking up and down the street, and I can't even get arrested!"

"That's partly your fault, you know, Berge," Hil said, explaining to Janine that it had been Bergeron Love, years earlier, who had been mostly responsible for rousting the homeless and the homeless shelter from the neighborhood. Civic duty was a Love family hallmark; there were bridges and schools and state parks commemorating the name. "Remember all those drunk bums?" Hil said.

"Pissing in our yards," Bergeron recalled, "leaving all their Sudafed trash in the park. You don't know the half of what I kept off this street. Next they wanted to turn that flophouse into an AIDS clinic. No, ma'am, said I."

"But Berge, if those guys were still around, there'd have been more action out there tonight. You'd have had company. They would have been ecstatic to see you coming." And Bergeron Love laughed appreciatively, conceding, still savvy in her deceptive absurdity, then wondered aloud what a person had to do to get a drink around here. "I had an open container until just a little bit ago," she explained. "There might be some broken glass out on your walkway, sorry about that."

Janine jumped at the chance to leave the room.

"*That* is a *big* old gal," Bergeron Love whispered.

Hil couldn't disagree; Janine was three times her own size, a woman who must have been eating most of the day to maintain her weight, and yet Hil had never seen her do it. Janine had her own shelves in the fridge and cupboards; plastic grocery bags came and went; and still Hil had never shared a meal with the woman.

"You're lucky *she's* not the nudie here," Bergeron said, then added, in her normal voice, "Where's your son? Out on a date? Raising some high school hell?"

"He's here," Hil said. Had he heard, from his bedroom? Declined to enter the fray? No doubt he was listening to music on headphones, reading a philosophy book, texting with his school-hours-only girlfriend. He led a quiet, self-contained life; his peers maybe frightened him; he wasn't ready, quite yet, to go unguarded into the night. It was he who every evening checked the locks and switched off the lights. After Hil went to bed, he and Janine would play complex and violent video games into the wee hours, keeping score, speaking a fascinating coded language with one another while adroitly operating their control devices, never taking their eyes from the divided screen. For this, and other, reasons, she was an excellent roommate to both Hil and Jeremy, her own social life nearly nonexistent. Like Hil, she went to meetings to discuss her defining, overwhelming weakness; in the kitchen now, she would no doubt be devouring a frozen candy bar in addition to mixing fresh gin and tonics. She insisted on keeping the chocolate frozen hard, despite the broken crown she'd incurred just last week. Addicts, Hil marveled: so dedicated!

At a different AA meeting, earlier in the week, Hil had started the story of her longtime neighbor Bergeron Love at a different point. "So my neighbor the busybody once reported another of our neighbors to the child protective services." This meeting was one composed solely of women; there was no friendly blind man upon whom to settle her eyes in this group. In fact, they were an altogether tougher audience, overall, than the meetings that included men. Less likely to forgive rambling or giggling shares, readier to call bullshit on somebody's tears. "After my neighbor reported this guy, this huge tattooed Hispanic guy who was supposedly abusing his daughters, he started stalking her son." Bergeron's then-ten-year-old boy Allistair. Allistair the fair and pale and earnest and brave, who'd later walked Hil's son around on Halloween, utterly unembarrassed by holding a five-year-old's hand. Allistair was a good boy. Reporting the alleged abuse had been a lesson in minding your own business, Hil thought; Allistair had had to be moved to another school. Restraining orders had been required. Bergeron Love's front yard had been egged, her car graffitied, her most beautiful live oak killed by mysterious means. The tree had fallen on her porch, her gentle awkward son had been separated from his familiar friends, she never knew what to expect when she opened her front door in the morning. That man still lived in the neighborhood. His daughters and wife, to this day, had never said a word against him.

"But my neighbor knew," Hil told the group of women. "She'd heard him through the bathroom window with the girls. 'Don't, Daddy, don't! It hurts, please, Daddy!'" Bergeron Love had gone from one house to another, pleading her case, her car with its windshield covered in red spray paint parked at the curb for all to see. *Racist wore!* it said. "I know it's him because he didn't spray the *car*! He cares so much about cars, he couldn't spray the metal!" It was true that the man loved his vehicles; the house and yard were shabby, but his classic sedan and truck sat sparkling and cherry in the drive.

"It just seemed so unfair that her boy was suffering because of her," Hil went on to the roomful of women, most of them mothers. Little Allistair Love, studious, dutiful, always alongside Bergeron at the polling stations on Election Day, shirt clattering with campaign buttons. "I don't know exactly what I'm trying to say, I guess, but she came to my house just the other night, *bing-bong*, most likely lonely for her boy, I'm thinking now. He's all grown up now, living over in Austin. I mean, I can imagine how it'd be, having your son move away . . ."

Occasionally, on a bad night in the past, she'd heard teenaged Allistair trying to negotiate with his mother and Boyd when they took their drunken disagreements public, to the street. With a few drinks in him, Boyd could overcome his timidity, like a person in the woods encountering a wild animal, acting bigger than he was, defensive yet false bravado. Their issues were forgettable—certainly to them, tomorrow's amnesia—blame and counter blame, outrage shouted upon outrage, insult on insult, but Bergeron's son's entreaties were always the same: *come inside, please get out of the street.* Heartbreaking, that pleading, unforgettable adenoidal voice.

"Every time she came to my door, it was, you know, like, 'What fresh hell is this?' I mostly only saw her when she was drunk, but I know she had some kind of wits about her, since she got shit done in our neighborhood. Since she seemed to bring up a pretty great kid, mostly by herself." Bergeron the pitiful, whose first and only marriage it was rumored had not lasted more than a summer, that gold-digging, sperm-donor ex-husband who'd left her both pregnant and poorer by half. Also, Bergeron the bully, who'd driven off the homeless and their shelter, who'd prevented the presence of probably harmless AIDS patients. Bergeron the hypocrite, who'd fought and lost many a zoning battle from the confines of her own sagging antebellum monstrosity, in need of paint and roofing and porch repair, not to mention the proliferating cat population, inbred and unhealthy. And Bergeron the legend, debutante, socialite, donor, the Love name a lingering Houston institution, she some sort of mysterious yet powerful black sheep.

But at the evening women's meeting, Hil didn't mention what had happened that very morning. The ambulance and fire truck had roused the block at daybreak, pulling into place at Bergeron Love's front walk from either side, a dozen uniformed people hopping to action, everybody else stepping out in their sweatpants and bathrobes and mussed hair, arms crossed over their chests, curious about what, now, mercurial Bergeron Love had set into motion.

On that earlier, naked night, Hil had excused herself briefly to Bergeron and Janine. In the hall she was grateful for her son's resolutely closed door. She dialed her neighbor's number, making her way to the study, the window of which looked out on the street. From there, Hil could see the Love house, the shape of Boyd through the tall front window watching television. But he wouldn't answer the phone, on the first call. "Oh, hell no," Hil murmured, dialing the number again. She could almost hear it ringing over there. Could almost hear Boyd's mighty reluctant sigh as he rose, this time, and picked up. "Hello," he said hopefully, as if he hadn't already seen who it was on caller ID. As if he had no idea what he was going to be told. He was a chinless man who had routinely and voluntarily let himself be bossed around, made small. Bergeron wouldn't marry him—"Fool me once, shame on you," she'd said on the subject of marriage. "Fool me twice? No, ma'am"—wouldn't let him be anything other than her aging sillily named *boyfriend*. "You maybe want to come retrieve Bergeron?" Hil said to him.

"She told me she was setting out to get arrested."

"That hasn't come to pass just yet. I guess I could call the cops, if you really think she needs all that drama." Bergeron would not fear authority; her family was superior to most forces. "But it takes so long when there's uniforms involved. The paperwork."

Five minutes later Boyd stood wearily at the door. Wearing clothes, Hil was grateful to see. But instead of pulling Bergeron out of Hil's house, Boyd accepted the reluctantly offered invitation inside and sat in the second of the blue chairs. "Want a drink?" Janine asked him, probably dying to sneak another chocolate bar for herself.

Now that there seemed to be a party going on, it was impossible for Jeremy to ignore the strange ensemble in the living room. Hil hated to hear his bedroom door open.

He greeted Boyd first, Boyd who'd ferried Jeremy many a time across the busy lanes of traffic to his elementary school, whistle shrieking, hand protectively on his back, sign waving. Then Jeremy spotted Bergeron Love in his favorite chair wearing no clothes. He immediately turned away, blushing, a gesture Bergeron pounced upon.

"You can't be shocked!" she declared. "Give me a break! I betcha you've been all over the Internet looking at porn!"

Boyd provided Jeremy with a grimacing shrug; Bergeron Love, in her hat, on the chair, was nothing like Internet porn.

"What are you, on drugs?" Bergeron demanded, faced with Jeremy's silence. "Are you high?"

"No, ma'am," Jeremy said, now turning on her his sober, scornful glare. Did she know he was telling her, in his way, that he was fully aware that he was the only unintoxicated person in the room? He next fixed his eyes on the television screen, where the bullet through the heart remained like a new piece of art on the wall, that mesmerizing solar system of bloody mayhem.

"Oh, don't get all saintly," Bergeron said, smiling suddenly at Jeremy's indignation. "Be patient with your elders. Cut us some slack." She added fondly, "You're just like Allistair. All serious and all. You remember my son, Allistair?"

Jeremy said he did.

"He didn't like to be put on the spot, either, didn't like a direct question, didn't like a big to-do. Played things pretty close to the vest. He was embarrassed about his mom, too."

"He's not embarrassed," Hil said. Jeremy glanced at her in what she hoped was agreement. After all, it wasn't Hil who routinely grew drunk and then was driven to getting a few things off her chest with anybody who'd listen. Hil had not, tonight, exited her house wearing nearly nothing to parade around in public. Jeremy went to Al-Anon meetings because his father had made it a condition of their custody arrangement. "They're OK," he'd reported to his mother, concerning those meetings. "Lots of hugging. A little too much god talk, for me. I don't say I'm an atheist anymore, though."

"That's a good lesson to learn wherever you hear it," she'd agreed.

"Allistair was embarrassed, but he loved me," Bergeron went on. "He'd of done anything for me. Not like Boyd here. Boyd doesn't love me. The people who love me are all gone except Allistair. Mother and Daddy, my brother George Junior, although not my brother Allistair, that's Allistair the first. Everybody dead and gone except Allistair the second."

"I love you," Boyd put in.

"But," Bergeron said, taking a few breaths, "sometimes? Sometimes, it's like Allistair might as well be dead, for as often as I see him. For as often as he seems to think of me."

Janine cleared her throat quietly.

"He thinks of you," Jeremy said.

"Bless your heart," Bergeron told him, "but how in the world would you know?" She then turned to Boyd. "And as for you, Boyd, *you* just learned how to say the words *I love you*. I taught you those three words, and how I wish I hadn't. I might as well live with a parrot, for all they mean to *you*. Hey, where's your dad, anyway?" Bergeron turned back to Jeremy. "Whatever happened to him? How'd you end up with this big gal in your house instead?"

"Hey now," said Hil. "No need to be bitchy, Bergeron. You can be naked, and you can interrupt our TV program, but no getting flat-out rude." Poor Jeremy. What would he tell those hugging teenagers at the next Al-Anon meeting? Did they, like AA, warn of the forbidden thirteenth step? Was it frowned upon to date one's fellow members?

Jeremy moved to take a seat next to Janine on the couch, loyal to his late-night gaming buddy. As for Janine, she was studying the coffee table, the part in her hair a bright humiliated red. Like many an obese woman, she tended to her hair and makeup fastidiously. Hil tried to remember if this was the same coffee table she and her husband had brought when they moved into the house, twenty years ago. Was it the same one on which Bergeron Love had stood, during her first visit to them, giving her city council campaign speech? Perhaps.

"Do you remember when you were running for city council?" Hil asked.

"Which time?" Boyd said. "She's run more than once. And lost." He added this last quietly, somehow vindicated.

"A real reformer is never popular!" Bergeron declared.

"Nineteen ninety or so," Hil said. "You guys were canvassing the street, Bergeron stumping for herself on the Democratic ticket, and you, Boyd, signing up Republicans. You got up on this very table to give your speech." Boyd standing aside with his clipboard, as if knowing Bergeron was a perfect argument for the opposition.

Jeremy and Janine laughed.

"Oh, make fun," said Bergeron. "Go ahead, Bergeron Love's a crackpot and a nuisance." She struggled out of the blue chair now, glass of ice in one hand, toothbrush in the other. "Nobody was ever grateful for anything I did, nobody, not you homeowners or your kids, not you, Boyd, you damn cringing mynah bird, not even my own son, Allistair, not even *Allistair*, everybody's a fucking ingrate. Why run for office? Why give a shit? Why have children?" She turned to Jeremy, who blinked at the force of her fervor.

"Well," he said, taking a moment to put it politely, "it's not exactly like he asked you to do it."

At the meeting that was mostly men, mostly professional men in the medical district, they'd laughed to hear about the naked social call, appreciating the ludicrous image, the backstory details of previous drunken escapades featuring wild card Bergeron Love, even admiring Jeremy's visit-ending remark. That innocent teenage observation had defused poor Bergeron Love, and Boyd had then been able to rise from the matching blue chair he'd been occupying so ineffectually and guide her limpily out the front door.

"Wow," Janine had said. "Talk about true crime."

"Yeah," Jeremy had agreed. He'd seemed to be studying the paused image on the television.

At the front door, Hil had hugged Bergeron Love, taken into her arms that molten clammy body.

"Don't tell Allistair, will you?" Bergeron had said into Hil's ear, no longer angry, no longer an incendiary force, no longer anything but very tired. "Don't tell my boy."

After she'd told the medical district AA group all about it, after she'd acknowledged their applause, the mild smile still on the blind man's face, Hil and her friend Joe went as usual to their favorite Mexican restaurant to debrief.

Joe said, "You didn't share the part about Bergeron Love being dead now."

"Yeah, that part would kind of ruin the fun. It doesn't feel like a satisfying third act. Everybody would get all ashamed when they found out they were laughing about a dead person, right? In between the naked visit and the heart attack was only about five days."

"Short shelf life, for a crazy story."

"Exactly." Joe didn't care that Hil ordered a beer at Chuy's. It was his opinion that beer didn't actually count, as it took so much of it to provide a buzz. He hadn't had a drink in five years, but it had only been two hours since he'd downed a few Xanax. He was checking his watch to see when he could have another.

"You could tell the dead part next time, like it just happened. A follow-up on the first story, next installment. Chapter two."

"Could do. You know, if it wasn't for you and blind Jim, I'd quit this meeting."

Hil had first attended because the meeting was near the medical center and coincided with happy hour. Divorced, she'd thought she might meet a doctor. Instead, she'd found Joe, a guy she'd known in high school, gay, also looking for a doctor. "But *I* wanted to meet doctors because my dad was a doctor, and I like the fact that these guys are just like him, and also, hello, they're no better than me."

"A syllogism," Hil had supplied. "It makes perfect sense."

"Sort of. Maybe you can tell me why I've chosen to live with a porno addict?" he'd then said.

"Same reason I live with a morbidly obese woman? It's good to have somebody else's bad habits around to put your own in perspective?"

"Agreed. Also to compare and contrast. To get a little clarity."

"I should have known doctors wouldn't think of AA as a dating opportunity. In fact, the opposite."

"Live and learn," Joe had said. "Or, live and don't."

Bergeron Love had been on the gurney, led out feet first, just as she might have predicted she'd exit that formerly lovely home, that place where she'd been born, raised, loved, and abandoned, only five days after having gone roaming naked through the street on which she'd lived forever. Her last jaunt. On an unusually clear Wednesday, less than a week after that strange nocturnal visitation, the emergency equipment had screamed into the early-morning quiet, halting at the gates of Bergeron Love's beautiful ruin. Boyd the boyfriend had come out to undo three generations of fence: the faded white picket one that matched the house; the black iron one with its spiky tips; and the hideous yet effective chain-link with concertina wire, the enclosure of the most recent vintage. Suicide, Hil had predicted; Bergeron Love had been making a farewell tour of the neighborhood, exposing herself, putting herself at risk because she no longer cared what happened.

Also watching the action was the man who'd been reported for abuse. What was going through his head, Hil wondered. *Good riddance, racist whore.*

Hil lied at AA meetings. She led a life of sobriety, there; there, she had not had a drink for eleven months now. It was soon going to be her fictitious one-year mark. Telling the story of her neighbor was at least the truth. But was it a story? Twenty years' worth of half-known information. She'd told it at two different meetings, starting at different places. The naked visitation. The phone call to CPS. She could tell the version that began with Bergeron campaigning for city council, using the coffee table as a soapbox, Hil and her husband horrified and amused by their new neighbor, as yet still newlyweds, their moving boxes unpacked, their son a few years in the future; or she could begin with the homeless man who'd been discovered lying beside Bergeron's kidney-shaped swimming pool one night, the man who'd somehow breached the various deterring fences, empty bottle of isopropyl alcohol in hand, and who would have died had Bergeron not summoned the ambulance, had she not moved with surprising speed to get him aid, screaming for assistance, summoning it on the phone; or Hil could begin with the cocktail party Bergeron had once interrupted, pushing into Hil's house wearing an ivory evening gown and trying to seduce her husband. "He's flirting with me!" she'd gaily shrieked, laying her head on Hil's husband's chest. "Look out, Boyd, you've got competition! Careful, Hil! You'll lose him!" Hil and her husband later laughing together in bed. As if he would be attracted to the likes of

Bergeron Love! Or to *anybody* else, he'd then declared tenderly to Hil, holding her close and naked, romantic, affectionate, still hers.

Not a suicide, the neighborhood learned from Boyd when the vehicles had driven away soundlessly, their lights extinguished. Heart attack, very sudden, there in bed. She'd grabbed his earlobe, he told one neighbor, illustrating by grabbing it himself, his face a shocked white, more mouse-like than ever. She couldn't speak, said Boyd. That neighbor told the rest of them, and that was the end. Everybody went back inside.

Bergeron's son would come home, Hil thought. He'd have to. It would be up to him to decide what to do with the Love estate, that grand squalid monument in which he'd been raised, the mosquito-ridden pool, those many cats, the lingering boyfriend.

Meanwhile, Hil had found a new meeting nearby, one so close to her house she could walk there. Handily, there was a pub situated on the route home. Maybe she'd tell the story of her curious neighbor by starting with the son as a teen-ager, Allistair, him trying to keep his mother from trouble at two or three or four in the morning, shouting at her uselessly, "Please come back inside, Mom! *Please* get out of the street!"

# FUNNY ONCE

THIS YEAR, ON THE anniversary of their first date, Phoebe had said to Ben, "You know, now I've been with you longer than I wasn't with you," and he had found that wonderful, not only the fact—the twenty years *with* trumping the nineteen years *without*—but Phoebe's having kept track. Prisoners also kept track, Phoebe did not say. Her not finding it wonderful was the problem between them: she couldn't be happy.

Not happy then, not happy now. She hated Houston, yet she'd also hated Boulder. "You said you wanted to see fat people," Ben said. "You said you were sick of polarized sunglasses and tourists and . . ."

"Kayak skirts," Phoebe said. "I fucking loathe kayak skirts." Before hating Boulder, she'd hated Austin, where they'd met. She'd been raised by critics, pessimists; she was genetically disposed. Ben knew by heart the long vast list of what she hated, her unhappiness at the top, and then other, more minor things, including her parents—those progenitors—her paranoia, her pessimism, herself, and her self's inability to imagine anything but the worst-case scenario.

"Stop reading!" Ben had ordered her, exasperated. "Quit going to school! Get off the Internet! No more paranoid phone calls from your dad! Everything you do just makes it worse!" The lectures and research, the sad art and sadder science. Novels, newspapers, textbooks, her father's conspiracy theories, all of it evidence of a dismal downward trend. She was highly credentialed in disillusion.

That very morning, Phoebe had found her car in the drive with a flat tire, and Ben, naturally, was gone on some long salubrious run. "Fucking hell," she had said to the vehicle. Her father had long ago told her that an impenetrable rubber had been invented but that tire companies were on purpose withholding the product. "That's how they get you" was his mantra. Doomed to be late to her first appointment with the new therapist, Phoebe hadn't been able to trust the tattooed man who'd suddenly appeared in the street, this large, menacing stranger in his cabinet-of-wonders panel van, suspiciously well prepared for a problem such as hers.

"People are generally good," Ben often instructed her. The man had changed her destroyed tire in a matter of minutes, the lug wrench a blur in his meaty hands, the spare doughnut tossed about like a toy. From the ruined rubber he'd removed the blade tip of an X-Acto knife, presenting it to her like a gemstone held between his thick, begrimed fingertips. Ben couldn't talk Phoebe out of believing that the man had been the one to stab it there in the first place.

"Like the arsonist who's also the fire chief," she said. "He had facial tattoos, those kill-somebody teardrops. I just know he was casing our place. I wrote down his license plate number so you can tell the cops when you come home someday and find me all slashed up." She abruptly lowered the passenger seat to recline, put her feet on the dashboard. They were in his car, the one she called the Penis Mobile. She hated it, too, and thought Ben was neither young enough nor old enough to be driving it. Plus, she hated rush hour, as well as the sudden sodden spring humidity. She also hated that they were headed to dinner at his friends', the two Louises', which was a monthly ritual, but most of all she hated the fact that tonight she did not have her usual sport bottle of gin and tonic in the car console. The therapist had suggested she stop drinking.

This was all she'd told Ben, so far, about her session. He'd immediately volunteered to also quit drinking. "Solidarity," he'd said, making a fist and offering his knuckles for her to bump.

"Big of you," she'd said, and watched him, with satisfaction, flush red. They had been very, very high and drunk when he'd accidentally lit her hair on fire. That had been last weekend. A wake-up call, they named it, afterward, tending the blister on her scalp, trimming away the singe. There'd been other wake-up calls—a bloody spill on the sidewalk, a trip the wrong way down a one-way street—and then some ensuing forgetfulness, a sort of mutual snooze button. But the burst of heat near her eyes. The alarming pungency of charred hair. The image of her head, topped by that wavering flame, reflected in the window over the kitchen sink, just before Ben shot her with the spray nozzle.

May was always a bad month, and this one was no exception. First, Ben's old band, the Brutes, had finally, finally gotten their big break—nine years after Ben had quit! As usual, he and Phoebe had shown up for the release party back in January, had driven over to Austin and slept on a futon, sprung for two of the cheap domestic kegs, wandered the loft space poking gentle fun, Ben feeling sincerely pleased for—and modestly superior to—his old bandmates, and they vaguely chagrined by the low-budget look of their CD, if not also by the gray in their ponytails, their ragged concert shirts, and the faded state of their fan base. Ben's latest replacement on drums was the hostile fifteen-year-old son of the lead guitarist. Leaving the party, Ben had drunkenly thanked Phoebe for talking him into quitting the group.

Now everything had turned around. Instead of being a motley crew of losers who'd refused to move on, the Brutes had become the lucky performers of a high-rotation single with a replete backlog ready-made to reissue. "I can hear my influence," Ben insisted every time he heard "Wally's Gone AWOL," jacking the bass to emphasize his point. And then he couldn't help adding that Wally had been *his* basset hound, way back in high school, the lost dog who'd inspired the song.

He missed his band in Austin. He missed the mountains in Colorado. The jagged Houston skyline made of high-rises did not compare, nor did air-conditioning seem refreshing; the flow of traffic did not make him think of rivers; the cynical ways of grackles, the stupidity of pigeons, the skittery paranoia of squirrels and certain knowledge of rats did not wildlife constitute. They'd come here because it was their hometown, they had family here; they'd moved back because Ben's old college roommate Louise could get him a job. He'd shaved off his beard and put away his hiking boots, making the best of it. Now he wrote grants, and received a percentage. "You're good at begging," Phoebe told him.

"I'm a professional idealist," he would claim.

"Don't do it," she warned, as Ben reached for the car radio. "That's just what we don't need, right now."

"You're right, you're right," he said, sighing; it was the Brutes' success that had led to the long night with the pipe, to the fire on her head. "I freaking *named* that band."

"I know. And the dog. Ask me what the therapist asked me."

"What'd she ask you?"

"He. He asked me if my husband demanded rough sex."

"*What?*"

"I know. Right after 'What brings you here today?' and me going, 'I'm terminally unhappy,' he asks about rough sex." A strange opening gambit; Phoebe hadn't mentioned marriage, husband, sex, or violence; she'd thought "terminal unhappiness" might sound sufficiently suicidal. She'd looked down, frowning, at her clothing, to see if something about it had led to his strange question, then thought perhaps he'd mistaken her for another patient, that scrawny young girl in the waiting room, for example, the one cleaning her teeth with a business card. "Maybe because of the scarf. You think?"

"Like I tie you to the bed with it? Gag you?"

Mentioning the scarf made her head suddenly itch. She used both hands and scrubbed the whole apparatus angrily. In public, she'd taken to using the stems of her glasses to poke beneath and scratch. Undone paper clips. Plastic forks. The good news was that her hair appeared to be all growing back, the prickly stubble of uniform coverage, no permanent reminder of what had gone wrong. After they'd extinguished the flame, Ben had marveled at its swift uptake. "I've had a few mishaps," he'd said, "mostly just eyebrows or knuckle hairs, but wow, that was extreme."

"Product," Phoebe had informed him. "I think my mousse is made of napalm." But maybe she was simply more volatile than he. Laid-back, people labeled him.

"He's not my husband," she'd finally replied to the therapist, which wasn't even the beginning of a coherent answer.

"How do you self-medicate?" came next. So he did know a thing or two about her, after all. She recited in daily chronological order: caffeine, Prozac, nicotine, white wine, Adderall, red wine, vodka, nicotine, Xanax, Valium.

"Occasionally coke," she added. "If it's a gift." He was writing on his yellow tablet. "And pot. Under duress." He did not seem shocked, but then again, he'd asked about rough sex. There were toys scattered on his desk, inviting, mismatched objects, probably toxic with children's germs. Children who sat here, and told him awful things with these toys.

"Let's start with the alcohol," her new therapist said.

"The only good part about dinner with the Louises is the drinking," Phoebe complained as Ben whipped the Penis Mobile into their drive and engaged the hand brake. She hated how he set the brake, some piece of smug punctuation. Through the large plate glass window she saw their hostesses—Ouisie and LL, they were called, nicknames they'd adopted when they'd hooked up—awaiting them, the matronly elder, Ouisie, wearing a condescending smile and her apron, and LL, the ingenue, with her chin lifted, hands on her hips, tongue stuck out. "This is the last time I'm going in that house."

"You always say that," Ben said cheerfully, collecting the flowers they'd brought tonight instead of the usual wine.

Phoebe turned the car's rearview mirror to check her scarf. "Yeah, but this time I mean it."

In her relationship with Ben, Phoebe had been the ingenue, once upon a time: young, winsome, on display. She understood the rules. Couples bent this way: The one who not only tolerated but adored the outrageousness of the other. And the one who would fall headlong into a chasm if the other weren't there to hang on.

She and LL had in common the fact that they were not the smitten. They had taken up with surrogate parents, fallen into the buoyed fathomless atmosphere of those people's unconditional love.

It would be another dozen years or so until Ben could claim he'd been with Phoebe longer than he'd been without.

The Louises' place smelled of all its complicated and competing contents: children, old man, art studio, dogs, cats, cooking food, wet hair, moldering basement. The aesthetic was chaos, riot, extreme. They hosted dinner every Friday evening, and their guests were various: colleagues, neighbors, relatives, stragglers. Their home was one where you might be greeted with the information that the pet snake was loose. Or that an intervention was soon going to be staged. Ben had been the elder Louise's, Ouisie's, roommate long ago at UT; now he was godfather to her two children. He was godfather but Phoebe was not godmother. In the instance of the two Louises' untimely demise, Ben would be the official parent. And what was Phoebe's part supposed to be? "It's statistically practically impossible that they'd both die," Ben consoled her.

"Actually," she said, "it's a hundred percent certain they'll die."

"At the same time," he amended.

Phoebe often wondered what the younger Louise, LL, had demanded in return for bearing those two babies. She'd not been a happy pregnant person; she'd resented the sacrifice of body and bad habits. And as a mother she seemed diffident, maybe even jealous, usurped. The Spankies, Phoebe called the kids, grimy cherubs in saggy diapers, uncivilized, as lovely as their biological mother, blindly beloved by their other.

LL wore a halter top and a long skirt, costumed tonight like a belly dancer. The raw onion odor of her sweat was not quite covered by the fruity oil she'd smeared on her skin. Younger than the rest of the adults, she moved around the house as if preparing for an upcoming performance, dance or gymnastic, or maybe settling for a nap, head tipping sideways, arms reaching behind her back, feet flexing. You could not not attend: to her half-closed eyes, her jutted breasts, her small satisfied smile at physical pleasure, a little creak or pop, the audible sigh. Catlike, she preened, self-contained yet watchful.

And like a cat's, her attention was suddenly riveted by novelty. "That scarf is *fab*ulous!" she said.

"Not too Aunt Jemima?" Phoebe asked.

Before presenting the bouquet of sunflowers to Ouisie, Ben knelt and handed a single heavy stalk to each of her nearly naked children. They ran away slapping the floor with the flowers' faces. Ben followed with his eyes. He wanted a baby. Before that, he'd wanted to get married. Desire for what he wasn't going to get led him to reach for his shirt pocket, where he'd tucked his iPod. He was tempted to spring "Wally's Gone AWOL" on Ouisie now. He was dying to share his outrage with his old sympathetic friend.

"No!" Phoebe said, and his hand dropped automatically. The Louises exchanged a surprised glance. "Later, OK?"

Old friend Ouisie had advised Ben not to date Phoebe, back when. Phoebe's grudge against her, therefore, felt bulletproof. "She's cold," Ouisie had told Ben, tears in her eyes. "She's selfish." But too bad what Ouisie thought; Ben loved her. He couldn't be talked out of it. And when Ouisie had asked him to be the sperm donor for LL's pregnancies, Phoebe had been pleased to announce that she wasn't comfortable with such an arrangement. If she was going to be accused of coldness, she might as well mete out an icicle now and again.

Everyone made for the kitchen table, that official hub of this casual universe. At the stove stood Ouisie's grand-father. "*Ciao, Pep,*" Ben called to the old man, who was mostly deaf and did not speak English.

"*Ciao, bellas,*" he rasped in reply. Bent with some degen-erative back condition into a nearly perfect right angle, he had to turn his head to give them a glance and smile. His physiognomy was geological, one unique formation patched upon another. He'd relocated from Florence when his wife had died. You'd think it had been yesterday, so tragic did he seem, broken in half as if kicked in the crotch. He next navigated so as to gaze upon his granddaughter, as if she were the only thing he continued to live for. Perhaps she was.

By habit, Phoebe aimed for the sink, to wash her hands. In the window glass above it, she surprised herself with her reflection, that bundle of cloth she'd tied upon her head.

Superimposed, in another kitchen window, she stood aflame, woman in the glass like a burning torch. She shuddered involuntarily, then turned off the water and patted her hands dry on the wrap.

"Bonus," she said to Ben, who was watching.

"It's a fabulous scarf," LL repeated, studying the thing with a curious smile, extending a martini glass filled with icy pink liquid.

"No, thanks," Phoebe said, swallowing palpable desire. "Just water."

"You hate water," LL said. The story Ben had proposed was a bad dye job. A cosmetic disaster brought about by economic hardship—Phoebe still temping, still attending school in order to put off student loan repayment, all leading to home hair maintenance rather than professional, a lesson learned, Ben contributing by misreading the instructions. Middle-aged eyesight. Ha, ha, ha.

"Also?" Phoebe had warned him. "You are forbidden to say that I can *rock baldness*."

Dinner was a hodgepodge. LL did not eat food that had once had a face, and the children, for now, agreed to only the color orange. Pep required Mediterranean essentials: pork, cheese, tomatoes, olives. The neighbor, sad-sack Dennis, hapless bachelor, had shown up with a foil tray of raw venison, just the kind of offering he frequently made, something that looked like a gift but was actually a demand for labor, if not an outright insult to the vegetarian in the house. Regardless, Ouisie, aggressively amenable, accommodated all of these quibbling, truculent whims, perhaps even encouraged them. She needed her own orphanage or halfway house, Phoebe thought; this mob of only mildly needy people, this call for the simplest service and goodwill, this was hardly a challenge to somebody whose reserves had only begun to be tapped.

Because of the kids' day care, they all clasped hands around the table and mumbled a prayer. LL took Phoebe's right hand, Ben her left. Each gave her an extra squeeze. Under the glow of a drink or two, Phoebe liked flirting with LL. Sober, it seemed vaguely pathetic.

"Ahhh!" Pep declared, as he always did, after taking his first delighted bite.

"She's gonna get dumped," Phoebe had predicted to Ben, concerning Ouisie. It hurt Ben's feelings that Phoebe could only see impending disaster, and he'd been stricken when she'd suggested Ouisie ought to be warned; two children and an aged emigrant grandfather weren't enough to prevent devastation. They wouldn't stop the likes of somebody like LL.

The four-year-old child now insisted that her new name was Potion. "Hello, Potion," said Ben, gamely.

"Why Potion?" asked Phoebe. "Why not Zippo or Sparky or Spanky?"

"Spanky!" said her little sister. "Spanky!"

"Dennis's lions were stolen," LL said. "We've been driving around hunting for them."

"I thought something looked missing over there," said Ben.

"Goddamn juvenile delinquents!" said Dennis. "Right off the front porch. But really, why aren't those little freaks at home watching TV, where they're supposed to be?"

"They ought to be shot," Phoebe said. "You have a gun."

Ouisie was translating the conversation for her grandfather, who offered his hoarse opinion that it wouldn't be teenagers who stole decorative statuary.

"Goddamn," said the two-year-old around her gummy cheddar cube. "Goddamn."

"I agree, not kids," said LL. "Kids would have thrown the lions in the swimming pool. Or through a car window. It was a homeowner."

"Someone stole my grandmother's gravestone," Ouisie explained, Pep continuing on about the abomination. "There's a black market for reengraving them," she went on. He finished murmuring either a curse or a prayer; in another language, it was hard to tell.

"You know what?" asked Potion. "People on TV don't watch TV."

"You know what else?" Phoebe said. "People in books don't read books."

"That's right," said LL. "But it's better in books when people don't read books than it is on TV when they don't watch TV."

"Why?"

"Because the book is always better." And since she'd been drinking, LL had to repeat the line three times, delighted with herself, showing her teeth and her smooth throat as she laughed. Phoebe made a mental note, in case she went back to drinking: it's only funny once.

Ouisie spent dinner jumping up and retrieving food from the stove or refrigerator, filling glasses, bending to interpret the demands of her grandfather or children. *Martyr*, Phoebe thought; Ben would be thinking *Saint*. It was sort of the same thing, wasn't it? While LL relished the attention garnered by being desirable, Ouisie relished that garnered by being helpful. Just because she was generous didn't mean she wasn't also just as narcissistic. At least LL was beautiful.

Another insight Phoebe probably ought not to share with Ben.

The odor of searing venison made everyone lift their noses and widen their eyes at once, like a herd of startled animals. The two dogs, forbidden in the kitchen during meals, entered nonetheless.

"What is that bad smell?" the four-year-old asked her mother.

"Bambi," LL replied. "A harmless woodland creature." The children's spoons clattered into their plates; they turned horrified faces to Ouisie, the mother who did not tease; Dennis barked out a laugh.

"You sure tickle me," he said to LL, rising to evaluate the smoking meat. "Funny thing is, it *did* come from out near the Woodlands. Ran right into my buddy's truck on 45 North. You should see his grill." Dennis had been slow to realize that his neighbors were a couple; he had guessed that LL was Ouisie's daughter, Pep Ouisie's father, the household composed of several generations of single parents. Dennis had been under an inexplicable delusion that LL would someday return his leering admiration. It was Ben who'd been charged with setting him straight. Over a beer on the deck some past Friday communal dinner night. "No shit?" he'd kept saying. "No shit?"

"Pep," he yelled now from the stove, "you want yourself some of this Woodlands roadkill?"

"*Carne di cervo,*" Ouisie shouted at her grandfather, whose sitting posture was only slightly less painful-looking than his standing. He nodded agreeably.

Drunk, Phoebe was not depressed by this monthly dinner. Drunk, she would even consent to sitting on the floor with the Spankies, stacking some tiresome blocks or dreaming up dialogue for the stuffed toys. Drunk, she moved through it as through sleep, vague snippets later recalled like pieces of dreams. Sober, and time seemed unforgiving, unmoving. Sober, she could barely contain nausea when considering Pep's distorted arthritic hands and blue-veined skull hanging there over his plate.

"All the fingers are for something," Potion said. She held up her thumb.

"Sucking," said Phoebe. Masturbating, she would have gone on, of the pointer, next rage, then wedding rings, and, finally, a little pinky for cleaning out the ear. A handful of assistance. She used her pinky now to scratch at her stubbly temple.

"Why is that on your head?" Potion asked her.

"To protect the fleas," answered Phoebe. Potion then fashioned her own little messy turban of her napkin. And then she made one for her sister. And everyone else was charmed.

How she pined for a drink.

As usual, Phoebe and LL would walk the dogs while the others took a turn cleaning up: dishes, pans, babies, Pep.

Naughty, they walked around the block smoking Camels. Drunk, Phoebe would have been exchanging complaints with LL about their partners, stumbling on the live oak roots, cursing the wayward tangle of the dogs on their leashes, lamenting Houston's muggy intimations of the summer to come. Tonight, she asked LL's opinion about the man who'd fixed her tire.

"This therapist I went to said there were three ways to look at any situation," Phoebe told her. He'd said, "A man fixes your tire. No attitude whatsoever, just a straight description of what happened."

And then Phoebe had said to the therapist, "But he was too well prepared to be some random Dudley Do-Right," at which point the therapist had said, "A man sabotages your vehicle in order to then rescue you."

"So I go, 'Right. Exactly.'"

"I wouldn't have trusted him, either," LL said. "No fucking way."

"Who would? But then the therapist tells me, 'You have a need to see him as bad.' That's part three, *I need* to see him as bad."

"Wait. What?"

"I know. That's nuts, right? I mean, sometimes people are just bad. Right?" LL now went off on a long complaint about a gallery owner who'd first encouraged her to submit her work there and then become completely uninterested when he discovered she wouldn't consent to date him. Her stories frequently went this way: people with whom she flirted made a pass at her. Drunk, Phoebe generally ignored the juvenile tiresomeness of LL's ensuing indignation, her youthful self-righteous belief that she could have it both ways.

Sober, however, she was thinking about what had most baffled her about the whole baffling appointment this morning, which was that at the end of it, the therapist declined to take her on as a client. He said he could not help her. He didn't seem even remotely embarrassed to admit it, nor did he seem to think Phoebe should feel offended. All along, she'd thought *she* was auditioning *him*, but apparently not. On the way home, she tried to construct the same trilogy he had about the tattooed fix-it fellow. *The therapist declines to treat me. The therapist doesn't like me.* But what was the third part? If only she'd stuck around long enough to ask.

To deflect from either further discussing her own business with LL or acknowledging that she hadn't been listening to LL's, Phoebe moved on to Ben's. "So this lame-ass band he was in back in the day . . ."

On the deck steps, LL had breath mints and hand sanitizer for them both to hide the smell of cigarette smoke. "Hold on, hold on," she said, reaching for Phoebe's head. "Your flea cover is slipping." Phoebe wasn't quick enough to keep her from touching the exposed skin above her ear. "You *shaved* your head?"

"Chemotherapy," Phoebe said. In her mind, she went to the image of herself in the kitchen window. Unnatural, emblematic. Tears were easy now. "Colon cancer. No hair, no drinking." She shrugged.

LL dropped the dogs' leashes in order to embrace Phoebe. "Oh my god," she said. "Holy shit!"

"I'll be fine," Phoebe told her. "Really. And don't tell Ouisie till later, OK? Ben and I are so sick of talking about it."

"I can't believe you didn't tell us!"

"It'll be fine." In her arms, Phoebe felt the pleasure of being brave. Maybe this was the solution to unhappiness.

Inside, they found Dennis and Pep sharing a single plate of meat, eating with greasy hands as the dishwasher rotor thumped repeatedly on some tall utensil, and Ben in the steamy bathroom sitting on the toilet while Ouisie knelt over the tub. She wore earbuds, listening to the offending song, stirring the two children around in the water. The sunflowers were in there also, their faces bedraggled, their hairy stalks bent.

"It's great!" she yelled. "Sounds just like the old days!"

"See?" Ben said to LL and Phoebe, in the bathroom doorway. "That's *my* band! Wally was *my* dog."

LL gave Phoebe a sympathetic pout, then lowered herself gracefully next to Ouisie, plucking one of the earbuds out to insert in her ear, their two heads together there over the splashing naked children.

"*Chemotherapy?*" Ben forced a laugh, as if Phoebe had been leading to a punch line. They drove through Houston's surface and back streets by habit, avoiding the freeways, although neither had had any liquor tonight. The traffic lights were synchronized, a pathway of green that would suddenly begin turning yellow, coming at them in a flashing row. Inebriated, this was a sensation like an invitation to flight. Overhead, the clouds broke around the highest high-rises, swift and ethereal. The sharpness of detail impressed Phoebe, the absence of blurred edges. Impressed, and depressed her: unaltered reality was monotonous, predictable, and very slow. She would remember every part of tonight tomorrow. But so what?

"I thought we were going with the hair dye story?"

They'd stayed at the Louises' through the elaborate process of bedtime, the hugs and crying and book reading; foul herbal tea in lieu of the usual whiskey, and Ben's walking Dennis next door to stare at the two spots on the porch where the lions had sat; Pep's oxygen hookup and night-time meds; LL's marijuana, which could only come out when the neighbor and the children and their great-grand-father were safely tucked away. The four remaining gathered in LL's art studio, sitting knee-to-knee there on paint-splattered wicker furniture for the shared bowl. They all knew Phoebe didn't enjoy weed, but tonight LL held the pipe out to her. "You probably have nausea?" she said on an in-held breath, then slapped her hands over her mouth.

Ouisie guessed, "Pregnant?" and Ben simply looked blank.

"I'm sorry," LL murmured, although Phoebe didn't believe it had been an accident. She was a troublemaker herself; she might have done the same.

"I told LL about the cancer and chemo," Phoebe said apologetically to Ben.

"You have to tell them you were joking," he said now. *Take it back!* he'd texted from the bathroom, then.

"What if I don't?"

"Then you're either crazy or a liar!" he said.

"You can tell them the truth," Phoebe said. "How about that?"

"What was wrong with the hair dye?"

"In the end, it just seemed too boring. Boring, and also a lie, by the way."

"If I tell them the truth . . ." He couldn't seem to finish the thought.

"We could say you pulled my hair out while we were having rough sex."

"But really, Feeb, we can't go around saying you have cancer."

Drunk, they'd have been proceeding home as if through a video game, alert to the sudden challenge of a darting cat or unlighted bicyclist, the obstacles that could catch and doom you. Sober, he sighed, and Phoebe ground her teeth, sitting there the perfect picture of disgruntlement, stubbornness, self-loathing. "There's another option," she said. "We could never see or speak to them again."

For a long moment he was speechless. "Honestly, that's what you want?"

"I don't know what I want," she said. "What do you want?"

Sobriety might have explained what happened next, or maybe Phoebe's simple question. At any rate, they went sailing through a stop sign. Drunk, they'd never have missed such a predictable snag. Several things happened simultaneously: Ben stomped on the brakes, fifty feet too late, causing an empty X-Acto knife to fly from the center console and land at Phoebe's feet. Also, he instinctively threw his hand out across her chest, that useless parental gesture to protect the nowadays nonexistent child in the passenger seat.

"Wow." Ben sat blinking, stopped in the middle of the empty street. No cars, no witnesses, no cops or lights or cameras. No consequences, it seemed. Maybe, Phoebe thought, he'd have run that same sign drunk, and they'd not have noticed the fact. It was complicated to sort out the variables; she'd always found that to be true. Life was so little like a science experiment and so much like a cluttered drawer where you tossed things just to get them out of sight.

"That really hurt," she finally noted, putting her own hand where Ben's had slammed into her. At her left breast. Right about where her heart probably was.

# THREE WISHES

## 1. *A Clean Record*

No one ever pronounced their last name correctly. "*Panik,*" the three siblings said in unison, "as in panic."

"*Pan*-ick," nodded the woman in scrubs, as if that explained everything. The group was gathered on the driveway of a yellow brick ranch-style house in Wichita, Kansas. The place did not look like a nursing home, which was one of the only advantages. It was a late-summer dusk, and the woman in scrubs used her hand as a visor when she addressed the Panik father, the patriarch, owner of the name to begin with. "How are we, Sam?" she called. He blinked down at her furiously from his recliner. The chair sat like a throne in the back of his son's pickup truck, and the old man was duct-taped across the chest and lap into it. The expression on his face—furiously twitching lips, blazing eyes—suggested that his children had also duct-taped shut his mouth. Which, for the record, they wouldn't have done. But he hadn't spoken to one of his living offspring since they'd announced their intentions. When the time had come to execute these plans, he'd grabbed the chair's arms with surprising strength, gone rigid as rigor mortis in its seat, wrapped his toes behind the perennially sprung footrest, and clung like a sloth.

He'd spoken the name of his long-dead son Hamish; when he'd been found, out wandering near the river, he'd introduced the cops to his dead son. His living son, Hugh, owner of the pickup truck, wondered if this was where his own habit of addressing the dead came from.

"I thought he'd been drinking all day," Hugh's older sister had accused.

"And since when has drinking made him docile? Grab that side," Hugh had instructed his sisters wearily. And they wearily obeyed, the three of them carrying their father through his home of fifty years, wedging him briefly in the doorway while they took a breather, and then continuing out into the drive, his daughters on one side, Hugh on the other. He was not as heavy as they might have expected, but he was three times as enraged. That was the taxing part.

"I see you," Hugh called to Holly, the younger sister. "I see her right through your head, old man."

"I see Hugh," replied Holly, gamely. But their father wouldn't be teased. The hippies next door looked up placidly as the family went by, nodding, smiling in a shared stupor. Just last week, they themselves had employed skateboards to move a sofa into the yard. They sat on that sofa now, waving, stoned and useless. Why were all the world's old sofas burnt orange and made of velveteen? "Bye, Mr. Panik," they called. *Dude*, they'd said to him, when he felt an urge to spray the hose on their withered grass. He sprayed the water in memory of his neighbor, Hugh believed, a salute to the man who'd kept his yard immaculately green, his hedges trimmed square, his walkway edged, lawn maintenance a kind of religious or military fervor. This man who'd nonetheless died and left his house to his careless children, one of whose offspring was among these hippies, and was letting whatever happened happen.

What would old Mr. Roosevelt have thought today? Hugh paused on the drive, imagining their former neighbor, a man dead a dozen years now. Hugh often felt outside himself, watching his behavior as though through the eyes of some witness. Did it mean something that these witnesses were often dead? And if it were the dead who watched him, why wasn't it his mother he invoked today? She whose husband was being taken, via La-Z-Boy litter, to the highly inappropriate bed of Hugh's truck? Or his brother, Hamish, he whose ghost had been summoned by his father only an hour earlier? Whose hallucinatory body was frequently appearing in Sam Panik's presence, derailing his days, leading to dangerous decisions.

"He'll jump," the older sister, Hannah, predicted. Hugh and Holly were accustomed to being bossed around by her—also, to improvising. Hence, the duct tape.

Across town they drove, parade speed, avoiding major thoroughfares. "If we get stopped," Hannah said, "it's me who'll be ticketed. Just so you know."

"Poor you," Hugh said. He hadn't wanted to drive because he'd joined his father in having a few drinks this afternoon, their last together as roommates, and he was terrified of receiving a DUI. Holly, the youngest, not only was crying but also had never learned to drive a stick. Which left Hannah to take the wheel. "What would they cite you for, though?"

"I think it's illegal to ride in the back of a truck."

"People do it all the time."

She whacked him with the backs of her fingers. "What, were you absent the day everyone learned how lame that excuse is?"

Holly, in the middle riding backward on her knees, had opened the sliding window between the cab and the bed, and she reached through to locate her father's bristly cheek, which she swatted awkwardly. "Poor Papa," she murmured, sniffling. "It's like we're kidnapping him."

"Don't mention that," Hugh said. "He already has a whole story line about kidnapping, something to do with Mom. That's when he locks himself in the bathroom."

"I feel so bad," Holly said. To Hugh, she still seemed stranded somewhere in her midtwenties, though if he was thirty-nine, merciless time dictated that she must be thirty-five. Still, there she stayed stuck, a postcollege drifter, skittish and lost, with terrible luck in love. She wasn't finished, a project still under construction, unconfident, acne on her chin.

Hannah kept muttering, "Sorry," as she jammed the gearshift into her sister's leg, and Holly kept replying, "It's OK."

"Why in hell would you prefer standard?" Hannah demanded of Hugh.

He shrugged. He liked shifting gears? He liked old-fashioned things? He was stubborn? Mostly, he enjoyed the sensation of neutral beneath his palm, the way the knob floated briefly in between options while the engine took a breath and then he smoothly gripped and chose. None of this could be explained to Hannah. She continued to upgrade his life for him, bestowing upon him her secondhand laptop, gifting him with a laser measure on his last birthday, hauling both him and their father off for their annual flu shot.

Hugh opened the passenger-side window (crank handle), letting in more of the warm August evening. They might be making a tortured journey, but Wichita was peaceful enough tonight. Perhaps it was best that they'd been detained in their errand; rush hour had ended, and the cicadas sawed on tiredly, the shade trees heavy with deep green leaves. Summer had had enough of itself, was just about to give up and let go. Riding three abreast in the front of Hugh's truck reminded the Paniks of high school, as did the sound of the pavement beneath the spongy tires, the wind in their hair, dusk settling its melancholy self. Even the radio played the songs they'd known back when.

"Just imagine," Hannah said, "just imagine this was the first time you heard this song"—Tina Turner, "What's Love Got to Do with It"—"and somebody told you that in, oh, twenty years or so, you'd be listening to it again while your dad was riding in the grody bed of your truck, duct-taped into an easy chair. Would you believe them? Could anyone ever predict this was where we'd end up?"

"I'm glad Mom's not here to see this," Hugh said. "She'd say, 'Shame on you.'"

"I hated how she said that," Hannah agreed. "It might be the worst thing to say to a kid. I would never say such a thing to mine."

"I probably would. Have. Will. Right?" Holly said, looking freshly guilty. She was exempt from exactly nothing, when it came to feeling bad. "And I sure wish we'd given Papa a haircut," she went on. "He looks crazy back there with his hair flying around."

"A stylist comes to the home every week," Hannah reminded them. "One of the perks, Day of Beauty."

"Friday," Holly added miserably.

"He is so going to hate it there," Hugh said.

"Say it enough, he will." But none of them felt like arguing. They'd already done that. This was the result. What *did* love have to do with it, anyway? Despite loving their father, they were taking him to live with strangers, against his will. It was a one-way trip; the police, upon bringing Sam Panik once more to his and Hugh's door like a wandering dog, had specifically threatened legal intervention. With the exception of perhaps passing the place on long aimless drives (sitting inside, in the passenger seat, like a normal doddering old father), he would never visit his home again. This year, Hugh speculated, would most likely be the one in which he died.

And if he didn't, finances dictated that Hugh and his sisters would have to move him somewhere worse, downgrading all the way to the hot, hot oven where he would eventually arrive.

"Hell," Hugh said.

"It's not hell," Hannah corrected. "It's the best possible solution to an insoluble problem. Deal with it." She was practical, his sister Hannah. Practical like a kitchen tool, dispassionate as an appliance. She made Hugh want to try to make her cry, just to see if he could.

Holly changed the radio station. "Buttons! Your car is so old!" she informed him. "How can you stand not having 'scan'?"

"You would love XM," Hannah added, and Hugh could almost hear her congratulating herself on solving the problem of this year's Christmas gift to him: satellite radio.

Hannah was the mother of two teenage boys; she knew a lot of things about the contemporary world. Nobody was going to pull a fast one on her.

Hugh wasn't as aware of that world. Certainly he didn't seem like somebody eager to embrace the twenty-first century. He felt comfortable dwelling not in the past, exactly, but in a familiar place that happened to be the past. Since high school he had lived, off and on, in his childhood home with, until this very day, his father, and, when she was alive, his mother. He'd brought no wife into this arrangement, spawned no offspring, opened no savings account, planned for no retirement from a job that paid an hourly wage and provided no health plan. So no, he had no XM radio. His job beeper still alarmed him when it went off in his pocket, an exciting little surge in the groin.

Every few years he took himself to the mall and bought six pairs of khaki pants. When J.C. Penney had quit carrying the ones he liked, he'd switched to the Gap. That was as much progress as he had made, evolutionarily. A woman in his past had believed the source of his trouble to be metabolic; she'd thought he ought to medicate. Hugh hadn't had enough interest, or energy, to pursue the matter—exactly what she'd meant to cure him of. He lifted his ankle to check the status of his pants cuffs, reassuring himself that he was still presentable.

Slowly, they left Riverside behind, crossing the river at McLean, then sneaking down the winding residential streets to the home, which was a one-story, sprawling suburban-type place three miles from the Panik family home. It was located in a neighborhood not physically far from their house, but not in any important way close to that landmark. Hannah took the last corner faster than she should have, and they all felt the weight in the rear lurch ponderously as the chair tilted. "Sorry!" Hannah said savagely. She was always anticipating criticism, even when none was forthcoming.

"They're gonna think we're awful," Holly said, meaning the keepers at the home.

Hannah tapped Hugh's instrument panel, pulling out the keys. "Your odometer just flipped."

"Damn," Hugh said. He'd meant to be paying attention when that happened. Two hundred thousand miles. And he'd driven most of them.

"Back to zero," Hannah said. "A clean record. Papa?" She called to him as she climbed from the truck. "We're here. Your new home."

"*This* is my home" had been his simple plea. In the face of every piece of evidence presented, every argument laid out, every solid illustration of logic, his line had remained the same. It could have broken your heart, to hear him. Without Hannah's relentless reminding, Holly and Hugh would have succumbed to that voice, that simple plea, his case for convenient inertia. He'd have eventually wandered into traffic naked and been rolled over by a bus, or simply disappeared, had it been up to Hugh or Holly.

"Don't cry, Holly," Hugh said. She now sat with one leg on either side of the gearshift, hunched forward, a palm over each eye. Outside, Hannah was laughing with the aides, gesturing toward the truck. Hannah had enough maternal instinct to lead an army. That seemed to have left Holly with a serious deficit. Although biology had handed her a son, her very own, she often had no idea how to proceed. "Let's get Dad out," Hugh prodded gently.

Like the hippies next door at old Mr. Roosevelt's, the nursing home staff didn't seem all that shocked to see a man riding in the bed of a truck in his recliner. Stuffing was escaping along both faux-leather sides of the chair. The ride hadn't improved the looks of it or its passenger. "Hello, Mr. Pa-*neek*," called out the buxom aide named Brenda. And, in unison, the siblings corrected her pronunciation.

Someone had to have died to make moving in possible, Hugh thought suddenly. Just yesterday, he'd been called: an opening. He hadn't quite put it together that an opening meant, for someone else, a closure. His father had been next on the waiting list. The waiting list: there was a big one in the sky, and everyone was on it.

"Oh, we'll be so glad to have a *man* around the house," claimed Brenda, holding open the front door. It was wider than the one at the Panik house, fitted for chairs and walkers and apparatuses of all stripes, including the gurney from the morgue. Through it the Paniks passed, Hugh once more gripping one side of his father's chair, his sisters the other. "Over there," directed Brenda, scurrying after them. They'd chosen this home for its homeyness. And so it should have been comforting to see the space that had been made, in the circle of similar chairs arranged around the television, for Mr. Panik's. That must have been where the dead woman's chair had sat. "We haven't had a man since Junior."

"Junior," scoffed a different scrub-dressed aide, crossing her arms, curling her lip.

The circle was made up of old women, six of them. They shared the three other bedrooms at the home. Each and every one of them had a memory problem, victims of stroke and Alzheimer's and other flavors of dementia. Hugh had visited last spring, when his father had been hospitalized after a collapse and the inevitable had suddenly been upon them. He recognized a few of the women—the one with the unidentifiable plush toy she petted and praised; the one who'd thought he'd come to visit her and named him her son Sonny, reciting to him all of her pertinent, contradictory data; and the one who'd sat at the table with her forehead on its surface, crying softly, unreachable.

Last spring, there'd also been a chatty woman named Mary, one who'd cheerfully rolled her eyes and thrown up her hands when she'd forgotten what she was saying. She'd been the liveliest tenant, treating her role at the home as that of hostess at a cocktail party, the person who'd convinced Hugh that his father would have some worthy company, should he move in.

"Where's Mary?" he inquired.

"Oh, she passed," said Brenda serenely, smiling benignly, saintly as a nun. "Just yesterday morning. That's her room your dad will have. A single." She added, "It's usually the men who prefer it. They find it harder to live with others, I think. But Mary liked her alone time, that's for sure. Sometimes she needed to get away from the other girls."

Hugh hadn't really known the woman, but like all the dead he was aware of, she turned in his mind from substantial to opaque, wavering there like a sheer curtain with her image sewn upon it. When he closed his eyes, the faces of the dead would appear like this, a laundry line of wind-blown sheers, sepia toned. He watched them, behind his eyelids, he listened, he concentrated, he guessed at what these phantoms would think. They were his audience, his attendants, his witnesses.

His father's delusions featured these same players. He was simply more receptive to their demands.

"He's a good roommate, aren't you, Papa?"

His father turned his acid gaze on Hugh. His eyes were still furious, burning embers in his gray stricken face, but he was obviously straining under the burden of rage. It was exhausting to be as angry as he'd been, as forsaken. Hugh felt sorry for him. Surely he'd like to surrender, get untaped and explore the new digs. Settle at the plastic-covered table and eat something that hadn't come from a can or takeout box. Change the channel, perhaps, flirt with Brenda and her chubby coworker, who seemed so prepared to do his bidding. He'd always been a curious person, quick to find the humor, easy to live with.

"You can relax," Hugh whispered into his father's ear. "They're going to be nice to you here."

Very softly, nearly inaudibly, his father said, "*Fuck you.*" Hugh literally stepped back.

"I hope that's not the last thing you say to me," he said.

"What'd he say?" Hannah inquired.

"Papa?" said Holly. But the old man had turned his evil gaze toward the television screen.

On it he was greeted by a black-and-white movie. This boded well, Hugh would tell his sisters later, at the bar. At least the old ladies weren't watching the usual drivel, the humiliation shows. No embarrassing dirty laundry being aired here; no judge scolding a feuding set of neighbors, no smarmy talk show host keeping at arm's length family members who wished to kill one another. Instead, the gals were watching a movie. And an old one, at that. The past would comfort his father, Hugh would say to his sisters, although he and his father had rarely watched old movies at home. They'd tended toward historical material, documentaries and nature shows. At a certain age, Sam Panik had grown impatient with make-believe. He wanted facts, history and nature. Period.

*Fuck you.* In the immediate wake of those stunning words, Hugh left his father with the women—all the women: residents, aides, his own sisters—and padded down the hall to the room at the end. Unlike the three other bedrooms, it was undecorated, tiny pinpricks in the walls where tacks had held up mementos. Until yesterday, someone else had lived in this room. And then had died there. Like in a hotel room, you had to make peace with its publicness. It was not like your house, exactly. But, unlike in a hotel room, you weren't going to get up in the morning and drive away from the temporary squalor you'd indulged yourself in. No, his father was not "passing through." Not passing through, but passing, as Mary, its latest inhabitant, had just done.

Hugh sat on the bare bed; a puff of scented air wafted up, something familiar and sad. Mary's lotion or perfume. He pulled a hip flask from his khaki pants pocket and slid it between the mattress and the box spring. Irish whiskey, better quality than what his father generally drank. He'd brought it so that he could make a guiltless exit. He'd imagined the gesture—his leaning close to his father's ear, whispering into it, letting him know that even if Hugh weren't here, even if they were no longer roommates and drinking companions, Hugh had not forgotten him. He'd not forsaken his father; his father was wrong on that count. But then his father had preempted Hugh's ongoing fantasy, uttering those awful words. *Fuck you.* Everyone said it—teenagers, women, office managers, radio DJs, professors, delivery boys—everyone except his father.

"Shame on you," murmured Hugh's dead mother as he paused on the newly made bed, taking in the blank walls and the cheerless ceiling fixture. A large box of man-size diapers was the single personal touch, placed beside the bed like an end table. Hannah and Holly would accessorize; they'd already made plans to come back tomorrow with a mirror, a lamp, a few pictures. But the room would always sadden Hugh, no matter the props.

Moreover, what was he to do with his father's room at home? That was the real question. The man could move here, could sleep here, hang his clothes here, tack up his own memorabilia, but what, exactly, was Hugh to do with that venerated, complicated space waiting unoccupied back at the house? When his mother had died, he and his father had been similarly perplexed: now what? They'd slowly removed the evidence of her presence there: drawers that had held her clothing eventually filled with tax documents and photographs and warranties; her feminine trinkets went to Hannah's and Holly's homes. Without her there to open the windows or their shades, they simply stayed closed and grew dusty and stuck. As a result, the room began to resemble a kind of cave, the entrance of which Hugh passed daily without paying it much mind, sometimes aware of a sour stench. Only in the last few months had he been forced to turn on the overhead light, wrestle his father from the filth of his own bed into the bath, and then sit beside the tub to prevent his drowning. His dad in the bathtub like a small child, breathing while aromatic bubbles (dish detergent) popped in audible whispers around him, accusing Hugh of conspiring with the kidnappers, the killers, the figures who wished him harm and led him astray. Perhaps it was one of them to whom he'd addressed his fury?

"I want the cops," Sam Panik was saying, in the nursing home living room. The ladies looked alarmed, but Hugh knew what to do.

"Channel 325," he told Brenda, motioning toward the remote, then checking his pocket watch. "It's almost over." His father liked to watch the police videos, the evidence of idiocy and mayhem, captured on film. In general, he and Hugh watched with the sound muted, making up their own dialogue and commentary. Since last spring, his father had been failing, then recovering, then further failing, then recovering less fully, a two-steps-backward, one-step-forward kind of dance, his nightmare hallucinatory land slowly encroaching upon his normal one. But it wasn't like Zeno's paradox; he would reach the end—even if at first only by half steps—and then be utterly and wholly felled, lost to ghosts and illusion.

Now he wouldn't meet Hugh's eyes; he was ashamed, Hugh could tell, still in possession of the wherewithal to regret what he'd said, and for once, Hugh wished for an onset of dementia. Let the moment evaporate in a crazy scramble. His father's most frequent—could you call it "fantasy"?—was that Hugh was conspiring with others in an elaborate plot to poison him and steal his fortune. During these bouts, Hugh would have to taste his father's food, sip first at his drink in order to convince him that the offering was safe, and reaffirm with his right arm raised that he was telling the truth, the whole and nothing but. Of course, there was no fortune, although Hugh sincerely wished there were. He'd be happy, now, to confirm some false notion his father entertained, assist in the old man's passionate conviction of phony persecution. Better that than the actual betrayal.

His father stared at the television as the end of the police show blared on. Its narrator liked to yell over an absurdly dramatic soundtrack; the ladies looked alarmed, the one with the stuffed object in her lap suddenly petting it frantically. A little smile pulled on the old man's upper lip. Amusement defused his anger, and he could still give in to it. The duct tape instantly became irrelevant, in terms of escape; it seemed, instead, as if Mr. Panik were being held upright because of it, even vaguely entertained by his trap. Hugh had always thought his dad would have been a wonderful comedian, if only someone had aimed him in that direction.

Immediately Holly and Hannah set to undoing their father, pulling the sticky stuff away. His loose skin wished to stay with the tape; peanut butter was retrieved from the kitchen in order to help with the separation, smeared gently upon his forearms. He was half the size of his former self, a skeleton in a freckled hide, an old man sitting in a diaper. His chair was ragged, its upholstery leaking its stuffing, once clawed mercilessly by a cat now long dead. Blanche: run over and crippled by a car, killed with a merciful bullet by Sam Panik.

Now there was nothing to do but leave. The keepers were checking their watches, ready to carry on with their duties. Four Paniks had come in, but only three would go out.

Holding the wad of gray tape, shirt stained with peanut butter, Holly knelt to speak into their father's slack sallow face. "Papa? Please, please forgive us."

## 2. *Ugly's*

It was a good bar only because they were regulars in it, all three of them, and the bartender could say, if he wanted, "The usual?" and they could agree. Agreeing, this evening, might serve to undermine what wasn't usual. Usually, they wouldn't have just consigned their father to purgatory.

"They say it's not good to drink when you're depressed," Holly said. "They say that alcohol only makes depression worse."

"'They'!" Hannah scoffed, flicking her hand as if to slap Holly in the face. "Red wine," she had long ago instructed the bartender. She always drank wine, even in dive bars like this. Sometimes she inquired about the quality. "What reds do you have by the glass?" she might ask, at an establishment that clearly carried wine by the box, if at all. Ugly's was such a place. Then her companions were treated to a wince after her first swallow. In Hugh's experience, any red wine whose color was actually purple was not a good wine. Never mind those other considerations the wine snobs made, legs and nose and tannins and leather, the swirling and sniffing and puckering: look for purple and politely say *No, thank you.*

"Awful," Hannah said, as usual.

The bartender had pulled a draft for Hugh and was reaching for a martini glass when Holly said, "I'll have sparkling water." He heaved a sigh, which made her revise her order again. "The usual," she said, and he paused, waiting for her to waffle once more, as was her nature, then fixed her a cosmo. For Holly, drinking had always been optional, whereas for her brother and sister it was required. They drank every day. It was built into their schedules like a religious practice, perhaps more faithfully than meals. This would be especially true now that he was to live alone, Hugh thought. His father had been his last drinking buddy, and Hugh had already imagined the future, when he sat by himself before the television, chewing on his ice cubes. (His rule was to eat the ice, all of it, before making himself his second or third or fourth drink; "Does ice count?" he'd asked his physician when polled, at last year's checkup, about how much water he drank in a day. Yes, it turned out, ice counted, but not tonic. Not coffee, either. And he knew better than to ask about gin.)

"To Dad," he said, raising his beer bottle at Ugly's.

His little sister's eyes filled, once again. "We're mean," she cried.

"I could have locked him inside," Hugh speculated once more. "I could have hired somebody to keep him inside."

"You could have hired *me*!" Holly said, freshly guilty.

"Stop that," Hannah insisted, pulling out a pack of cigarettes and offering them around. This was to distract Holly, for whom smoking was required, whereas for both Hugh and Hannah it was purely recreational, now and again. Hugh marveled at the peculiar ways the human animal loved its bad habits, grew dependent on one while indifferent to another. The only one he understood was alcohol, but understanding it meant he sympathized with all the rest, be it heroin, or slot machines, or Jesus, or little rodent-like dogs.

It was illegal to smoke in bars, but the owner of Ugly's, a former mayor, wasn't having any of that.

His sisters blew out streams of smoke at the same time and, for a moment, looked alike, as if Hugh were a magic mirror between them, one woman making kissy lips, breathing fire into her kissy-lipped reflection. Then they resumed their ordinary, individual faces, and did not look so similar. Whenever Hugh considered Holly's appearance, he twitched. It was a peculiar reflex, one he'd acquired in high school when his friend Jeff Frick had remarked within Hugh's hearing that Holly was "such a mutt." That phrase—*such a mutt*—echoed in Hugh's head still, and as soon as it did, he flinched, a hot sensation in his chest, as if a BB had struck his sternum, so that the result was this mild twitch, like a repressed half-assed sneeze. Shame, he supposed. *Shame on you.* Holly had all the same features as her older sister, but they just weren't lined up as well, as if something had gone south on the assembly line in the eight years between models.

Hannah, forty-three, perched like a flirty bird on her bar stool and wrapped one leg around the other. She had the tired elegance of marriage in her body, a slackness to her limbs and flesh, yet the expression she wore said, *Try me, I'm game.* Holly, thirty-five, painfully single, looked fresher, somehow, but less comfortable. Her posture was terrible, and she was sighing morosely, gazing into a nether distance. She often seemed lost, as if she'd come in on the tail end of the joke and didn't quite understand why everyone else was laughing. Her left-behindness was sometimes endearing, sometimes alarming, and sometimes, like tonight, purely enervating. She had a bad habit of worrying her chin with her fingers, so there was frequently a patch of acne there. She startled too easily, and her mouth trembled; her obvious lack of confidence in herself made others lack it in her, too. This was unfortunate; she'd been without love overlong. A person could get out of the habit, lose the knack.

"This whole day has been like high school," Hugh said. "Even now, being at Ugly's, just like high school." Jeff Frick had suddenly come to mind; and this was the place where they'd drunk when underage. Out in the parking lot, there'd been fights in the gravel, sex in the cars, vomiting and pissing behind the Dumpsters. Rites of passage all over the place.

"I was thinking of high school, too," said Holly. "Remember when you first brought me here? I was such a moron." *Suchamutt.*

"What I remember is your fake ID," Hannah said, smiling indulgently. In an uncharacteristically sly and bold move, at age fifteen Holly had marched up to the DMV window and announced that she'd lost her driver's license. She'd claimed to be Hannah Panik, age twenty-three, and then provided all the pertinent info as if it were her own. She'd been studying her older sister long enough to have the facts cold. Those fooled folks at the DMV had shot her photograph and stuck it on a replacement license: voilà, of age. "Inspired," Hannah said, as she always did when the anecdote floated up. "I can only hope Leo doesn't get wind of it." This was her fifteen-year-old son, famously delinquent these days. He, too, had an older sibling. Hugh cheered a bit upon hearing one of his nephews' names. Unlike his grandfather Sam Panik, Leo had all of life ahead of him, a Panik with a future. Oughtn't that to provide some relief from their sad errand tonight?

"To Leo," Hugh said, raising his glass again. Leo's mother cast him a dubious glance.

"Whatever," she said, swilling down the last of her first drink, grimacing again, then ordering another. "If I didn't already drink, that kid would have driven me to it." Hannah reapplied lipstick in between glasses of wine. Funnily enough, she, the married sister, seemed more on the make than the unmarried one. Hannah had a nervy awareness of her femaleness, the way the den of men had vaguely stirred, straightened its collective spine—math nerds, slackers, divorced professors—when she and Holly had entered. His older sister looked like a woman who knew how to have fun in the world, whose smile came from zealous desire, whose mind was worth investigating, who wouldn't reject you without a test run.

His little sister looked like somebody who'd threaten to kill herself if you broke up with her.

Beside Hannah a stool opened. On it, Hugh imagined the ghost that haunted him most frequently, the one with which he was most intimate. His brother, Hamish, animation suspended at age nineteen. There ought to have been four Panik siblings, and the fourth ought to have been sitting there, on the other side of Hannah, first in line, the one who would have led the other three, graciously assuming the lion's share of masculine responsibility and thereby allowing Hugh to simply follow like the little brother he was fated to be. Their older brother's absence had been the center of their lives for as long as Hugh could remember, a kind of black hole into which all confusing emotion got pulled, and which was, coincidentally, a source of explanation for that same confusing emotion. Looking at Holly now, Hugh realized that though she had known Hamish less well, had had the fewest years in his company, and had been fully ten years his junior—only nine when he died—it was possible that her life had been most profoundly altered by his death. Not by grief, which had been the others' damage, but by a sudden change in course. The family destiny had been abruptly disrupted.

He had been the most attractive Panik, Hamish. The best of both gene pools had gone to him—and he'd thrown that bit of luck away, along with everything else. Earlier, Sam had told his three children that if Hamish were alive, none of this nonsense about the nursing home would be afoot.

Holly had let her cigarette grow a long wobbly ash. Her mind was still occupied by their adventure at the home. "That one lady thought Papa was her sister," she said.

"No," Hannah corrected, "she thought the *chair* was her sister. She couldn't see him in it; she was patting the back of it. 'Is that Sophie? Is that you, Sophie?'" This had been the crying woman, who ceased her sad business only long enough to come hopefully address the back of Sam Panik's chair.

"What was that thing in the fat lady's lap?"

"I don't know. She was killing it with kindness. It could have been taxidermy."

"Her face looked like flan."

Hannah's cell phone brrred then. She held it up. "Look at this text." Her son Leo had sent @ *mall L8r*.

"Huh?" said Hugh.

"He's back at the mall. Despite the restraining order." There'd been an episode with a paintball gun. Fifteen-year-old Leo had explained it to Hugh, to anyone who would listen, something about the universal appeal of a large splatter of red paint on a wall. Hugh must have been a disappointment, as an uncle, as a man. Not the same kind of disappointment as Leo's father, but not someone who would relish shooting at objects and watching blood appear as a result. "Leo's a dues-paying member of the Live and Don't Learn Club," Hannah said, snapping shut her phone.

"Me, too," Hugh offered. He didn't mention his night school class that would start the day after tomorrow. For more than a year now he'd been taking classes at the U that were offered during what would otherwise have been happy hour. It was his current attempt to curtail his drinking, going to school in the early evening a few days a week.

Failed attempts over the years had included stopping cold turkey; allowing himself only three drinks a day; only drinking after dark; and not drinking on Sundays. But college was sort of working. Advanced Creative Writing, Prose met on Tuesday and Thursday from five thirty to seven P.M. His sisters did not know he had returned to school. Hannah would have wanted him to be aiming toward a master's degree in something practical, and Holly would have bemoaned her own inability to finish her B.A. Hugh's path was eclectic, the only consistency the hour at which the class met. He'd done car repair, poetry, and pottery; now it was Advanced Creative Writing, Prose.

Ugly's was across the street from campus. Both school and bar were located in a neighborhood that had been going to the dogs for decades. During the day, the neighborhood was still relatively benign, but at night it became a kind of battle zone. Hugh always drove home marveling at the way the streets had turned menacing, both in his lifetime and during the hours of his college course, when the sun set and the wild things came out. On the evening news, if someone had been shot in Wichita, nine out of ten times it was here.

"You know what Papa said to me?" Hugh decided to unburden himself of his father's words. They were ugly, and it was growing dangerous outside the door of this bar, called Ugly's. One had to have cohorts when darkness and despair set in, when one was sowing the seeds of a hangover, when one was staring at the empty seat where one's brother should have been sitting, where his ghost hovered in a not-so-innocent fashion, smirking from teenage 1989.

"What?" Holly asked.

"'Fuck you.'"

His sisters' eyebrows shot up; they were shocked. "He never said that before," Hannah said.

"I know."

"Maybe he was saying it to one of his phantoms?"

"I don't think so."

And Holly began to sob and sob, her shoulders heaving monstrously, her cosmo glass knocked over, the bartender ready with the bar rag and the wagging head. *Suchamutt.* The men who'd perked up at the entrance of women now turned back to their drinks, relieved, perhaps, at having dodged the particular bullet of histrionics in public.

"Sometimes, Holly," Hannah said, "I think you use crying like a weapon."

"I'm sorry," Holly sobbed, face buried in her hands.

"It *is* kind of like a weapon," Hugh agreed, thinking about it. The bartender, the patrons, everyone was keeping a timid distance from the tears, averting their eyes. "Or maybe like a secret power."

"Most men can't take it," Hannah said.

"You don't use it much," he pointed out.

"I take pills to prevent it."

Holly blew her nose in a bar napkin. "I should try those pills. I'm gonna be just like that pitiful lady at the home, weeping and weeping, mistaking a chair for my sister."

"Dead sister," Hugh said.

"Not dead yet," Hannah said, bristling. "Here's what we'll do," she went on. "We'll bring Papa his stuff tomorrow. We'll go there every day to visit." She looked to Hugh.

"Right," Hugh said. Beyond that, a blank. He was tempted to ask his sisters to come visit *him* every day; his father at least had delirium to fall back on, and a houseful of distracting ladies. The larger change, maybe, was going to be in Hugh's life. He would talk to himself, he predicted. Although it would appear that he was occupying the air before you, he would more likely be wandering memory and speculation, those palatial spaces too seductive to forsake, no matter the uselessness of them.

This was the problem with drinking all day, the exhaustion and discouragement that followed just after relaxation and nostalgia.

"I hope he never says 'Fuck you' to me," Holly said.

"Excuse me," said a voice behind the three. He'd placed a hand on the bar beside Hannah, steadying himself, sending ghost Hamish swirling away. A portly professor with the stereotypical wardrobe: striped seersucker jacket and a plaid shirt beneath, neither of them particularly clean, and on his face very thick eyeglasses that completely obscured his eyes. He was an Ugly's regular, and he also hosted a public access show featuring his various hobbies. Saltwater fish aquariums. Brewing beer at home. Model trains. Around his basement, the television viewer roamed. Something about the lighting on that show always made him look insane, his eyeglasses like headlight beams shining from his fat skull. It wouldn't have been wholly surprising to see a caged animal down there, an alligator, say, or a feral child. "Can I buy you all a round of drinks?" he asked.

"Sure," Hannah agreed instantly. If she were single, Hugh thought, she would be pickier about who bought her drinks. Holly, meanwhile, was furiously wiping her eyes and nose with a new cocktail napkin the bartender had slipped her way.

"I'm Sid Kivich," the professor said.

"I've seen your show," Hugh answered as he shook Dr. Kivich's hand. "Did you ever make wine?"

"I did," said the professor. "Dandelion wine. Delicious." He confided, "The secret is letting it ferment in old Scotch barrels."

"Hmm," said Hannah, interested. Or pretending interest. She flirted within the safety of marriage, her husband, Thomas, a man Hugh didn't particularly feel like standing up for. Thomas and Hugh had not really hit it off, as brothers-in-law. Thomas was a lawyer, a runner, a man with a schedule. His hours were billable. He seemed to find Hugh pathetic. Whenever he was forced into a visit to the family house, he acted as if he might catch something there, or as if he were making a scientific inquiry, archaeological or anthropological, inspecting the lair of a curious species.

Hugh now imagined himself returning to that very same home this evening, the way there wouldn't be any lights lit. In his father's usual location, in the living room, would be the crusty space where his chair had been. Beside it still sat the other easy chair, Hugh's mother's chair. Like his father's, it was a ratty pleather model, its arms shredded by that dead cat Blanche. Its headrest was still stained by a henna-colored patch where his mother's brightly colored head had rested for so many years. She had died in her chair. But she'd also lived in it—eaten there, slept there, read her fat paperbacks there. Drunk her vodka and grapefruit drink there. For that reason it had seemed proper to deliver their father to his nursing home with his chair; even now, it was holding its owner in its lap, familiar when nothing else would be. But hers, their mother's model, Hugh was not sure what to do with. At the Salvation Army store, he and Holly had recently come across a whole section of donated recliners, rows of empty chairs as expressive as a row of human inhabitants, empty laps, indented headrests. Hugh had said, "Somebody died in every one of these."

"Ugh," Holly had said, her eyes filling. "I'm sure you're right." They'd gone for a couple of lamps, but came home empty-handed.

"What brings you all out on the town?" asked Dr. Kivich. *Out on the town?* He had wedged himself on Hamish's stool between Hannah and a stranger, leaning his large soft chest against the bar. His eyeglass stems had dug deep ruts on either side of his face, trenches from eyes to ears. He was in his early sixties, Hugh thought, a man in between the ages of his father and himself. His basement and his hobbies suggested perennial bachelor-hood, seclusion and freedom. Hugh, too, was a bachelor, yet he could not really identify with Dr. Kivich. He would never have walked up to a group of three strangers and offered to buy them drinks. In no way would he conceive of Ugly's as "out on the town." He wouldn't have let a camera crew into his home, never mind standing in front of them being filmed. And why *brew* beer when it was so much easier to *buy* it? Dr. Kivich, he realized, actually made an effort. Dr. Kivich, despite his mismatched cloth-ing and unfashionable eyewear, despite his big belly and advanced years, his bad breath and his boring conversa-tion, was still a social animal, doing the things that bachelors were traditionally supposed to do. Hugh looked down at his own lap as if to measure his testosterone. A bar stool did not encourage good posture. Moreover, his thighs spread unattractively.

On what could he blame his desire to go home, lie on the couch where he always lay, and watch television until he passed out? He looked up to see Holly watching him. She leaned forward and he followed suit. "You want to go home," she said under her breath.

"I do."

"Me, too."

"But we're in one vehicle."

"The nutty professor will take her home."

Hannah looked up and frowned when her brother and sister rose from their stools. "We're off," Hugh said.

"You're good to drive?" Hannah squinted as if she were able to perform a Breathalyzer test with her nostrils, as if the results would display in her eyeballs. Dr. Kivich, meanwhile, had noticeably brightened at the possibility of having her to himself.

Hugh shrugged; he could navigate the back roads, proceed with caution.

"I can give you a lift," Dr. Kivich said to Hannah. "I have an Austin-Healey." And when Hugh popped back into the bar thirty seconds later to retrieve his car keys from Hannah, the two of them were deep in conversation about recent films. Apparently, Dr. Kivich's newest hobby and accompanying public access programming involved reviewing movies.

The energy that guy had, Hugh marveled, climbing dispirited and exhausted behind the wheel.

## 3. *Ms. Fox*

"No knitting," said Ms. Fox, the first day of Advanced Creative Writing, Prose, swinging back over her shoulders a large load of tangled black hair. She was very small and exotic under that hair, wearing her pointy black boots, pacing in her tight black pants before her group of students.

In the room of plump midwesterners she looked like another kind of being, like a wiry black ant addressing a fleet of roly-polies and ladybugs. "No snacks in Tupperware. No ringtones. No single-spacing, no font size smaller or larger than 12. And no nail biting," she went on. Her own creepily long nails were painted different shades of pink, like an advertisement for a line of polish colors. Hugh had written poems for his first creative writing class, a year ago, using Pittsburgh Paints sample chips. Whisker, Silver Bangle, and Pearl Dream—they were sufficiently specific yet prettily imprecise enough to work well in poetry.

They were also, basically, gray.

Ms. Fox seemed on the defensive already, and she hadn't even discovered what to defend against. Her workshop was filled with people Hugh was coming to recognize as regulars, recidivists; he could have told her a few things to beware. Three of the women had been in his poetry class and waved happily when they saw him. He was one of two men in the room, also not an uncommon situation for these classes offered at happy hour.

Ms. Fox was a new instructor this year, and not what the group was accustomed to. For instance, she had started calling roll at five twenty-seven P.M., sighing heavily when someone came sheepishly through the door ten minutes later, tiptoeing, as only a heavy person can, to an empty seat at the table and snuggling quietly into it. Ms. Fox hadn't exactly said so, but the impression she gave was that she was not in Wichita by choice. If anything, it seemed as if she'd been abducted from some big city on one coast or the other, brought here under duress, and marched at gunpoint across the campus into continuing ed. Here, she found her students, all of them adults returning to school after the hours they'd spent at work, and most of them late. "Motivated," Hugh would have labeled him and his classmates. But perhaps also a little calcified, as learners, a little more willing than your average undergraduate to express mild scorn concerning wild artistic notions imported from the same place that Ms. Fox had originated; they were not afraid of projecting a tolerant dismissal of their instructors' assertions, the same patient reaction they had to their teenage children's wacky phases, knowing that eventually those children would grow up and get over it, whatever it was.

Hugh had not taken Introductory Creative Writing, Prose, but neither had anyone else in the group. Ms. Fox had sighed upon discovering this, muttering about prerequisites and permission-of-instructor forms, taking down the name of the registrar who'd blithely signed them up. The U was flexible, Hugh might have been able to explain to her, and that was one of its virtues. Prerequisites were for nitwits.

"Why does this building smell like a hamster cage?" she asked, in the middle of calling roll. The class as a group sniffed the air.

"I don't smell hamsters," said one student.

"It's a little like the zoo maybe," said another, helpfully.

Hugh didn't say so but thought it was probably because of the homeless man who lived in the building. He showed up in the evenings, while the doors were still unlocked to let out the students of the last classes, yet after the official staff had left the grounds. There'd been budget cuts recently, so that the janitors only cleaned once a week instead of every night. As a result, the homeless man usually had the place to himself, a series of bathrooms and classrooms and vending machines, even a telephone, a few couches, and some magazines, if he was interested. He hugged the wall when he entered, skulking by with his head lowered, the only real giveaway his plastic bags instead of a backpack. Otherwise, he could have been a student, scruffy, sullen, pensive. Hugh had only taken notice after a few semesters. He was always one for a good scam; he never pulled them but he enjoyed conceiving them, and witnessing this one. If he hadn't been afraid of spooking the guy, he'd have asked his name and brought him a sandwich on class nights. In lieu of this, Hugh had planted a jar of peanut butter and a loaf of bread behind the third-floor couch last semester.

Ms. Fox had moved on to other issues concerning her new job. "Is it really named Hiney, this place?"

"Hiney," the group agreed, nodding. The Hiney Building, for Ed Hiney, the man whose statue greeted you at the door, extending its bronze hand into which somebody was always placing unlikely items, condoms or a cigarette.

"Unbelievable." She continued down her list of students, calling names and having those names amended ("Call me Babs," said Barbara Kilcox; "I go by Nettie," said Antoinette Myers). Again, Ms. Fox ran her hands under her hair and lifted it from her shoulders, heaving it over. If it annoyed her as much as she made it seem it did, why wouldn't she simply cut it off?

Now she went around the circle, asking everyone to briefly ("*briefly*," she emphasized) say who they were and why they were here. The other man in the class was younger than the usual demographic for continuing ed, and had hair almost as long as Ms. Fox's. He had his hands in it as well, flipping it, as she had, over his shoulders. The rest were women, the assortment Hugh had grown comfortable with, wives and office professionals, dabblers, hobbyists, brainy high school girls, mostly kind, and for the most part very pleased to find Hugh in their midst. You did not have to do much to be the favorite man in a classroom of continuing ed women.

And among the college creative writing faculty Hugh was known as "Good Hugh." There was a "Bad Hugh" whom Hugh had met at a poetry reading several months earlier. The faculty had tried to banish Bad Hugh from their classes, but the threat of litigation and a timid dean had prevailed.

"Hugh Panik?" Ms. Fox asked, eyebrows raised in what looked like dread. She didn't pronounce the *H* in his name, yet she also did not pronounce his last name correctly. *You Paneek.* Sometimes the teachers knew only to beware a middle-aged Hugh. There'd been confusion concerning the Hughs until both had shown up at the end-of-semester poetry reading in May. Bad Hugh was a retired professor from the college. He wasn't quite old enough to have retired in the usual way. He'd been forced out by a series of strokes that had left him somewhat diminished and odd. Half of him appeared to have been short-circuited, fried like a faulty machine: one eye blinked like a Christmas tree light, and he held his left arm with his right while dragging his left leg behind him. The poetry he'd read that evening had been populated with biblical characters, and, like a child, Bad Hugh had seemed titillated by naughty words and bodily functions. He could hardly make it through "Flatulent Jesus" without bursting into guffaws. When the other students read, he blurted out random reactions, immediately slapping both hands over his mouth. "I'm a bad boy," he murmured repeatedly. "Bad Hugh."

"I'm not Bad Hugh," Hugh assured Ms. Fox at break. For the last forty-five minutes she had been casting stern glances in his direction.

"'Bad Hugh'?" she said.

"There's another Hugh," Hugh explained, understanding now that she hadn't been warned by her colleagues in creative writing. This meant several things. One was that the other instructors didn't like her. Another was that her stern glance had to do with so-called Good Hugh himself rather than an instance of mistaken identity. And, very unfortunately, he was only complicating matters by trying to explain Bad Hugh. Maybe now Hugh was going to become Ms. Fox's own private Bad—and banned—Hugh.

A woman in class at just that moment stepped in to save him. Not on purpose. But nevertheless.

"Excuse me," she said. "I've locked my keys in my car." She wasn't a regular. She was new, more or less Hugh's age, and looking very frazzled.

"Class isn't over," Ms. Fox said, lifting the wrist that sported a watch the size of an alarm clock.

"But my dog is in the car."

"And . . . ?"

"It's very stressful, having to think about my dog in the car, locked in, I mean. I wanted to get it taken care of so that I could relax and pay attention." She would cry, Hugh saw; life with his sister Holly had taught him the signs, the reddening nose and cheeks, the fluttering eyelashes, the little storm just on the verge of breaking.

"I'll help," Hugh said. They left Ms. Fox giving them both her fierce eyebrows.

"Her thought balloon says, 'Humph!'" Hugh told the

woman as they trotted down the echoing steps of the Hiney Building.

"Do *you* think it's cruel to leave a dog in the car?"

"Not necessarily." She was pretty, although Hugh hadn't really noticed her during class. He'd been preoccupied with how he'd rectify what he'd thought was a mistaken identity situation. He himself wasn't particularly bothered by Bad Hugh. At the poetry reading last spring, Bad Hugh had applauded with genuine enthusiasm, wiping his eyes when Hugh had read his piece about his mother's death, heckling—"Oh, hot mama, hot mama!"—in a very charitable and mostly sympathetic manner.

"Some people think it's cruel," she was saying. "Sometimes they give me grief. Isn't it so weird how total strangers will walk up and tell you what they think? I really do not appreciate that." Her dog had his nose at the back window, which had been left open an inch. The evening was less mild than the one two nights ago; a breeze tossed around the parking lot trash. On a night like this, it would have seemed sinister to convey a man to a nursing home in the back of a pickup truck. It would have looked like hazing, or Halloween. The clouds were hurrying overhead, the sky yellow-tinged, a situation that could lead to tornado.

The woman explained that she left the *back* windows cracked instead of the *front* so that if the dog wasn't enough of a deterrent (he was big, black, extremely hairy and enthusiastic; the window was thick with foggy nose prints), a thief would have a harder time getting to the driver's seat.

Why would it matter, Hugh thought idly, which door you came in through? But never mind. Now he had to help her break into her car. Her spare set of keys was the set locked inside (she'd lost the originals *ages* ago, down a sewer drain after a fender bender), dangling there in the ignition, an outrageously large bangle of objects that it seemed would be difficult to forget when exiting a vehicle. How, Hugh wondered, did she fit her leg beneath that chandelier of trinkets and keys to press the gas?

The dog leapt about, rocking the car, ecstatic to see the woman. She knelt to speak into the open slit of window. "Bozo," he was named. She was desperately trying to calm him. "He'll have a seizure otherwise," she explained to Hugh. "Honey, honey, honey," she crooned into the opening. A flash of lightning snapped overhead, followed quickly by the boom of thunder.

"Baby, baby, baby!" the woman pleaded. But she and the storm had succeeded only in agitating the dog further. She began to cry, worked up like her pet, bouncing from foot to foot, hands at the glass, fingers at his nose. Sure enough, the dog's enthusiastic anxiety suddenly became something else—he turned a full, albeit circumscribed, circle and fell on his side, then lapsed into a spastic jerking and twitching on the seat, mouth gone rubbery, legs kicking out as if swimming, testicles, Hugh noted, as big as chicken eggs. The first drops of rain began splattering the parking lot.

Hugh responded to the woman's crying, he thought later, rather than the dog's seizure or the storm, the distressed human rather than the flailing animal and angry sky, when he picked up a rock from the decorative parking lot landscaping and crashed it through the driver-side window.

He failed to notice the clues—not so subtle: french fries on the floorboard, pacifier in the ashtray—of this woman's life: wife, and mother of three small children. Instead, he focused on putting her into contact with her pet, getting them both out of the rain. "This is *just* what I kept imagining," she cried to Hugh. "That whole time while Ms. Fox was talking about the five senses, I was imagining Bozo having a seizure out here and me not getting to him." Bozo's seizure only lasted sixty seconds or so, but it was a long minute. The woman had rifled around in her purse in search of the dog's pills, chanting a harmless bit of profanity, the profanity of a parent, "dang, dang, dang," and not finding the meds.

All four doors hung open now, rain spotting the interior panels, Hugh sitting in the passenger front seat while the woman laid herself alongside the dog in the back. Her skirt was hiked up on her thigh and Hugh just stared. She had soft white flesh, with small veins of pink and blue. He could see the point, just above her knee, where she drew the shaving line. There was a sack of groceries on the front floorboard, and a jug bottle of wine, which Hugh touched reflexively, seeing if it was too warm to drink. The rain was evaporating on the parking lot pavement as it hit; sunshine pierced through for a moment, then disappeared. This woman's car was filled with stuff, as if she and Bozo lived in it. No wonder she'd begun thinking of it, as that had been the prompt for their first writing exercise. *Using the five senses, describe a place with which you are very familiar.*

Lulu, the old lady, had raised her hand to say, quite certainly, that she believed there was a *sixth* sense. Ms. Fox had given her a look like a lizard's. Poor Lulu; she was the one who'd brought her bag of yarn and needles to class and gotten them all off on the wrong foot with Ms. Fox. A distant rumble of thunder had then startled the group, and Hugh had bet it would probably make its way into all of their assignments.

When the dog had quit twitching, the woman sat up behind Hugh and scowled at herself in the rearview mirror, picking at her disheveled hair. The dog sat up beside her, dazed, his tongue exploring his teeth, his enormous black testicles a fascination on the seat. Hugh's hand was bloody, which was also something they'd learned about in the first half of Advanced Creative Writing, Prose class. A sudden appearance of a complication, a visceral result and detail. Here was that "happy accident" Ms. Fox had predicted, a bleeding hand to deal with now that the dog was becalmed. "Put enough tangible business in your work and a happy accident might occur."

The happier accident was the woman's willingness to—insistence on—take Hugh to the emergency room for stitches. Apparently his fist had followed the stone through the glass. Yet he hadn't felt particular pain—it was as if the sound of breaking glass, the sight of the writhing dog, the proximity of the woman's distress, the storm brewing overhead, as if an overload of other sensations had masked this one. In a way, Hugh was relieved to discover how absentminded he was even when he wasn't drinking. His drinking began these days after he'd returned from class. Before his going back to college, cocktails had been creeping up on him and his father. Who knew what might happen, now that he lived alone? Taking classes had successfully delayed his first drink at least a couple of days a week. And creative writing, so far, had been better than car repair or pottery. Had he been drinking this evening, he would have blamed that for his ripped knuckles.

While the doctor pulled the thread through Hugh's hand, Stacy—they'd exchanged names on the way to Wesley Medical Center's urgent care—took Bozo on a walk around the parking lot. Over the white dividers of the ER cubicles, through the slats of shades bisecting the stormy sunset, Hugh could see her pass back and forth, the dog dragging her, her arm outstretched and her legs stumbling along in his wake. He was a big strong animal, utterly untrained, unneutered, Hugh recalled, and the wind was fierce enough to make Stacy's skirt fly up. She could not control both things at once. She kept squinting in the direction of the automatic doors, waiting for him, Hugh thought.

"Ms. Fox will think we hated her class," she said when he finally came out, coaxing Bozo back into her car, tugging at her skirt.

"Maybe that'll make her nicer to us next time," Hugh said. "Or maybe whoever she's hiding from here in Hicksville will find her, and shoot her in the head."

Stacy's window was broken, and the big white bandage on Hugh's hand made his arm look as if it were a butcher-wrapped turkey drumstick. The dog was drooling more than usual, Stacy claimed, because of the seizure. Still, this turn of events didn't trouble Hugh. There was no one to whom he'd have to explain his weird appendage, since his father had moved away, and he'd probably been due for a tetanus shot anyway, which the ER doctor had insisted upon. Three hundred dollars was a lot of money, but Hugh didn't have many expenses, so that part was OK, too. Stacy was likable and her dog's loud moist breath on his neck was vaguely comforting. Something ripe and recently picked—tomatoes?—sent up its earthy odor from the grocery sack at Hugh's feet.

"Hey," he said. "Your wine is gone."

Stacy slammed on the brakes. "Jeez Louise," she said, without rancor. A car behind them honked, and she jerked back into motion. "I have bad luck," she told Hugh. "Ever since I was little, very bad luck. I used to think it was because of this mole on my face." She put a finger to her upper lip. "Then I had it removed and the luck was still no good. It was sad to say goodbye to my mole. I left it at the doctor's office, on his little tray. It embarrassed me my whole life, that mole, and I used to beg and beg my mom to get it removed. She said my dad said he thought it was sexy—do you think that's sick?—and anyway, it would make a scar. So when I got old enough, about ten years ago, I had it done. Then I had to leave it at the doctor's office, in its little bloody gauze. I actually waved goodbye to it. Bye, mole. I thought that would be the end of my bad luck."

"Turn here," Hugh said as they were just about to pass the last entrance to the university. They had driven along Twenty-first, passed Ugly's, almost passed the Liberal Arts parking lot and his truck, and had been headed off toward Highway 96. Hugh wouldn't have minded, but he didn't want Stacy to cry again. "Sorry," she said, swerving without signaling. "Bad luck, and no memory. Also, however, no scar. He was a good doctor, that guy who took my mole. I wonder what he did with it?"

There Hugh's truck sat, alone in the dark. The building would be locked now, the homeless man stretched out on a couch or sponging himself with paper towels in the men's room. Hugh would have to bring more peanut butter and bread next week. Maybe Nutella instead, just for variety.

"Already I'm glad I signed up for creative writing," Stacy said. Hugh opened his door and the interior light came on, so they could see each other. Tears had left a couple of trails through Stacy's makeup. Hugh himself wasn't handsome. He knew that. He was soft and lacked ambition. But men didn't have to be handsome. They just had to be presentable. And kind. And to smell halfway decent.

"Me, too," he said.

"See you next time?"

"Yes. Goodbye, Bozo." The dog licked him on the neck, which sent an unsettling erotic charge all the way down Hugh's spine.

She was wrong, Hugh thought, as she drove away; there was a small pale mark, a fingernail sliver of white flesh, just above her lip. That's where her bad luck mole had left a slight scar.

## 4. *Liquid Smoke*

A couple of weeks later, before his creative writing class, Hugh stopped in to visit his father. For the remaining days of August and the beginning ones of September, he'd allowed Hannah and Holly to go in his stead, let them take pictures and lamps and a small television. To them, he lied, claiming he'd visited. His father could neither reliably deny nor confirm it; the aides wouldn't tell. But Hugh was still mulling his last encounter with the man. Time had taught him to trust its passage: wait and see. He was waiting to see how he felt about his father now, weeks after leaving him.

He felt the same: guilty, hurt, confused. The home looked innocuous, nestled there among other ranch models on the street. The only giveaway was the wide drive where extra vehicles could park. That, and the lengthy note beside the bell explaining the rules concerning illness—no coughing, please wash your hands—and identifying oneself as a visitor and making sure the door was latched upon entry or exit.

"Hey, Pop," Hugh said when the aide had buzzed him in. His father's chair had been moved to a corner where it was not in the sight line of the television. In it, his father sat slumped, asleep, his large head tipped sideways on a neck seemingly too weak to support it. "You in time-out?" Hugh asked, kneeling, placing a hand on his father's leg.

Sam Panik looked up, surfacing from the dreamy depths of his nap. He took a variety of medications, and some of them left him stupefied, reacting as if in slow motion. Had it not been for the milky saliva on his chin and the stubble on his cheeks, he might have seemed graceful as he awoke. As it was, Hugh could not bear it. He used a Kleenex to wipe his father's mouth. From his father's expression he knew Sam did not recognize him. Which was worse, being told "Fuck you" or being regarded anonymously? And were these the only options Hugh could expect, blasphemy or blankness?

He settled in on the floor beside his father's recliner and let the old man gather what he could of his wits. His shabby chair faced the others, as if there were teams, or as if he might be the object of a question-and-answer session. The women, arranged in their semicircle across the room, around the television, each occupied an entirely other universe, it was clear. The aide chattered as she moved among them, including Sam Panik in her routine.

"He's a little fussy," she confessed to Hugh. "Aren't you?" she shouted at his father. He rolled his eyes. Hugh hoped he wouldn't say something scathing; Sam Panik had the ability to say some very wickedly pointed things about women. Everyone believed him to be a kindly old man, but there'd always been a streak of eloquent cruelty beneath. Now he moved his mouth but nothing emerged. The aide trundled on, delivering meds and crackers to the others.

Hugh decided to check on the hip flask he'd left between the mattress and the box spring, telling himself that he was only curious about whether it was still there, whether his father had found it. Even as he entered his father's room, he was scolding himself for his real motive: taking a little snort of the Irish. The flask was where he'd tucked it, and apparently his father had yet to discover it there. Hugh took a long drink, joyful at the early pleasure of an unexpected treat. He'd resigned himself to after-hours alcohol on Tuesdays and Thursdays, yet here was a nice surprise, a melting warmth seeping throughout his limbs. He smiled, tucked the flask back into the bed, and returned to the living room, where he lowered himself to the floor beside his father again. In the hallway, he'd passed the aide, who was leading a woman with a walker into the bathroom. He'd smiled, awkwardly—on tiptoes, arm well over the heads of the women—held open the bathroom door, nodded his polite encouragement. Visiting the nursing home would always be like this, he thought: much better under the influence of alcohol.

Hugh sat at his father's feet and just watched. His father was breathing heavily, shifting his legs about, grabbing blindly at the chair handle that would jerk his headrest forward. Soon enough he would speak. He would explain why it was he chose to put himself on the other side of the room, why he was in the corner facing the ladies rather than sitting among them, watching television. But Hugh already understood why. Sam Panik was the only man in this house. He didn't want to be one of its inhabitants, pudding-face women, nonentities. He had put himself in this corner so that nobody would mistake him for one of them.

For creative writing class last week the assignment had been to write a personal ad. This was supposed to teach the students to invent characters. Hugh recalled a personal ad he had actually written, drunk, a few years earlier. His interest then had been Ms. Fox's interest now: in what way did a person reduce himself to acronyms and salesmanship? She might have been impressed to learn that he'd revised the real ad for a long while, memorizing his brief synopsis of self, tweaking a word here and there. It had been a mildly entertaining endeavor. But although he'd enjoyed a few of the ads run by his peers—men who'd clearly understood their status as sad-sack bachelors with none of the ordinary requirements for courtship—there hadn't been a single personal ad written by a woman seeking a man that Hugh had felt even remotely tempted to answer. They emphasized age and weight, a preference for movies and twilight walks and Christian fellowship. They did not tolerate much, or if they did, it seemed they would be prickly and insistent, *Two-stepping or else!*

Stacy, who sat beside him, had composed a very long personal ad. Perhaps she'd never read a real one. Maybe she did not understand the pricy-ness of being thorough. Hugh was providing acronyms, and their scandalous meanings, when Ms. Fox gave him the hairy eyeball. But creative writing class had become, for Hugh, about Stacy. Who cared if the teacher didn't like him? All that first weekend, as his stitches had healed and itched, and while they were being removed a week later, he'd thought of Stacy's murmuring to her dog, of her behind the wheel of her vehicle, hunched forward a little nervously, as if she couldn't see very well yet refused to wear glasses.

Stacy's hair was the same color as Hugh's mother's, dyed red. Stacy's was probably done professionally, and was probably brown underneath, whereas his mother had dyed hers in the kitchen sink to mask straw-textured gray. For class, Stacy wore the kind of clothes women wore to go on dates—tight jeans or short skirts, low-cut blouses, jewelry and makeup. Most of the other women in the class had on their ordinary outfits, office-wear or casual things. Lulu the old lady wore what Hugh's mother would have, a muumuu. Hugh did not find Stacy's fashion statements alluring—her clothing seemed slightly too small for her, as if she'd recently put on a few pounds but felt certain enough that she'd lose them to not purchase a new wardrobe—but he was interested in her notion of creative writing class as a social occasion worthy of dressing up for. He himself wore his only real outfit, his khakis and his shirt.

Their homework for tonight was to go grocery shopping for their lovelorn creation and produce the bag of goods for the group. Like the personal ad, the shopping expedition had a formal limitation imposed upon it: ten items, no more, no less. These would further develop their character. Their *third-person* character, italics Ms. Fox's.

"Do not bore me with the endless chronicle of *moi*," Ms. Fox had warned them.

"Who is Mwaw?" Lulu the old lady had asked. She'd been in a couple of classes with Hugh. In substitution for her knitting, she'd begun bringing the makings of a rag rug, tying knots all night.

The punk rock girls, "gifted" high school students, had looked at each other with menace in their eyes. They would bring handcuffs, a Taser, Vaseline, some other satanic object that would alarm the room as much as their piercings did.

Hugh sighed heavily at his father's nursing home. He pulled back Sam's shirt cuff to check the time on his watch.

It was a model that lit up in the dark, if his father could remember to poke the stem. He liked to know the hours of his insomnia, as if knowing the time took some pressure off not knowing his physical location or personal identity. Although Sam Panik's mouth was moving, no sound yet came. "There's a flask," Hugh whispered into his ear. "Under your mattress. Some Irish." Baffled, his father blinked, closing his mouth as if to ingest the information without losing it. This permitted Hugh an exit, which he greedily took, patting his father's arm, waiting at the front door to be buzzed out. The aide gave him a large false smile, which, with a belt of whiskey charging him, he could return. Outside, Hugh held the smile, pausing. He was so pleased to be on this side of the door, headed toward class, and Stacy, a steady happy flame inside him, the evening ahead of him an unknown quantity. He shivered giddily in the oaky sunlight of dusk, free and autonomous, living the exact opposite existence of his father's, with unpredictability and possibility beating all around him. If he let it, guilt would overwhelm him, so Hugh made a note to keep guilt at bay this evening, and he practically ran to his truck, so eager was he to meet Stacy in the Liberal Arts parking lot. They were going to Safeway together before class.

"I actually need these things," Hugh told her at checkout. They'd driven in her car so that she could keep track of Bozo. The front window had been repaired; her husband was fanatical about such things, she'd explained. Upon hearing the word—he hated that word, *husband*, although he did not hate its companion word, *wife*—Hugh took in the detritus around him, her life. No wonder she was baffled by personal ads: she was safely out of the running. He could use another shot of whiskey, he thought, something to both buoy and blunt his new feelings.

She laughed at what he put in his grocery cart: Circus peanuts. Pimiento cheese spread. Tinactin. Toothpicks. A night-light. Liquid smoke. Wicker basket of apples. Dill pickles. Two lottery tickets. Depends. Everything except the liquid smoke was for his father, at the nursing home. These were the idiosyncratic items the home did not supply. Having just visited, Hugh had been reminded of his father's particular desires and as a result now found himself shopping for his father's character. His own was liquid smoke, in which he marinated steaks. Liquid Smoke, he thought. He ought to name a character that. He ought to find a way to compress it into a personal ad, or a license plate. LQDSMK. Whiskey, he thought, was some kind of liquid smoke.

In Stacy's cart was a mousetrap, a Tupperware tub, a *Mad* magazine, a can of Mighty Dog, a fennel root, and beer. "My character thinks a six-pack is not one object," she explained.

"How many objects does your character think it is?" Hugh asked at checkout.

"This doesn't count," she explained, feeding the Mighty Dog to Bozo, filling her car with the nauseating scent of canned meat. Having popped open one kind of can, they somehow decided to open the others, soon settling themselves back in the parking lot of the Hiney Building drinking 3.2 beer.

"I was going to write a character study about Bozo," Stacy said. "Except he would be a person instead of a dog. He would be large and loyal and overexuberant, and everyone he lived with would be tired of him, or afraid of him, or plain old mean to him, except a character like me. Who loves him. He would be like that guy from *Mice and Men*, the giant idiot who always crushes the bunny."

Bozo had finished his food more quickly than Hugh could have imagined possible and now stretched out on the backseat to chew on the can, a rhythmic metallic *chunka chunka* that did not appear to worry his owner. Hugh certainly wasn't going to worry, if Stacy didn't.

"I'm writing about my sister Hannah," Hugh confessed. "She said this thing to me about my neighbors—'I hate those hippies'—and I keep thinking about it." *Hannah said, I hate those hippies.* "It's the alliteration, I guess, but I'm changing her name to Helen." "I *hate* those hippies," Hannah had declared when she'd seen Waffle and Bob (the girl) out chanting in Mr. Roosevelt's yard.

"Why?" Hugh had asked. "They're harmless." *Helen hated the harmless hippies.*

"They're *also* incredibly *bor*ing," Hannah said. "And they don't even know it, they're totally self-righteous." Once upon a time, Hannah had been a hippie. She'd spent a summer riding around in a school bus with a peace sign painted on its hood, traveling from coast to coast busking at coffeehouses. "And filthy? Please. It's disgusting."

There were maybe six hippies. They lived in old Mr. Roosevelt's house. Somebody in the group was his descendant, a twentysomething fuckup sent to occupy the deceased man's home. They did not seem to distinguish between outdoors and in: furniture migrated back and forth, as did guests and animals and music. Sometimes they slept on the lawn; sometimes they rode their motorcycles or skateboards through the sliding glass door into the family room. Hugh didn't mind them, but he was apparently alone in this opinion. His other neighbors were plotting against them. Nobody liked hippies anymore.

"I found a hippie on the wall one day," Hugh told Stacy. Waffle, perched there like a gargoyle, overlooking the neighborhood. Hugh had stood studying the boy, his unconscious grace, his unfortunate facial hair. It took years to figure out proper facial hair. Long ago Hugh had decided on clean-shaven and he'd stuck with it. Mustaches were for playboys; beards were for political types. The low-profile preferred a daily scrape with the razor. What was that boy doing on the wall at six in the morning?

"He told me he had climbed up there to watch the sun rise." Waffle had shaken his confused face. "That's kind of sweet, huh? Watching the sunrise? How can you hate that, in a person?" Hugh didn't tell Stacy that the boy had been looking north, where the sun would never rise.

"Mr. Roosevelt would shit a brick," Hannah had told her brother.

Hugh agreed. His neighbor ghost weighed in now and then, tsking around in Hugh's head.

"Well, Mr. Roosevelt was actually an asshole, too," conceded Hannah, "but at least he was tidy. At least he kept his assholic self inside the house. Assholish?"

Since signing up for creative writing, Hugh frequently felt the urge to take notes. People often said very useful lines of dialogue; he now thought in quotation marks. Only when he told Stacy about substituting *Helen* for *Hannah* did he realize he'd used his mother's name instead of his sister's. It was just like Ms. Fox said: your life would pop up unbeknownst to you. Like dreams blurted out benignly at breakfast—full of trains, tunnels, explosions— and then the big blush when his sisters interpreted. You could learn to withhold your dreams. But he decided he would leave his mother's name in his creative writing assignment. She was dead, and *Helen* sounded felicitous next to *hippies* and *hate* in dialogue. *Helen said, "I hate those hippies!"* He might use their real names, too, since how could he possibly invent something as good as Waffle and Bob (the girl)? Hugh popped open another Coors Light, having drunk the entire contents of his first in two swallows. Jesus God, Coors Light from the grocery—why bother drinking it, why not just pour it into the toilet, thereby eliminating the middleman action of letting it pass through his digestive tract?

"I have mints," Stacy said. She opened the compartment between the seats to reveal red-and-white peppermint disks. "So we don't smell like we went to a bar."

"Good thinking," he said, although if anyone saw them out drinking in Stacy's car it would be worse than having gone to Ugly's. He chugged down the second beer. It was his experience that the first three ought to be drunk very rapidly so as to actually obtain some sort of high. The next eight or ten could be consumed at a more leisurely rate. Stacy's character should have bought a suitcase instead of a six-pack.

"Oh, look, there's Ms. Fox." Ms. Fox clicked along the sidewalk in her boots, dressed in her habitual black. "She's so pretty, isn't she?"

Hugh didn't think so. He tried to see what Stacy found attractive. The enormous hairdo? The angry energy? No, he deduced. It was the thinness. He knew enough about his sisters' complaints about their own weight to see where the "prettiness" of Ms. Fox lay: in her tiny body. "You're much prettier," he told Stacy. It was not only true, it was kind.

"My husband is always making comments about my thighs," she said. "He thinks he's being all subtle, but I know better."

"What does he say?"

She tilted her head back, thinking. "Well, it's not so much what he says but the way he looks at me when I put on certain clothes. Like: *You're going to wear that?*"

"I think you're very attractive," Hugh went on, helping himself to another beer. Lulu the old lady passed before them, then the rest of their classmates. Hugh and Stacy would be the last and latest, reeking of beer. The thing about drinking was that it made the consequences of drinking seem less burdensome. Hugh's thought, as he swallowed the last of the third can of beer, was: I'm happy. Right here and now, happiness. He popped open a fourth beer without really thinking about it. Stacy had finished her second and now checked her watch.

"We're really late."

"You want to share this?" Hugh held out the can. Stacy stared cross-eyed at the can's opening as if trying to decide whether or not to wipe it before drinking. She didn't, taking a long, manly snort, holding a fist to her mouth afterward to contain a belch. In the backseat, Bozo still chewed on his can, now down on the floorboard behind Hugh. He could feel the animal's head as it bumped against the seat, the vague nuzzle into his organs, especially his full bladder. "We're going to be absent," he said.

"I guess so."

"You want to go to Ugly's?"

"I don't think I should come home smelling like a bar," Stacy said. "I think that would be a problem."

The solution was to visit the liquor store and obtain a bottle of wine. Then to return to the liquor store in order to purchase a corkscrew. Back at Liberal Arts, they parked at the far end of the lot, where an overhead light had burned out, leaving a useful void for them to snuggle into. Stacy also enjoyed circus peanuts and pimiento cheese spread and pickles, so in addition to the wine they had treats. She told him about her husband and children. There were three children, two girls and a boy, and their order was like the birth order of Hugh's family—girl, boy, girl. Coincidentally, Stacy had had a miscarriage before her first daughter had been born, so perhaps there was supposed to have been an older brother, this ghost child in her life, like the one in Hugh's family. Stacy chattered easily and happily along, taking only the occasional swig of wine, allowing Hugh to enjoy both her voice and her presence, and most of the wine. Outside, Indian summer had arrived. It was warm in the way a dying fire was warm, an orange glowing that promised future chill, an odor of dying leaves in the air, the vague threat of tomorrow's ash.

They covered the yes and no questions, matters of identity and affiliation. The answers to these were irrelevant; he was watching the way she gave them. Did he care that she'd grown up on the east side? That both of her parents were real estate agents, that she had disappointed them by becoming a stay-at-home mom, and that her siblings were the other two members of a set of triplets? He did not. He cared that her fingernails had been chewed to within a half inch of her cuticles, that her mascara had been applied in a sweat, leaving black dots on each upper eyelid, that she did not ask him to repeat himself or look perplexed when he spoke, as so many did, because he tended to speak under his breath. She watched his mouth instead of meeting his gaze, her lips parted, eyes vaguely crossed, head nodding, as if she were coaching him or as if they were together recalling the lyrics to a song they both had once known.

She'd graduated from East High two years after he'd graduated from North; she'd gone to K-State and earned herself an MRS while he was wasting time out west. "Every Kansan has to go look at the mountains," she assured him, understanding his odyssey. "And the ocean," he responded. "The Grand Canyon." Skyscrapers, subways, monuments and museums—the million things that Kansas couldn't claim and that Hugh had needed to go gawk at. But they'd both come home to flat Wichita—a little grudgingly maybe, yet they'd stayed, hadn't they? And by choice? He liked that she didn't complain about the city. Everyone complained about Wichita, locals and visitors alike, about the whole state of Kansas, its monotonous landscape they were forced to drive through or fly over, its backwater reputation they felt free to ridicule. Yes, the place lacked a lot, but Hugh had already heard about it a thousand times.

"I even like the worst days of summer," Stacy confessed. "When it's so hot and the grasshoppers jump on your ankles and the cicadas won't shut up and it seems like you might just scream naked into your neighbor's pool. My husband keeps saying we're going to move to Alaska."

They would kiss, Hugh predicted. The wine bottle that passed between them would act as agent, introducing their lips to each other via its shared one, their fingers touching as they traded off the bottle, meanwhile its contents lubricating them sufficiently to allow a kiss to seem the only logical wobbly next step. And nothing more than a kiss, because Advanced Creative Writing, Prose was only an hour-and-a-half-long class.

"I have a crush on you," Stacy admitted. The bottle was empty; class was letting out, the door opening across the lot to reveal their classmates exiting.

"Me, too," Hugh said. He knew he ought to make the first move, but she was married, and that was the excuse he would cling to in letting her be the one who leaned toward him. It was his side, the passenger's, that she crossed into. Of course he leaned to meet her, but it wasn't halfway. He hadn't kissed anybody in a long time. He loved the shared taste of wine between them.

"My husband has a mustache," she whispered when they broke. "I like your clean upper lip."

He vowed anew to shave it every day. Stacy's lipstick had worn off on the bottle's opening, so that Hugh had already gotten used to a slight waxiness. This time when they kissed, their hands were at work, and Hugh rested his at her straining neck. Like other vulnerable, unexposed places on the body, her skin was very soft here. He wanted never to have to move his hand from the place where her neck met her jaw, below her ear, this place where he could feel the bone beneath, and sense the heartbeat. He wanted never to have to leave this moment. It was the moment before all the things that could—and would—go wrong. This was the beginning, which was always best. Like the evening's first drink, by which all the others were inspired, though they never measured up.

And then they mutually realized that more than an hour and a half had passed and it was time to go, as if to meet curfew. Which was fine by Hugh; he was exhausted from liking her so well, from finding no fault. "I should head home," she whispered. "Class is way over."

"OK," he said. He had to think a moment: was tonight Tuesday or Thursday? Would he next see her in forty-eight hours, or in five days (and how many hours was that, anyway?).

"I wonder what they thought about us not being there. Not there, together?" Stacy said, not yet moving away from Hugh. Suddenly she put her cheek next to his and held tight to him. "I like you more than I should," she said into his ear. "I don't know what to do about that." He was alerted to that secret weapon, tears. "This doesn't happen to me very often," she said. "I'm scared."

Hugh did not know what to say. He could have responded with "Me, too," if he'd wanted, because it was all identically true for him. Fortunately, he was drunk. Fear was for later. He kissed her again. From experience—and not enough of it—he knew that this kiss ought to be savored. There would never be a better one. He told Stacy that she was wonderful and that he felt lucky. He reminded her to eat a couple of breath mints before walking into her house. When he opened the door, at last, she recoiled at the sudden dome light, and he looked away, collecting the empty cans and bottle to take with him, only much later wondering what she would do with his character's groceries, while he was wandering around Safeway repurchasing them, the Depends and the liquid smoke. He had, it turned out, five days to relish their first kiss. He loved those one hundred twenty hours.

## 5. *Say It: Divorce*

Like most people's, Hannah's brother's worst traits were also his best. He could not care less what anyone thought of him, so he didn't mind if his sisters visited his house when he wasn't there. They could take for granted his hospitality.

It had been their house, too, after all; they still had keys to its doors and garage, although half the time, Hugh forgot to lock up.

Forgot to lock up, declined to pick up—the phone, the floor, the magazines and half-done projects, a jigsaw puzzle in perennial postponement on a card table one leg of which was a former broom. The place was not messy, exactly, but neglected. Dusty. Sat upon and then not fluffed; books read and not reshelved, teetering in towers, splayed on chair arms. Spiders left in peace to ply their trade. If Hugh had visited her house, he wouldn't have mentioned any of the things she'd failed to do there; he wouldn't have noticed any lapses in housekeeping. His disposition disallowed it. Hannah sighed in wonderment; the place truly had not changed since childhood, nor had she. Alas.

She'd come today after visiting her father. Sam Panik had requested a photograph of his wife. Maybe because she was separated from Thomas, Hannah had been uncharacteristically moved upon hearing her father's simple desire. She'd taken herself to the nursing home and sat with the old man who was her father, who'd once upon a time been the man whose temper she was tuned to, whose favorable opinion she cultivated; they could sit for a long time, saying nothing. Hannah meditated on her middle-age problems while smiling wanly at the vaguely surreal existences going on around her, the woman stroking her stuffed animal, the woman crying at the table, the woman reading the children's book, reciting single lines over and over and over again. They were religious tales. They probably had morals, but you'd never find out. "Jesus loves the little children," the woman said, so many times there seemed to be a kind of ominousness to the phrase; you were almost waiting for the verb to change, or the inflection to subtly shift, as if Jesus might, upon deep speculation, not be such a benevolent lover of children.

Hannah was tempted to find the place a kind of philosophic hell; she turned to her father to ask him how he liked his new roomies, these existential muses.

"I miss Helen," he replied, simply and lucidly. And Hannah's heart swelled, returning from brooding to the flesh and blood of her mother. It appeared she would never be in the same state of mind concerning a spouse; hers had moved away.

Now she picked her way through the mess of her parents' old bedroom in search of a photograph. Hugh was undoubtedly at his job. For over twenty years he'd been working in the same capacity, gofer to Junior Wheeler, head of Wheeler Construction. It didn't seem to bother Hugh that he'd gone to school with Junior, that Junior was two years younger than Hugh, and that Hugh was on call to the man 24-7, tethered by a beeper that still made him jump when it went off in his pocket. His errands, to Hannah, occasionally sounded suspect—pickups in the middle of the night, objects transported across state lines, co-workers who all seemed to be ex-cons or under restraining orders. Hugh had no health insurance nor a retirement plan. Of course, Hannah scolded herself as she ransacked yet another drawer full of papers, neither did she, at the moment. And if she wanted to get technical about legal troubles, it was she who'd escaped by the skin of her teeth.

Stealing a scrip pad: she was lucky to have been merely fired. And she'd only shot for *Adderall*, she countered in her own defense of herself to herself, rolling her eyes. Not that big a deal. A little pick-me-up, a diet plan, something dispensed to kids like candy, why not her?

Hugh had apparently shut the door of their parents' ground floor bedroom the day he and his sisters had taken the old man to the home and not opened it since. There were drinking glasses on the nightstand and a basket of sour clothing in the corner. The bed was a vicious tangle of its various layers of coverings—plastic mattress protector, quilted pad, filthy flowered sheet, holey woolen blanket. The headboard tilted downward, as if ready to fold up on the next person who lay there, and the closet was spilling over, not a single garment hanging. The wire hangers clanged when Hannah swept her palm inside, searching for the chain to the light. The bulb was burned out. The wallpaper near the overhead-light switch was black with the oil of hands, and that light was also burned out. Hannah finally tugged open the heavy curtains, exposing to merciless daylight the true horror of the place. It was a cry for help; it was condemnable. She sighed. Maybe this was her new role in life: the person who showed up and disposed of things, applied the crowbar and mop and sponge and unsentimental eye, energetic, a fanatic when it came to order—no matter how disorderly her own life might appear.

She tore down the drapes and jimmied open the windows. They screeched when she flung them up, paint chips scattering at her feet. Out went the curtains, rods and all, onto the drive; in rushed the cool fall air. Her mother had sewn those drapes, stitched O-rings along the tops, hemmed the bottoms, inserting lead weights every few inches so that they would hang smoothly. They'd complemented the wallpaper, salmon-colored birds of paradise. Out everything went. Two hippies from next door at the

Roosevelts' old house stood watching as objects were ejected. "Can I have this?" one asked, picking up the wicker magazine rack. It was stuffed with reading material from a decade past.

"Anything you want," Hannah replied.

"Awesome."

Then there were a half dozen youths, holding up clothing, trying on shoes. Their dog, a mongrel, stopped only long enough to urinate on the broken automatic shoe polisher. Hannah winged out the stained lamp shade, then set the ceramic lamp itself gently on the ground below the sill. No lightbulb there, either. Her father had apparently lived in the complete dark his last days at the house, hibernal, neglected. Hannah supposed that her own son, Leo, would opt for a similar circumstance, given the chance. What became of such men?

As if in answer, her brother pulled into the drive at that moment, home for lunch. He appraised the situation from the driver's seat for a moment before emerging from the truck. Hannah could hear a voice from the radio, some bloviating political commentator. XM, she reminded herself; she'd borrow his truck before Christmas and have it installed. "How's it going?" Hugh asked his neighbors rhetorically, swiping his palms against theirs in some ritualistic greeting, then, to Hannah through the bedroom window, "What are you doing?"

Hannah put her head out. "I was looking for a picture of Mom."

"There's one on the mantel."

"Help me with this goddamned rug," she said. She'd rolled it up and was trying to lift one end to the windowsill. Her back ached from having had to pick up the bed, her toe throbbed from having dropped the box spring on it, and the rug, beneath the heavy dilapidated disaster, was blotted with urine from some long-dead cat. The neglect was infuriating, unending. Under the rug: a rotted floor.

"Can it wait till after I eat?"

"No!"

He joined her in the bedroom and they slid the old rug out the window, scattering more chips of paint both inside and out. Instantly the hippies descended upon the rug, hauling it to Mr. Roosevelt's front yard and unrolling it there, walking around on it and admiring it, sitting on their burnt-orange couch to see how it looked from that perspective.

"Jesus Christ," Hannah said. "This place is a perfect example of entropy in action."

"I don't even know what that means," Hugh said. "Come have a glass of wine. You'll feel better."

Despite being lazy, and not caring about most material goods, Hugh did stock decent wine. It was perhaps the only addition, in the way of furniture, that he'd made to the house: a large wine rack, always with at least a case on hand, a heavy professional corkscrew also within reach. But when Hannah opened a kitchen cupboard to retrieve a glass, little bugs flew out. She screamed.

"They're just moths," he said mildly.

"Disgusting!"

"I kind of like them. They're like company. Low-maintenance pets."

Hannah had selected a bottle of white from his rack and now pulled out an ice tray to cool down the drink. In the freezer were several bags of lima beans. "Good lord, Hugh," she said, "I cannot believe you've saved these."

"It's hard to throw them away."

"She's been dead three years."

"I know." The lima beans had been their mother's hemorrhoid cure. She'd sat on them, in her easy chair, changing one package for another as they defrosted. The chair also remained, resting there in the living room, their mother's orange hair dye staining its headrest. Were men more sentimental about their mothers? she wondered. Did that explain her husband's recent fleeing to his mother's home? Did it provide a reason for Hugh's inability to locate a wife? Move on? Grow up?

Could she actually claim to be a grown-up, push coming to shove?

Hannah returned the antique metal ice trays to the freezer and shut the door, declining to cool her wine, and then thoroughly washed the glass she pulled from the buggy cupboard. Hugh was right, however, that a drink relaxed her. She was an anxious, moody, annoyed person; she needed to calm down. That's how her marriage had gone bad: restlessness, agitation, irritation. A need to make things happen, a desire for change, an urge for upset even if what ensued wasn't necessarily for the best.

Maybe Adderall had been the wrong drug?

"I need a vacation from our marriage," she'd told Thomas. "I will probably come back from it, but I might not."

"I will probably not be here when you do, but I might be," he'd eventually sort of replied. Or so she'd interpolated.

Hugh retrieved the mantel photo, blowing off the dust as he handed it to her.

It was a glamour shot from the sixties, taken before any of the children had been born, before their mother had been worn out by pregnancy and labor and concern for others. Her hair was dark in it, and her young shoulders exposed, the angle of the photographer somewhat above her, as if capturing her face as she swirled in a big-city ballroom, in an era just before the one wherein everything went wrong. Hannah had spent hours torturing herself, seeking out a photograph, and Hugh had been on the job for exactly five seconds before solving the problem. Now he opened a can of soup, plopped it into a hideous bowl some child had apparently made, thrust it inside the filthy microwave, and poked a few buttons. The old machine whirred into action, causing a brief dimming of the kitchen lights, and Hugh poured himself some wine. In a pickle jar.

"I finally get what you mean about chardonnay," he said.

"I told you so," Hannah said.

"Who was it who liked that really sweet wine, that German syrup at Thanksgiving?"

"Thomas's mother. Bea."

"Bea." He nodded. "How's she?"

"I have no idea. I haven't seen her in months. You know, Hugh, I've separated from Thomas. We might divorce."

"Really?" Something in the microwave popped, then another something. "That usually means it's done," he said, rising to retrieve his lunch. "Why might you divorce?"

"Boredom," Hannah said. "I get bored so easily, it's kind of crazy."

Hugh had built a little city around his ugly soup bowl, the jar of wine and Tabasco and salt and pepper containers, a stack of white saltines. The soup was split pea, of a color and odor that nearly made Hannah gag. "I don't get bored," Hugh said between spoonfuls.

"Yeah, I know. That's the same lunch you've been eating since grade school."

"I sort of like predictability. I find it comforting."

"That's pretty obvious. I mean, look at your pants."

Hugh literally looked at his pants. "What?"

"You only have one pair."

"I have six. They're just all the same."

Hannah conceded, "I guess there's something appealing about knowing what's going to happen next."

"Routine," Hugh agreed. "Find a dozen things you like to do every day, and then do them. What's wrong with that?"

"Finding the dozen things, I guess. What are your dozen?"

"Well, coffee. Then a crossword puzzle. Lunch, which you're looking at. I used to enjoy watching the cop-video shows with Dad, but that's not as much fun alone." He paused. Hannah scrutinized him. Something he wasn't going to tell her crossed his face, a pleasure in his daily routine that he was withholding, savoring just briefly. "Cocktail hour, naturally," he said.

"Naturally."

"And so on. You can build a day around those things, can't you? What's wrong with that?"

"You don't *get* anywhere."

"Where do you want to get?"

Hannah sighed. "I don't know. That is perhaps the precise goddamn crux of my problem." She poured some more wine; they'd emptied the bottle, which must be the advantage of the jar or tumbler as receptacle, each having had only one "glass." "Today, I want to clean that fucking bedroom. It nauseates me. There's a hole in the closet floor that a mammal could crawl through. A large mammal."

"Yeah," Hugh said. "I've crawled through it before. The joist under the bathtub seemed a little hinky. I had to go prop it up."

"With what?"

"Books," he said, adding, "Joke. Concrete blocks." He took his bowl to the sink and put the lids back on his condiments. They occupied a plastic lazy Susan that had sat on the kitchen table since Hannah and Hugh's childhood, a cheap antique object, ugly and useful. The whole house was like that, comfortable and shabby and full, for Hannah, of sadness. How was it that the place did not sadden her brother? Moreover, he didn't seem to mind her walking in and rearranging it, literally tossing pieces of the past out the window. He did not instigate anything, nor did he object when anything was instigated around him. Underneath, he crawled around propping the place up with concrete blocks when it started to grow spongy. Hannah had an image of the house returning to nature, rotting and moldering away like a dead body, grown over and gone. Already some greenery had bloomed in the rain gutters around the roof, flourishing in the mulch of last year's leaves. It reminded Hannah of hair that sprouted from old men's ears. Old men who had no women in their lives to keep them presentable.

"And how's our boy Leo?" Hugh asked.

"Seen my hair lately?" She grabbed a hunk and shook it. Her busy, bored son Leo, just like her, out raising hell. The other, Justin, had moved with Thomas over to Bea's house. Hannah happened to know that her brother didn't much like her husband. Or, since he wasn't actually energetic enough to dislike someone, it might be more proper to say that he didn't understand Thomas. Along with some kind of misplaced optimism concerning his wife and sons, Thomas also possessed what he would have called a *work ethic*, something that Hugh might have labeled *anal-retentiveness*, if he'd bothered to label it anything, that kept them from ever truly relating to one another. It was as if they were from different countries, with customs and habits and basic needs that simply didn't mesh, their conversation tools of the most rudimentary, broad variety. They could be polite to each other, but hardly anything beyond that. In high school, had they attended the same one at the same time, Hugh would have been the stoner in the beater in the parking lot, listening to a cassette tape of Led Zeppelin, watching in mesmerized perplexity as Thomas, wearing a very skimpy pair of running shorts, sprinted around a circular racetrack, trying to set a record in the Kansas spring heat.

"Dad'll like having that picture," Hugh said. "I should have thought of taking it to him. Sometimes I look around this place and sort of don't see what I'm looking at. You know what I mean?"

"Not really," Hannah said, looking around the kitchen. "I see everything, and it's all pretty repulsive. No offense."

Hugh laughed, then startled as his beeper went off in his front pocket. "Break over," he said.

"Is there anything in that room you want to keep?"

"Dad's room?" Her brother stared upward, thinking. "He might think those old tax returns mean something. Plus, I think the hippies will set a fire if you put too much paper out there. They get a little carried away sometimes."

"Noted."

"See ya."

He hadn't been out the door ten minutes—Hannah had just opened another bottle of his very decent pinot grigio—when the phone rang. Nobody but Hugh still used a phone like this phone, the square black rotary model that resembled a British taxi, also outdated. The ring reminded Hannah of childhood; the smell of the vented circle you spoke into was the smell of her parents, of her own youth, of all the breath they'd used and wasted talking into it, and on the other end was her little sister Holly.

"Huh?" Holly said. "I'm sorry. I speed-dialed wrong. Sped-dialed? I was trying to get Hugh."

"This is Hugh's. He's gone. Did you know you could still unscrew the two parts of this receiver?"

"Isn't that phone a trip? What're you doing over there?"

"Dad asked for a picture of Mom."

"Oh, poor Dad! That's so sad. Take him the one on the mantel. She looks so happy in that one. How come neither of us looks like that, all happy and pretty and festive?"

"Speak for yourself," Hannah said. "And anyway, that was hours ago, then I got swept up in a cleaning frenzy. You cannot believe the bullshit in that bedroom, plus those freaks next door who are scavenging it all. What do you want with Hugh?"

Holly paused. Had Hannah not been floating on a few glasses of wine, she would have been ruffled. Why would Holly phone Hugh? What business were they conducting behind her back? Hannah suspected that Hugh knew the identity of Holly's son's father, something Hannah had never been able to extract from her sister. Why did Hugh know, who could not have cared less, and not Hannah, to whom it mattered? It drove her mad. Holly now came up with some manufactured need to borrow Hugh's truck, but this was an ill-considered lie, given that she did not know how to drive stick. Then there would be the invention of a friend who knew how, et cetera, et cetera. Holly was a terrible liar, always had been, but Hannah let it go. "Hey," she said. "I guess I should tell you that Thomas and I are getting divorced."

"*What?*"

Thomas had not actually spoken the word *divorce* yet. Thomas was a lawyer, and he used words very carefully, as if he would be quoted, as if everything were future evidence. Hannah wasn't careful, at least not with words; her father had long ago accused her of "shooting off" her mouth. Fair enough; words could be weaponry. She'd first used the word *divorce* in her imagination, and then not again until earlier today, with Hugh, and now she said it to Holly. It was easier to pronounce with every repetition. Plus, she felt the need to trump her sister's phoning Hugh instead of her. See what she'd miss, if she didn't keep herself tuned in?

Then suddenly Holly was crying. Nobody cried as easily as Holly; she had hair-trigger tear ducts. But then Hannah recalled that Holly might be entitled to tears, suffering the impact of *divorce*. She'd been the maid of honor in Hannah's wedding when she was just fifteen. She'd been so young when she was introduced to Thomas that she thought of him the way she thought of other family members: she was stuck with him, hell or high water, a part of her life. There wasn't choice involved. And now Hannah was notifying her that there *was* choice involved, as a matter of fact, and that Thomas would soon no longer be a member of their family. "You know Thomas better than you did Hamish," Hannah said, startled by the insight.

"I know," Holly responded. "Hamish was just this guy who smelled like smoke and slammed his bedroom door all the time. *Thomas* taught me how to drive. *Thomas* helped me with my W-4s."

"He'll still do that, don't worry. It's not like he died. He's not going anywhere, that's for sure. So far he's gone as far as his mother's house."

"Why are you getting divorced? I don't get it."

Hannah swirled the wine in her glass. She'd told Thomas she needed a vacation and she'd told Hugh it was boredom, and it *was* a need of vacating, and boredom, but it was also something else. Her marriage hadn't required enough work. If their marriage was an education, then it was time for her to graduate, or skip ahead a grade. If their marriage was a band, they were in danger of parodying themselves, of having creative differences. She wasn't being challenged; she'd learned everything there was to know or say or sing about being married to Thomas. Remaining so was bringing out the brat in her.

"I don't love him enough," she said. "I love him better at a distance, like the distance between our house and his mother's." Hannah filled Holly in on the particulars, where and how the boys were, putting a spin on Justin's desertion of her by saying she'd insisted he go with his dad to Bea's, for the company. She told Holly what Thomas's mother thought—that Hannah was heartless, ungrateful, unwomanly—and the last thing Thomas had said to her: "You're making a mistake, and you'll live to regret it."

"But I feel like I'm waiting for something to happen," she confided. "I have this weird sensation of something coming."

"You're not having an affair?"

"No, I wish I were." A new school, another band, a fresh challenge. "But, no. That's not it, anyway, it doesn't feel like I'm waiting for a man, but for a mission."

Holly had to hang up and go back to work (substitute teacher, of course; Holly would only ever be the stand-in, the temporary replacement; no one would find her qualified to assume an official role). Hannah had realized, in talking to her sister, that she wasn't fabricating the sensation she was describing. It was as if her duty now were to wander the world available to messages, like a big satellite dish, or a magnet, attracting something to herself. Meanwhile, there was this half-emptied, half-cleaned room to embrace. She took herself back to the job, glass in hand. Many a tedious chore could be made palatable in the company of a good wine.

## 6. *Nigel*

Holly's son, Nigel, was the only grandchild who wished to visit his grandfather in the home. Holly was both proud and concerned. "I like to see Papa," the boy said, but when he was at the home, he spent most of his time studying its other occupants. This November morning he was pulling on his coat, each gaping sleeve carefully approached as if to avoid wrinkling it, as if he could wear a garment without the garment's knowing. Adults were often unsure what to say to Nigel. He was like a spy impersonating a child, whose agenda was unclear.

Holly knelt before him. He had no father, only her. She wasn't a very assured mother. She sometimes asked Nigel what his friends' mothers did, attempting to survey the behavior of her peers. But Nigel provided very little information about his classmates' parents or their actions, not because he didn't know but because his mother had said "friends." Those people weren't his friends. At school, as at home, it seemed he was a loner. Some days he rode to College Hill Elementary in a taxicab because he did not like to be late and Holly was nearly incapable of not being late. "Papa is sick," Holly told him the first time they went to the home. "He might not remember you." She hoped he wouldn't say *fuck you* to her son, as he had to Hugh. Nigel was sensitive; such a thing would wound him.

Actually? It was Holly whom it would wound. Nigel would most likely take it in stride, as he did most things.

He nodded. "I know. I want to see him."

"Why?"

At this, he slowly lowered his chin without breaking eye contact, as if ashamed on her behalf. She sighed. Despite not ever having met his own father, Nigel had managed to acquire his exact expression, an unblinking Eastern European gaze. His teeth, however, were perfectly American. He was a beautiful child, which did not endear him to his aunt Hannah, who also had sons. The two of them, the cousins, were always going through difficult, unsightly phases. Holly said, "Do you know what *senile* means?"

Nigel shook his head. She explained, aware that what she was describing didn't sound very different from any person's potential social facade. "He might be in a bad mood, he might think you're someone else instead of yourself, he might say naughty words. We can't take them personally."

"OK."

"Maybe we should pick up Hugh to come with us?"

"OK."

On the rare occasions when circumstances called for a man in Nigel's life—visits to public bathrooms when he had been too young to go alone, the father-son Robotics Club banquet, the facts of life speech—Hugh stepped in. There were still times when Holly preferred being the lone parent, preferred it the way one might prefer masturbation, for the simple economy, the utter efficiency. Then there were times like now, when she felt stunningly bereft, in need of backup, defense, somebody to agree that she was doing the best she could.

"He's curious," she said to her siblings, to explain Nigel's interest. "I guess."

Her son smiled reassuringly at her, perhaps letting her know that his interest in old people who'd lost their minds was not something she should worry about. His own father had grown up in the Ukraine. During the childhood years that Holly had passed sitting in a blissful daze before the television set with her hand in a bowl full of Cheetos, Ivan had been fleeing Chernobyl. He'd arrived at last in Kansas, salvation, sanctuary; he'd never understood why its natives were always scheming to leave the place. Holly had met him freshman year in the university cafeteria where he'd happily worn an apron, bused tables, waited on pampered coeds. Had Holly known anything about the world— anything about anything—she might have opted for an abortion nine years ago. Only later had she seen the photographs of children born in the disaster's aftermath, the missing limbs and stunted appendages.

Her own son, however, was physically perfect. Yet in his wise face and angular gestures you could apprehend some sadder landscape, history encrypted there that awed or confused the average American. His cousins, Justin and Leo, showed no interest in their grandfather's new home. The adults, including Holly, treated the outing as a burden— akin to others they had martyred themselves to as full-fledged adults: mammograms, parent-teacher conferences, tax payment. The burdens shifted during this annual impending slide toward Thanksgiving and Christmas, shopping, cooking, fighting throngs at the mall—and most children would have responded by hunkering down at home in front of the fireplace or the television or the computer screen. Nigel was always surprising his mother. His motives were impenetrable. He secured his coat now—dexterous hands negotiating each wooden button like a praying mantis—and then waited at the door with a patient inquiry on his face: shall we go?

At first, hosting Thanksgiving had seemed like a victory. Usually it was Hannah's house at which they all convened. Hannah had a large dining room, a beautiful kitchen, and a husband who knew how to carve a turkey. With an electric knife. She also possessed a warming tray, a gravy boat, matching cloth napkins, and a turkey baster. Meat thermometer, candleholders, crystal wineglasses. The list was endless and depressing; Holly had to quit thinking about it.

It also depressed her to think of why they weren't convening at that perfect table with that perfect husband: her sister was blowing up her life. Holly felt the personal affront of it, how Hannah would squander the thing Holly herself felt most in need of: the love of a good man. Thomas was the kindest, sanest, most solid citizen. And he had been good not just to Hannah but to all of the Paniks, smiling at his father-in-law's quips, tolerating—although a teetotaler—the heavy drinking at family get-togethers, being the driver, when that was called for, remembering, the next day, what had been said and done.

"I have to buy a lot of stuff before tomorrow," Holly said to Nigel.

"OK," he said. He sat in the back, buckled in the middle seat of the sedan (safest, he'd tell you), twisting a Rubik's

Cube around. His calm listening mode encouraged Holly to make lists; he had a fine memory, too, so that she could ask him what she'd said, when she'd forgotten later. "What did I want to buy here?" she would inquire, perplexed over an empty basket at the Big Lots.

"Pasta," he would say. "Paper plates. Mason jars. Mustard. You said to remind you to check on bras." Today, the day before Thanksgiving, she was enumerating groceries. In the rearview mirror, she glanced at her son. His head was the shape of a lightbulb; he didn't eat enough. Still, he was lovely. People tended to stare at him, to sense that he was in possession of more than the average sensitivity of a child his age. Holly often felt inadequate to the task of being his mother, as if she wouldn't know or recognize what he needed to become who he was destined to become. She felt like an inadvertent gardener who'd been handed a rare and exotic flower. She waited for him to shrivel, to fail to bloom or survive. However many times she explained this feeling, she never got the impression that anyone believed that she genuinely doubted her abilities. They always seemed to think she was experiencing normal anxiety. It could not be normal; other mothers grinned confidently and swatted authoritatively. Other mothers made firm rules and stuck to them. Other mothers did not expect their children to wake them in the morning. Other mothers did not collapse in weeping heaps when the ceiling leaked or the television remote wouldn't work. They didn't expect their nine-year-old to come over and pat their back, reassuring them that everything would be fine, then slap open the remote and replace the double A battery. Nigel had been the one to bring Holly the phone book and tell her to look under "Repair: Roof." He was clever! Brilliant, even. Yet also friendless, and very, very thin.

Last month he'd given up eating meat, so Holly was dreading what her sister would say tomorrow at dinner. "Shall I make a veggie loaf in the shape of a turkey?" she asked now, as they rounded the corner to Hugh's house.

"If you want to," Nigel said. He held up the Rubik's Cube so she could see it in the mirror. He'd already mastered the ordinary solution and now made checkerboard patterns. "Can we get Diet Coke and Mentos?"

"Sure," she said. "Why?"

"Experiments." The cube started clacking around again.

There was a fire burning in the Roosevelts' front yard. "The city won't let you make a bonfire," explained one of the hippies, "but they don't care if you barbecue."

"A loophole," Hugh said. He stood placidly drinking beer at ten in the morning, shifting the can from hand to hand to warm himself, while the Weber kettle seemed ready to collapse under the weight of the flaming logs it held. "Hey, Nigel." Hugh was the only person in the world who didn't care that Nigel wouldn't say hello or respond if you asked how he was. Nigel did not indulge in pleasantries. It wasn't personal; nor was it easily explainable, like autism or ADD. It was his old-soul personality, his disdain for small talk, for tedium. He wouldn't laugh politely at a failed effort in humor. He wouldn't hug you back unless he actually liked you. He liked Hugh. He liked Holly. He'd liked his grandmother Helen. When she'd died, he'd been insistent about going with the grown-ups to the mortuary, to have a last view.

The man who had counseled the family—the despondent widower, his three chastened adult children, a son-in-law, and the six-year-old boy—had been a consummate professional. Holly had admired his ease. She'd also recognized him: he had gone to school with her, a year behind her, and here he was wearing his suit, his very large manicured hands like statuary folded on the table before him, his voice not only solemn and deep and full of appropriate and well-crafted sentiment, but also sounding truly sorry for them. He did not need to claim that he felt their pain: his every gesture assured them it was true.

He alone did not seem to find it strange that her six-year-old son was there. What could startle a man who worked with dead bodies for a living? Who'd been raised in a family business of many generations? He was the son of one Kasenbaum Brother and a grandson of the original Kasenbaum. His twin, Holly recalled suddenly, had killed himself during junior year at North. Perhaps that explained this man's unshakable composure. It seemed to Holly that a lot of people at her high school had killed themselves. Her own class reunited every spring at the old alligator pit for a picnic, an event Holly generally avoided, but she'd been reminded, on the day, of the list of those who'd drowned, crashed, overdosed, or slit their wrists. The Kasenbaum had hanged himself, in a closet, with a belt.

"Is Grandpa going to be burned up?" Nigel asked Hugh, as if he, too, had been remembering the strange day at the mortuary. Or maybe it was just the mesmerizing fact of a fire.

"It's called cremation," Holly said.

"It *is* burning, though," Hugh pointed out. "I mean, he's right about that. And yes." He turned to Nigel. "He wants to be cremated. And then put in a vase like Grandma Helen and buried right beside her. His name is already on the stone."

That had been one of many negotiations upon their mother's death. The three children had wanted to include

261

their parents' favorite expression on the stone: *No Frenzied Bits!* This was the advice they had been given as they'd left the house on weekend nights as teens. It had been a fond saying, although after Hamish's death, it had fallen out of favor for a while. Hannah now used it with her boys. But their father hadn't wanted it on his wife's tombstone.

They could add it when he died, Holly thought now. Who would be there to object? Nigel, that's who. He would not do what the dead did not want done.

"When Grandpa dies, I want to see him," Nigel said now.

"Do you remember seeing Grandma?"

"Of course."

Holly and Hugh exchanged glances. In the chapel of the mortuary, where the living Kasenbaum twin had led the family, Helen Panik had lain beneath a sheet at the front. "I'll leave you now," the Kasenbaum had said in his solemn, authoritative, sympathetic voice. Had he been Richard or Ronald, Dick or Ron, Fuck or Run—wasn't that what the twins had been called?

"Thank you," the remaining Paniks had said in unison.

And there had been their mother, Nigel's grandmother, Sam's wife, on a gurney. Nobody did anything for a while but stare and sniffle. She had been cleaned up, her hair colored and curled, her lips and cheeks reddened, her eyes closed, her perplexity and sorrow erased. From the neck down, a sheet covered her. She looked like the subject of a magic trick, like someone who'd been hypnotized into a trance and then told to levitate, floating there in space beneath her plain white sheet, all womanliness gone, a Human Body. Nigel was the first to approach, touching his grandmother's cool cheek. The Kasenbaums had done a very good job of rehabilitating the matriarch's appearance. Gone were the unsightly skin growths, gone the unruly chin hairs, and concealed the wild frightened eyes.

"My kids would never do that," Hannah whispered.

"Maybe they should," Hugh said.

"It seems sorta ghoulish, to me," Hannah replied.

"He's a good boy," said their father. "He was Helen's favorite."

"She didn't have favorites!" Hannah was outraged.

"Yes, she did, of course she did. Hugh was her favorite of you all."

"Dad!"

Hamish had been his favorite. Everyone knew that.

When their father stepped up to pay his last respects, Hugh and Hannah and Holly shoved together on the pew and began whispering about the obituary. They'd written it days ago; now, as they contemplated the sobering fact of their dead mother, it seemed glib.

"'Returned to the angels. Lifted by Our Lord. Promoted to glory,'" Hannah read from the newspaper.

"She would have hated all of those."

"She would have laughed."

In the end, they went with "passed." Neutral enough without being too clinical, or too euphemistic. The Paniks could agree on that: no tarted-up sentiment.

A hippie brought out a stack of books to throw on the fire. "Let's go," Hugh suggested. "I don't think Nigel's ready for *Fahrenheit 451* just yet."

"What's *Fahrenheit 451*?" Nigel asked when they were back in the car.

"Go ahead," Holly said. "You know him, he won't let go of it until he gets to the bottom of it."

"I probably have a copy somewhere in the house," Hugh offered, then turned elaborately in the seat and described the book's premise to his nephew, keeping his beer can low so that the authorities wouldn't see it. Open container.

## 7. *Disciplinary Action*

Everybody was misbehaving. First, the nursing home aide phoned Hugh to say that his father needed to stop undressing in the community spaces.

"What's going on?" Hugh asked his father. They had adjourned to the back deck, which was as close to nature as the residents were allowed to get, a porch from which squirrels had dashed. The women inside stared out at the two men, as if being treated to some kind of theatrical spectacle. What a disappointing drama, Hugh thought, two guys sitting around talking.

"Nobody knows what's going on here," his father said ominously.

"I'm listening." Really it took so little to get along with people. His father needed a confidant, same as anyone else. Hugh did wish he'd fished out the flask from beneath the mattress. If he was going to participate in a paranoid delusion, he might as well be in the proper mood. In a past circumstance, before the fantasy had claimed the majority hold on Sam's mind, he and his dad had had a fairly good time inhabiting that wacky space: A submarine hauling chickens from Peru. A prison cell in Oklahoma, the two of them on bunks, their keeper a kind of mythical beast with horns and a tail. It was not unlike childhood play, that shared magical space in which a narrative came alive and thrived, fueled by reciprocal input from both parties. Charming, whimsical, not unlike love, Hugh realized, thrilling himself with the next part of his day, creative writing class. Stacy. The land of make-believe the two of them now shared.

His father told him that these women—he gestured toward the sliding glass door, toward the row of chairs that faced it—had abducted his wife, Helen, years ago, and that they planned to do the same with him. "You never met Helen," he went on confidentially, "but she had the information. I've got to find her first. Her and her purse."

"The information is in the purse."

"In the lining. She was a very clever seamstress. Also in her shoes. Mine, too." He lifted one foot, then the other, from the kickplates of the wheelchair. He stared at the mechanism as if some aspect of the world he was in had jumped track, or he was trying to make some part fit; Hugh could almost hear the internal logic shifting to sync up.

Hugh was torn: Pull his father from the fantasy, grab hold of reality—the kickplates, the frozen boards of the porch, the benign dying women inside—and insist? Or play along? He went with the latter. "But Dad, if they're going to take you to the same place, if those ladies are holding Helen hostage, and you want to see her, shouldn't you just let them take you? I mean, if Helen is already there?"

"Let myself be abducted?" His father shook his head at Hugh's sorry logic, then accused him of being as useless as everyone else. "I'm surrounded by idiots," he concluded, dismissing his son with a feeble wave.

"I'm sorry, I was just thinking out loud."

"Take me back inside, do you want me to catch pneumonia?"

Hannah had already been to the home earlier that day, attempting to correct her father's understanding, insisting on and explaining over and over again the facts of his situation, which had also failed. "Why do you indulge his delusions? I think that makes him believe them more."

"I subscribe to the rules of improv," Hugh had told her. "Yes, and?" He wondered now what percentage of his father's usual day was anywhere near lucid. In the past, these flights of fancy would come up, hang around long enough to be entertaining, then evaporate. His father would be asking for his shows, his dinner, his drink, his ordinary perfectly reasonable necessities. And would it be worse, Hugh wondered, to know that he wasn't a person of interest to a group of kidnappers? Would it be preferable to understand the truth, that he was just waiting around to die, that some stranger would take his place, whose son or daughter or spouse out there in the greater metropolitan area was hoping his death would be sooner rather than later?

Didn't everyone operate under the delusion that there was something else going on besides that sad fact?

Meanwhile Ms. Fox had sent an email to Stacy about her attendance—or lack thereof—and asked her to deliver the same message to Hugh Panik, who hadn't provided an email address.

"Why don't you have email?" Stacy asked him that evening while they were skipping yet another session. They'd had every intention of going to class, but somehow ended up talking and drinking in the parking lot instead. Hugh had picked up a bottle of the same wine stolen from Stacy's car in the beginning, a pleasant jug of Chianti. It had become their special beverage, its quality irrelevant; his sister Hannah would have been appalled.

"Who would I email? Ms. Fox?"

"You could email me. Except, knowing me, I'd probably forget to close the in-box window, and my husband would snoop around in there, and then he'd be furious—well, first he'd be super-surprised, he probably wouldn't believe it, me having a man friend to write to, he thinks I'm invisible now that I've had kids and gotten a little chunky—and then I guess we'd get in a big GD fight, and the kids would hear, our house isn't that big, we're all up in each other's business—and the nine-year-old, sheez, she would lose her crackers, she's such a drama queen—and next thing you know the whole weekend is wasted by arguing and crying and making up, and . . ." She sighed. "I guess it's just as well you don't have email."

"Nor a cell phone, either."

"Yeah, I've noticed that, because I always want to send you a message or talk to you about something, all day long, it's like you're hanging around in my head with me and I'm talking to you. A cell phone would be good for that, because now I try to remember what I want to tell you but I know I forget, I should keep a list."

"This is the first time a cell phone has seemed at all tempting. My sister's been trying to hook me up for years."

"I think it's sweet how old-fashioned you are."

"She also hates my wardrobe," Hugh said of Hannah, just so Stacy would compliment that as well.

Stacy insisted that she did not mind that Hugh wore the same thing every day. "You remind me of Ernie," she said. "From Ernie and Bert? They always wear the same clothes, too. It's very comforting." Ought he to have been insulted, being compared to a pair of Muppets? He wasn't. She went on, "I love Bert and Ernie. They make me cry sometimes, they're so dear." Her eyes teared, just thinking of it. Just looking at Hugh's khaki pants. On Sundays, he washed all six pairs and then hung them around the basement on hangers, on water pipes. There they swayed, drying from the cuffs up. Sometimes, on Sunday evening, he would wear a pair with damp pockets, slight detergent odor rising from his crotch. "Moist," he said now to Stacy, of his pants, of her eyes. "I hate that word."

"I'm going to use it in class next week, just to torment you," she said. "'The moist weather made the skin of Harvey McFarvey moisten like he was covered in moisturizer.'"

"I'm going to put 'cacophony' in again."

Stacy covered her ears and chanted "lalalalala" against her least favorite word.

Hugh's subject, in both the poetry and the fiction class, was drowning. A fear of it, and also just a lot of water imagery, unbreathable atmospheres, and the weird simple baffling disappearance of a boy in still black water. He'd disappeared at dusk. Setting like the sun, silently into the lake. Like an illusionist. Like a miracle in reverse.

*This better not be about Jesus*, wrote Ms. Fox. Her comments in the margins were interesting to Hugh, as they seemed to reflect her personality. She was sarcastic and had a short attention span. She had been living in Wichita only four months and didn't get it. Also, she was tired of teaching creative writing. *Oh, please* indicated this. When Hugh described his brother's (his protagonist's father's) disappearance into a lake as "like a cheap magic trick," Ms. Fox responded with *Fresh!* The exclamation mark made Hugh smile. That was good, both pleasing Ms. Fox and being able to smile about his disappearing drowner. He would write his way out of that old trouble. Then some other characters dragged the lake and didn't find the body. *Not credible,* penned Ms. Fox, a sloppy circle-and-slash drawn around the paragraph. Well, OK. But it had really happened. Yet Hugh had seen how ineffectual that defense was in Advanced Creative Writing, Prose, and knew not to mention that fact. She'd be all over that.

Hugh had been at the lake when Hamish had drowned. It had been his first (and last) camping trip with his older brother and his friends. They'd gone every year just before school started; when Hugh had started high school, he'd been invited to join them. Hamish was to head back to college within a few days. Instead, he'd walked into the lake. It was Hugh who'd driven the car home, after, in the full-blown dark of midnight. Did his brother walk in on purpose? Yes, said his arms, thrust cross-like in a T. It was the walking out—the failure of the return journey—that had always been a question mark. For hours, Ham's friends and his little brother Hugh had waded, swum, yelled, and floundered. Fourteen years old, with no real experience behind the wheel, Hugh had insisted on driving them home. He'd been the only one who hadn't been drinking, smoking pot, inhaling cocaine, and coming down from the same in the subsequent hours. He'd been stunned to discover that camping was, mostly, about intoxication. His sisters might have been proud of his tearful, raging, sober insistence on being the driver: back then, Hugh had been proud of it.

Now he could hardly recall that terrible trip, the highway a series of yellow lines he'd watched without blinking, devoured by the car hood, trucks roaring past angrily, rocking the vehicle, his brother's friends chattering and sobbing, Hugh recoiling against the fact of having left his brother behind. Betrayal: it had overwhelmed him for years, a hot sensation of shame, his failure.

Later, he'd come to believe Hamish had killed himself; he and his mother had agreed on this point. They had also agreed not to tell Hugh's father or sisters what they thought, absorbing the dark belief as if to prevent the spread of infection, the infection of despair. Nonetheless, the family had been altered by Ham's death: before, they'd thought themselves lucky, and after, they'd realized they were, at best, ordinary and, at worst, cursed.

When they sat around the seminar table reading their work aloud, Ms. Fox placed her elbows on the surface and then rested her face in her palms. This made her expression harder to read. Everything on her face was squashed into a sort of grin (grimace?) like a leftover jack-o'-lantern. She could be thinking anything, inside that mashed face. Hugh would try to practice this at home. It could be useful to be inscrutable like that. Right out in public. A face that could be smiling, smirking, or smoldering. Rotting, he noted, of the pumpkin comparison.

Stacy's story was told from the point of view of a dog.

"What, now you're Tolstoy?" said Ms. Fox. Hugh liked hearing Bozo's (Boris's) take on Stacy's (Laura's) life. Two of the three "small humanoids" in the house treated Boris kindly, but the third, the middle little biped, the only boy, was very unkind. He often experimented on Boris's body with pushpins or markers. He fed Boris suspicious concoctions, the ingredients of which were not all necessarily edible. For this and other reasons, Boris was brought along with his owner whenever Laura went out and about in her "quick-moving scary thing." This was more fraught in the "time of panting."

"'Time of panting'?" interrupted Ms. Fox. "Like being in heat? I thought Boris was a boy dog?"

"Summer," explained Stacy, blinking like an owl behind her round reading glasses. She had a strong reading-aloud voice; at one time, she'd thought she might make a fine newscaster, but somebody over in the Communications Department had disabused her of that notion.

Ms. Fox eased her cheeks back into her hands. "Proceed."

The seizures confused everyone except Hugh. He thought Stacy had done a good job describing the sensation of having a seizure from the point of view of the poor frightened dog having one, including a kind of hilarious interpretation of the pill that had to be inserted in the dog's anus so as to calm him. She was sensitive, he thought, and wasn't that a requirement for creative writing? He told her so in the car after class in between kisses.

Stacy had ended up in tears. This was a risk of workshop, Hugh had discovered. The class members themselves, with the exception of the two punk girls, had been very kind. It was Ms. Fox who had brought on the tears. Apparently the enthusiasm of the students—all but the high school girls had declared that they'd happily read a whole *novel* told from this dog's point of view, so charmed were they by it— had been too much for her to bear. "I cannot help you with puppy lit," she'd finally said. "I have no expertise in senti- mentality or soft-focus!"

That was why Stacy and Hugh were skipping class tonight. He'd brought Bozo a gift, one of the clay bowls he'd thrown last year during his ceramics class. He had a large collection, occupying their lumpen positions in the cupboard. Dog bowls, he saw. All last semester he'd been preparing for a dog.

The hippies had adopted a new one recently, too, and they didn't take very good care of it. Waffle had told him that the dog was part coyote, which certainly looked to be true. But maybe that was only an excuse for their not feeding it enough? More than anything, it looked hungry. Unhappily so. It stalked around like a cheetah, suspicious and jumpy. It had grown extra fur in anticipation of winter. The hippies didn't believe in fences, so the dog was at large all day. Hugh had seen Animal Control prowling along the street more than once, but the animal was wily, perhaps endowed with some native ability to blend in, become camouflaged and invisible when its enemies appeared.

"We can't go to a bar," Stacy said in the parking lot.

"We can go to my house," Hugh offered shyly. "It doesn't smell like a bar." What did it smell like, anyway? Old people? Since his mother's death three years ago Hugh had rarely made his bed. When had he last changed the sheets? Would those cupboard moths bother Stacy? And what, exactly, was she just now saying?

She was saying she would love to come to his house.

"I'll lead," he said, and climbed into his truck. They had not had sex, and they were going to. He wished he'd already drunk a drink so that this information wouldn't scare him so. It had been fine with Hugh not to have sex; he'd *wanted* to, but a phrase had been running through his head that stopped him short of making a request of her: *another man's wife*. She was Stacy, first and foremost, with her half-moon scar and her too-tight dress clothes and her ready laugh and squinted expression as she listened to what he said, but she was also that other thing: another man's wife. At night, when he was drifting off, happily thinking of her, the phrase would come in like an arrow through a window, an arrow with a message on its sharp tip that *wanged* into the wall and vibrated there, forcing his eyes to slap open and his happiness to flee: *another man's wife*, the message read.

Well, tonight he was going to sleep with another man's wife.

But that was not what transpired. Instead, Bozo had a massive seizure while left alone in the kitchen on the other side of the closed door (he wouldn't stay off the bed, and there simply wasn't room for the three of them, Bozo mistaking foreplay for roughhousing). The noise was tremendous, as if a far larger creature had fallen over, rattling the oven door. Stacy leapt naked from the bed, knowing at once what she'd heard. Again, the rifling through the purse, bouncing on her bare feet, this time locating the pills. "Hold him?" she requested of naked Hugh, who'd followed. He found himself squatting with the dog's gnashing teeth uncomfortably near his exposed privates, while Stacy lifted Bozo's tail to adroitly insert the pill.

Hugh was surprised how arousing *that* was.

"He's gonna go down pretty fast," she warned, standing to wash her hands, gazing with stricken eyes at Hugh and her monstrous pet. Hugh held the dog's shuddering shoulders at arm's length, registering the uncontrollable spasms rocking Bozo. "Just watch. *Poor ting.*" Sure enough, the beast fell, splayed flat like a bear rug, his mouth agape, tongue sideways out of it, shuddering still but no longer rigid.

"I like this linoleum," Stacy noted, joining Hugh on the floor. "Ooh, it's a little chilly on the botto, huh?"

"Original," Hugh told her. "There's probably nice wood underneath."

"Good colors."

"I used to race my Matchbox cars along here. This yellow line was the lane divider. My poor mom, trying to cook with me underfoot." Hugh stared at Stacy's freckled breasts while stroking Bozo's head, their hands running over one another's, grabbing for a moment, letting go, back in the dog's fur. Maybe it was because she had children that Stacy was so playful. Although that hadn't turned his sisters playful, anything but, actually. Hugh toyed with the passed-out dog's tongue, putting it through the front teeth so that the animal had the aspect of intelligence, alert as Lassie, pondering a point. When he moved it, to hang out the side of the jaw, the dog looked dumb, goofy and drunk as a cartoon. All from the position of the tongue. Stacy laughed, then cried. "Please God, don't let this one die," she begged. "They're always dying on me! I have terrible luck. I have to tell you a secret, Hugh."

He prepared to hear that she did not, in fact, wish to make love with him. That she had somehow engineered this seizure to interrupt them. He bowed his head. "Go."

"This isn't the original Bozo," she whispered, as if the dog himself might not know the fact. "The original Bozo got run over at an intersection when I opened the door to pull in my coattail."

"That sounds terrible."

"It was! He just jumped right out and got hit by a van, right in front of me, it was awful! And the van driver was so mean to me, just yelling and yelling about how irresponsible I was, who needs that? Anyhow, I couldn't stand to tell my kids, so I just went and got a new Bozo. I mean, that's the kind of thing you do with pets, right? I mean, before it was only gerbils or goldfish. But why not dogs? And the breeder still had his brother, thank the Lord, but to be honest I think this second Bozo was kind of a reject, maybe he's a little retarded? It took my husband a week to figure out what was different."

"You're doing the best you can, Stacy. Don't beat yourself up." These phrases, which in general disappointed Hugh, seemed to be de rigueur at this moment, terribly useful. "Do you think faux Bozo would mind sharing his Valium?"

"Oh no, he's got plenty, take two." Stacy shook out two of the yellow tablets. "Maybe I'll have one? For my nerves?" They swallowed their pills. "Bozo has this one great trick," she said. "Next time, let's go to McDonald's and I'll show you, he can take a hamburger into his mouth, the whole thing, and chew, chew, chew, and then send out the lettuce, untouched. Touched." She corrected herself. "But intact. Like a wrinkled dollar rejected from a Coke machine. Bozo." She sighed, running a finger along his gums. "Ah, for the love of monkeys, what am I gonna do?"

Next time, Hugh thought dreamily.

In his sleep, the dog suddenly threw his head up and sneezed, a sodden mess on their bare laps, his tongue now gripped between his teeth.

"Bless you," Hugh said automatically. Stacy clutched at his arm, her large pale breasts squashed against him, her hair on his shoulder.

"I love you, Hugh," she said, miserable. "I truly do."

Hugh mumbled his line into her forehead; it seemed a rule, was certainly a reflex, and, most important, in this instance it was true: he loved Stacy. A hole opened in Hugh's chest when he said those words, a place like a wound he'd decided to inflict upon himself, as if he'd suddenly drawn a target on his breastbone and invited the arrows to fly.

He loaded the sedated dog into her car, then stood at the driver's door unwilling to let her climb in and go away. That man she lived with suddenly enraged him. He wasn't used to being enraged. Its heat distracted him, foreign, novel, a companion to the vulnerability that had arrived with his declaration of love. He felt nearly proud of his rage, as if he might need to demonstrate it. How would that happen? How had love led him to rage? How had the dog led to love? The equation was mysterious. The sick dog equaled a clenched fist. A rock plunged through a window. That, too.

## 8. *Für Elise*

"Mama." Nigel stood beside Holly's bed. "Mama," he repeated. She hadn't heard the alarm, nor the telephone call and message about subbing at her elementary school alma mater, nor the second message, from the nursing home, concerning her father's antisocial behavior. Her sleep had always been scarily deep; her sister would claim it was the result of having been the family baby, the fact that some-body had always been around to rescue her from whatever she had blithely managed to sleep through.

But was it reasonable to think her nine-year-old son should be that somebody? Nigel was telling her that he had already called a cab and gotten money from her purse, and would bring her change, that he'd packed a lunch and gath-ered his homework. "You have to sign the permission form," he said, holding the paper on a DVD case, pen in his other hand. "Just sign here." She struggled out of her nest of pillows and did as he requested.

"I'm sorry," she told him.

"Why?"

"I'm a lame mom."

He blinked at her, having no particular response. Some other child might have reassured her she wasn't a lame mom, or would have forced her to quit being one, but not this child. The cab tooted from outside; they had a favorite driver, Ben, who liked to discuss chess. "Bye," Nigel called. "I'm locking the door."

When she'd first brought him home as a baby, Holly's mother had come to stay with them, so frightened had Holly been of caring for an infant alone. In their family, Holly was famous for spilling her milk nearly every night at the kitchen table. Who in his right mind would allow her to try to hold on to a baby, anyway? Every time she encountered a hard surface—tile floor, cement drive, bathtub, brick wall, marble counter—Holly was nearly incapacitated, so easily could she see her baby's head splattering onto it. Her family had named this postpartum depression, but Holly hadn't really gotten past it yet. And you couldn't legitimately suffer postpartum over a fourth-grader, could you?

She didn't even listen to the message from the drone at the Wichita Public Schools downtown office; she wasn't up to spending time with other people's children today, either (swings and monkey bars over gravel, lunchroom choking hazards, crosswalk mayhem). Instead, she called her brother, whose work schedule was extremely erratic and whose hapless existence could sometimes lift her out of troubled feelings about her own.

"Dad's being a bad boy," she said. "Should we do something?"

"Like what? Ground him? He's already grounded. Kick him out? Send him to jail? He's already in lockdown. Every single punishment that exists he's already suffering. And besides, so far it just seems like getting nakey-nakey in front of the old ladies. They're calling you now?"

"Last resort, per usual. Wanna hang, anyway?"

"You could help me pick a cell phone," he said, shyly. Holly smiled, taken out of her own vague distress by Hugh's news.

"There's a girl!" she said.

"Don't tell Hannah."

"Hannah who?"

He was dying to talk, Holly discovered. In the past he'd dated a certain kind of girl who'd lasted only as long as it had taken her to figure out he wouldn't move past a fixed degree of intimacy. He wouldn't bring her home to meet his mother, he wouldn't go on a road trip with her, there wouldn't be a ring or a wedding. In the past he'd been known to break up via postcard. These affairs of the heart had lasted, at most, a year, and usually less.

This, however, seemed utterly other. The beloved was named Stacy, and she was taking a class with him at the U ("I'm on the seventeen-year plan," Hugh told Holly. "I'll graduate in the same class as Nigel"). Not until they'd purchased the phone, gone to lunch, then decided to visit Ugly's—and had to wait for it to open at two, sitting in the parking lot with the other desperate regulars who were watching their clocks—did Hugh reveal that the girlfriend, this fantastic object of his affections, was married.

"Oh, Hugh." How could he seem so optimistic? Holly wondered. The married people never left their spouses, never. Well, occasionally, she supposed. They left for the more beautiful, for the better fit, for true love at last. In movies, in novels, in Hollywood, in glamorous celebrity history. But for her brother *Hugh*?

He gave her a wan, smitten smile. "She wants me to meet her children."

"*Children?*" Worse and worse. "How old are they?"

"Nine, six, and three. She says she and her husband mate every three years."

"Then she's just about due for another," Holly noted. Which made Hugh frown. The neon light buzzed on in the barred window and everybody in the parking lot jumped into action. "You know what Hannah would say," Holly couldn't help mentioning. "She would say this is because you're thirty-nine. Because now Dad isn't at home anymore. Because it's time for you to grow up."

"If I wanted to know what Hannah thought, I'd ask her," Hugh said. This was as rude as he ever got, so Holly apologized. Their bartender brought them their usual drinks and they sat not talking for a while, finding their way back into the subject, into friendliness. It was not Holly's job to argue with Hugh; she'd never been that sister. And she hated that she'd knocked the wind out of his sails. But seriously? She loved her brother, he was a great person, and maybe this Stacy appreciated all those qualities that made him who he was, but as for being husband material, not to mention stepfather material . . . "Has she been to the house?"

"Several times," he said primly.

"What'd she say?"

"She likes it." And then, because he was in love and because Holly was the first person he'd told about Stacy, he gave up his grudge against her and went on at length about some misadventure with the woman's dog. Holly was fascinated. She hadn't been on a date in more than a year, yet sitting around naked on the kitchen floor with a sick dog didn't sound in the least bit romantic to her. Maybe this woman was wackier even than her brother;

maybe she was the perfect soul mate for Hugh. Even though she could hear her sister's skeptical voice pounce on the notion of a "soul mate." This, despite the fact that their very own parents had been modestly happy together for roughly half a century. The evidence was solid—genetic—that it could happen, but it hadn't, not for any of the Panik offspring.

"I don't like it that Hannah and Thomas are separated."

"Hannah's always been hard to live with. And I can see moving in with your mom. Sometimes it's nice to live with your mom. She probably cooks. Moms make great room-mates. I still miss ours."

"I hope Nigel feels that way about me. I get the impression he's counting the days until he can go to college and be with his true tribe, the other geniuses who've had to tolerate life with morons all these years."

"So Stacy and I have been trying to figure out how I can meet her kids without making a big deal. I could rent a clown suit, maybe."

"How about you rent a clown suit and we go to the nursing home? Little shot in the arm?"

"How about two clown suits, and we rob a bank while we're at it? I mean, as long as we're renting clown suits. Might as well get our money's worth."

His new cell phone suddenly broadcast a song from his shirt pocket, right over his heart. *Für Elise*. Stacy had mentioned it was the only thing she could play on the piano. "My first call," he said. They'd copied all of Holly's contacts into Hugh's new device. "Hannah," he noted. "Not like we've ever been able to pull one over on her, is it?"

"Not once," Holly agreed.

## 9. *Goodbye, Sam*

Sam Panik had been evicted from the nice nursing home and now was at the not nice one, the large place that more closely resembled a hospital than a house, whose operations were modeled on factory rather than family dynamics. Patients here wore name tags because otherwise the staff would not know what to call them, and wristbands that identified their wishes concerning emergencies. DNR, some said. Their beds were lined up like trays containing parts, labels at the foot of each to identify exactly what parts were therein contained.

Their father's La-Z-Boy had been returned to the family house, back alongside its companion chair, two decrepit empty seats.

"For fuck's sake, stop crying," Hannah said tiredly to her sister. It was a refrain with Holly. "You're gonna get everybody all mopey," she said, then conceded, "Not that they aren't already." The place leaked despair, reeked of hopelessness and the dread and promise of death. And like Vegas, it seemed timeless, as much going on at three in the morning as at three in the afternoon, the clock on mortality a relentlessly noncircadian one.

"Mama," said Nigel, putting his hand into Holly's. The middle of the night; all Paniks had been summoned to the patriarch's bedside. Hugh smelled of beer and had failed to zip his pants. Nigel had deep purple circles beneath his eyes; he was a kind of living reproach, to Hannah; her own sons would never be so sensitive to the plights of their elders. Never. Had she roused Leo from his stinking teenage comatose slumber, he would be standing here like a bear pulled from hibernation, surly and snarling. Nigel's lovely slender fingers, his graceful lithe attention to his mother, his fragile tragic beauty. Hannah wanted to shove him over, for some reason. Sensitivity in men was starting to infuriate her. Was this the beginning of menopause, the disappearance of those syrupy hormones responsible for tears and sympathy and compassion, the end of love? Was this the next step on her journey, further scorn for softness, sissies, sentimental fools?

She'd always been accused of being cold; how much chillier could she expect to become? Woman: begun as mammal, moved through amphibious stages, landed eventually a leathery reptile, rolling dispassionate eyes from a rocky perch . . .

Her father appeared reptilian, now that she thought about it; maybe the evolution wasn't strictly female. Desiccated, tongue prominent, fingers crimped as if for clinging to a less substantial piece of ground. His lucidity had slipped; he no longer could be counted upon to come back from his purely private landscape to join his family in a shared one. Hannah kept thinking about the dozen highlights that Hugh had suggested she find in her daily life, those twelve ways to predictably be made happy. What might those be for her father? What, now, gave him any pleasure whatsoever? If it was difficult for her to locate her own joys, assuming that drinking only counted for one, how on earth would her father find his? At present, he was muttering a long monologue to himself, the kind of thing one observed on street corners and at bus stops, the unmedicated crazies of the world who created around themselves the force field of invisible companions, antagonists.

Into his grandfather's circle of anger stepped Nigel, saying, "Papa?" in his clear child's voice. Which seemed to penetrate whatever dispute had been going on, cut right through the crowd to the deeply submerged version of singular Sam Panik. He blinked as if coming to. "Papa," the boy said again, "are you having a bad dream?"

"It's *terrible*," his grandfather croaked, clutching at Nigel's hand. He'd been shouting for hours, the staff had said; no matter what drug they tried, he came out from under it at full volume once more, flailing and furious. He'd punched one of the nurses in the throat. Despite his emaciated condition, he was still fierce, his bones heavy, his right hook impressive. The woman had pulled down her scrub top to show the Panik family the bruise. Hannah wouldn't have let her own sons anywhere near the man, despite the restraints on his forearms and chest, despite the sedative drip. Watching Nigel, she had a terrible presentiment: he would die young, like Hamish. He carried the aspect of ghost in his graceful limbs.

"What's the bad dream?" Nigel asked.

"They tied me up, so I couldn't save him," said his grandfather. "I could see him but I couldn't save him." He'd stopped struggling against the very real belts that had been secured across his chest and legs and arms. Nigel was holding the old man's hand.

"Tell him about the prize," Holly coached her son.

"What prize?" Hannah demanded. "Chess again?"

"Something something humanitarian," Holly said. "It had to do with fundraising, I think? He wrote an essay? I didn't even know about it until the newspaper called. His picture'll be in there tomorrow." She shook her head in astonishment; this kid of hers was always surprising her. And not because she received phone calls from the police.

Effortlessly, he went around doing good deeds, like some kind of fucking saint.

"Maybe we could turn off some of these lights?" Hugh said. "No wonder he's having nightmares."

"He's talking about Hamish," Holly said.

"Hamish," agreed their father.

"Hamish," echoed Nigel. "I like to say it."

From the moment he'd moved into the new home, he'd refused sustenance. A kind of vigil was established, a member of the family or a hospice volunteer always present. But Hannah was alone with their father when he died. She thought it was a gift, that the person best prepared to accommodate a death was the one who did, in fact, show up to take on the task. Oldest sister, bossy little stand-in mother all her life. Only Hamish had been able to challenge her, only Hamish, long dead brother. Who would she have become had he remained where he should have, above and beyond her, that boy who skipped ahead mere inches outside her reach, taunting her authority, brazenly disobedient, naughty fox to her clucking hennishness?

When they'd removed Sam Panik from his home, he'd declared that Hamish would have prevented it. Maybe. He lay now deprived of fundamentals, by his own design. He'd stopped eating a week earlier, spitting the water and food from his mouth, unresponsive to any words or actions. Holding his hand, she had a strange wish: that her nephew Nigel was with her, the image of his spatulate fingers in her father's gnarled grip a lasting one. It appeared to her in a kind of vision, that the boy was the only other human available who would have appreciated the moment, the instant, of passing from among the living to the not. Nigel. That strange boy who shared in Hannah's bloodstream. Who gave her long penetrating looks from which she, by dint of pride, did not avert her gaze, although she wanted to. He was daunting. He was like her dead brother, she realized. "Who have you assigned him to, in the instance of your death?" she'd asked Holly. Who'd, predictably, burst into tears. "Make plans," Hannah had ordered, hoping that those plans would include her, yet assuming that it would be Hugh, bachelor alcoholic hopeless Hugh, given the gift of wise Nigel, reincarnated version of their beloved brother.

"Papa," she said softly. She had watched a litter of kittens die once, born too early; their mother had not been interested in them, dropped them from her body like excrement, then abandoned them to their fate, knowing they wouldn't survive, were not worth nursing. And they went like this, one at a time, tiny wet black chests heaving up and down, and then not at all, Hannah helpless witness. Her father's breathing had lengthened. It was something to focus upon, the long pauses in between, in and out. Not believing in anything beyond the here and now, it might be peaceful to enter death's chamber. The end of labor. The last difficult willed or unwilled drift into sleep, his daughter still helpless, yet there, here, to see him out.

## 10. *Hello, Ivan*

One day Nigel's father, Ivan, showed up on Holly's doorstep. It was the beginning of January; snow was falling; spring was ages away; Holly was an official orphan. "I saw the picture!" he shouted when she opened the door; she'd forgotten that about him, his overloud voice. "But you aren't in the phone book."

"Unlisted," Holly said; her number had been too close to a doctor's, and she'd grown tired of fielding messages. She smiled at Ivan. He was a nice man, and he looked exactly the same as he had ten years ago. He was far too nice to be her boyfriend; that had been the problem. Too nice, too serious, too reverent in his affection toward her, which was the kiss of death, finding her worthy. Too innocent and too worldly, at the same time. He liked to talk about politics and history; Holly had always felt like a spoiled idiot next to him. And also a cynic. Also? Bored. And then ashamed of her boredness. Making love with him, she'd been able to imagine their future arguments, which would end with him being profoundly disappointed in her, and her being ashamed, American ashamed, fat ignorant privileged shame.

"I could not remember the street, so I drove around and around knocking on doors, your neighbors might find me tiresome. I am sorry, the houses are so similar. But finally here you are!" He'd seen Nigel's photograph in the newspaper, had read about the award the boy had won for his Christmas essay, which had been used to raise money for hurricane victims. He'd first recognized himself in the image; next he had recognized Holly's name. He had done the math. At any rate, he wanted to meet the boy, whom he did not call "my son," which Holly appreciated. Men: they could have children they did not know about. How preposterous! An American man, Holly thought, would have sent a lawyer, or done nothing, hidden in fear of Holly's sending a lawyer, her brother-in-law, in fact, was a lawyer, to collect support. But Ivan merely wanted to meet the boy.

He was not going to make any claims. His new girlfriend, he said, had children of her own, and he had, a few years earlier, gotten a vasectomy, frightened of what his home-land experience would wreak upon a next generation. And so his offspring, this accidental, incidental, unknown-till-now child, was a complete gift, in his mind, a miracle, amazing! Exclamation mark! He had landed on Holly's doorstep with gratitude, solicitude, an homage rather than a court summons. He greeted her by holding her close, murmuring his thankfulness into her ear. He said, "He is exactly like my brother, exactly like Roman, who is gone. I couldn't believe it, when I saw it, I just looked and looked at my face, at Roman's face looking at me from the news-paper!" And Holly remembered how Ivan had always smelled faintly of raw onions. And had gray teeth. And hadn't known how to properly kiss her.

"He's exactly like my brother, too," she said when released from his embrace. "He's also gone. Hamish." Together they considered their dead brothers over a cigarette on the front stoop in the falling snow. Having a dead brother meant there would always be a sad space in need of filling. A specific space, one that her family had not particularly mentioned but that existed unstated among them just the same. Her father's death, in a strange way, had made Hamish's death less painful to Holly. The victims of their shared tragedy were disappearing, one by one, and that made the sadness recede ever so slightly, the inevitable fading of an important bad dream; Holly could feel it. And then, there was Ben the cabdriver, dropping off Nigel. The taxi parked at the curb, the man turned around in his seat to finish some animated point he was making, Nigel nodding thoughtfully in the back, chess technique, no doubt. Then he climbed out and beheld his father. At whom he smiled hugely, fully, her tall skinny beautiful boy. Holly had never seen him do anything like it before.

"Hello, Nigel!" said Ivan loudly. "I am Ivan. I hope you never smoke cigarettes, it is a terrible habit!" They shook hands. And then went inside to have a snack together, bananas, white crackers, milk.

## 11. *Easy Rider*

The man came to Hugh's door without a weapon, yet Hugh wouldn't answer, hoping against hope that he'd locked the thing last night, sometimes he did, sometimes not. This would be the husband; he recognized the expression on his face as it came toward him across the street and lawn, hostile red like a meteor speeding toward him, angry beyond reason, an utterly entitled, earned, undeniable anger, and if that weren't enough, the landed meteoric pounding. It shook the porch, the door frame, the cuckoo clock above the television. Never mind the doorbell, a doorbell was for a mere finger, not a fist, a doorbell could not convey the fury, a fury that could certainly bring down the door, locked or not, could knock down the clock upon the TV. And that would be fitting, a cuckoo for a cuckold. Hugh hid in the kitchen, having scrambled there as soon as he'd seen the man's approaching furious face; the slammed car door, the resonant bang of that, and then the ensuing bang on this second door, the violence done upon doors, now the booted foot.

The hippies would prevent his breaking it down, Hugh figured, flinching with every strike. He'd never been more grateful for his neighbors' benign witnessing presence, their choir of stoned opinion. Their gentle indignant voices now calling across the drive. *Hey, man, chillax, whoa, dude . . .* Hugh crawled to his father's bedroom window to peek out. The hammering at his door abruptly ceased, and then there was Stacy's husband, roaring toward Waffle and Bob, who had the good sense to scramble up the burnt-orange couch, raise their hands against assault, fall behind the sofa, and use it as a makeshift shield, from which protection they then began screaming at their nearly feral dog, who'd come blazing out from his lair under Mr. Roosevelt's porch in his own un-reined wild fury, to meet the man in his.

Hugh stood on the other side of the glass, shaking and murmuring, "No, no, no, no," fumbling the receiver from its cradle, impatient for the first time in his life with the over-long revolution of the rotary dial; 9, it slowly rolled along, then staccato 1-1.

They met at the zoo. The university semester was long over, Ms. Fox had failed them both, her husband was at work, her two older children busy at school, her husband would never suspect she'd meet her boyfriend with the toddler along. While the child stared transfixed at the penguins and flamingos and spiders and cockroaches, in a winding trek from one fictional natural habitat to another, Stacy and Hugh had what was designed to be their final conversation. "Why are you crying?" the three-year-old, Mavis, took a moment to inquire of her mother. The child was bundled in a snowsuit from within which only her chubby red face emerged, a face very like her father's, small-eyed and skeptical.

"I'm sad for the zebra," Stacy said. "See? No friends."

"The giraffe is his friend," said Mavis. "They both have funny skin. Don't be sad, Mama!" The child thumped Stacy's thigh with her mittened hand to emphasize her point.

"Don't be sad," Hugh repeated.

Mavis whirled, peeved. "Stop copying me!"

"Sorry. She's a pistol," Hugh said, glad to have his mother's word so readily on his tongue.

"I'll get a bruise there," Stacy said, of her thigh. "I bruise so easily it's ridiculous. I could have a case for spouse abuse, if I wanted to, nobody would doubt it if I said he was knocking me around, he looks like a brute what with that thick neck. But he isn't."

Hugh recalled the man's raging face, coming for him. He could never do a thing about that, not one thing; he'd done what came naturally, which was to cower. He was lacking an essential ingredient that would make him fight for her. It wasn't in him, whatever it was.

And she knew it. *Pussy*, said his dead brother Hamish, not unkindly, just factually, still age nineteen, sexy as the cover of *Sticky Fingers*, his favorite album. "I think I wanted you to come zooming up on a motorcycle or something," Stacy had told him on the phone. "Just like some crazy hellion from a movie, carry me away, maybe even hold a gun to my head, frigging kidnap me or something."

"I hate guns," Hugh had said. Because he did. He was fearful, and probably lazy, or maybe worse than lazy: insufficient to the labor of love. "I'm just not going to do that," he'd told her. "I don't even know how to work a motorcycle." He'd grown up terrified of them. Hamish had been that kind of boy, would have been that kind of man, daredevil, confident with girls, with women, brave to the point of destruction, fluent in the use of those loud flammable masculine tools . . .

"I know," she'd sniveled. "I wish you would, but I know you won't. Maybe that's why I chose you to begin with. I knew nothing would really happen, in the end?"

This was what his sister Hannah would have predicted: nothing. Holly, too, for that matter. She'd said as much, back when he was acquiring his cell phone. He wasn't the kind of man women left their husbands for. "You don't have a sister, do you?" he asked Stacy now, to make her smile. "An unmarried sister? Somebody just like you?"

"My sister is nothing like me," Stacy said. "She's real organized and skinny. And also a Republican, I don't think you'd like her at all." Then she laughed and laid her head on Hugh's shoulder. Mavis was busy stumping up and down the stairs at the otters' habitat, following the figure eights of the creatures' swimming pattern, from the glass tank downstairs to the exposed islands on top. "I'm lying like a rug," she said. "My sister's beautiful and single, but I'm not gonna tell you her name. I want you for myself. Even if I can't have you."

"What are we going to do?"

"I don't know, Hugh, I truly don't." Her husband had flung the coyote-like dog off his arm as if it were a creature half its size; his anger outranked the animal's, and his threats to the hippies shut them up. He'd pulled a phone from a holster, was punching in numbers himself. He had the law on his side; it was irrefutable. Cuckold: he wasn't suffering it in shame, that much was clear. His last words, aimed at Hugh's house, at Hugh, who was stationed back at his father's bedroom window: "Leave her the fuck alone. I know where you live."

"He would kill me," Hugh said now to Stacy, still marveling at that fact. She'd had to beg to get him to meet her; she'd had to cry and plead, his fear of the husband, and the arsenal of righteousness that surrounded the man, putting a distinct damper on his enthusiasm for being with her. But now that she was near him, her warm head on his shoulder, her familiar face and not invisible scar, well, the fear began to melt, to splinter, to do something metaphorically disassembling in his body.

"Yeah, he was pretty mad at me, too, he even broke our big wooden salad bowl, but then he started crying, which is . . . unusual. Highly."

"I don't want him to kill me," Hugh said.

"Me neither, that would be the worst! You'd be dead, and he'd go to jail. Then where would I be? Up a creek, that's where."

When her daughter came charging at her, crashing straight into her crotch, she explained to Hugh, "After my miscarriage I made three wishes: one for my first girl, next my boy, last this girl." Mavis growled, burrowing and churning against her mother in what looked like a painful manner. "Hugh," Stacy said, looking up from her daughter's hooded brutal head, "if I had another wish, I swear it would be for you . . ." There was a "but" at the end of this sentence; they both heard it.

Everything starts with an "if" and ends with a "but," Hugh thought. If his father could have stayed at home, he'd perhaps have been happier in his last days, but . . . If only Hamish would have walked out of the water, would have stuck around and overseen his siblings who needed their big brother, his parents who loved their boy, but . . . If Hugh had declined to follow Stacy out of creative writing and into her disaster, knowing as he should have not to risk falling in love with a married woman, but . . .

And everybody knows you only get three wishes.

"If . . ." she repeated.

"Yeah," he said. "But."

## ACKNOWLEDGMENTS

With thanks to Deborah Treisman, Anton Mueller, Bonnie Nadell, Steven Schwartz, Merrill Feitell, Kathleen Lee, Lillie Robertson, Laura Kasischke, Noah Boswell, and, especially, Robert Boswell.